1998   1st

THE PRINTER'S DAUGHTER

By the same author

By Honour Bound
(St. Martin's Press, New York, 1988; Robert Hale, London,
1989; Thorndike Large Print, 1990; Leisure Books, New
York, 1990 [paperback])

A Spy at the Gate
(The Book Guild, 1985; St. Martin's Press, New York,
1987)

THE
PRINTER'S DAUGHTER

Valerie Gray

The Book Guild Ltd
Sussex, England

The Book Guild Ltd
25 High Street,
Lewes, Sussex

First published 1998
© Valerie Gray, 1998

Set in Baskerville by
Rowland Phototypesetting Ltd,
Bury St Edmunds, Suffolk

Printed in Great Britain by
Antony Rowe Ltd, Chippenham, Wiltshire

A catalogue record for this book is
available from the British Library

ISBN 1 85776 203 7

For Dottie,
my extraordinary mother-in-law,
with love.

HISTORICAL NOTE

All the characters in this book are fictitious, with the exception of several prominent members of the printing and publishing world, including Rudolf Ackermann, William Clowes, John Hatchard, Charles Knight, senior, Charles Knight, junior, and his wife, Sally.

1

Two Gentlemen from America

It was a dreary December day, late in the afternoon, when two gentlemen descended from the hackney carriage in the Strand. The taller of the two men paid their fare, while the other lifted down their capacious travelling bags with easy strength and looked about him. The driver observed this independent action with mild surprise and resentment. In his experience most travellers expected help with their baggage and tipped accordingly.

'New in Lunnon, are yer guvnor?' he queried, fumbling in his pocket for some change. His sharp eyes missed no detail of his erstwhile passengers' attire, which was dark, serviceable and plain, perhaps a little crumpled and certainly in no cut that the coachman recognized as even moderately modish. He could not place them and he was puzzled. Could they be foreign? In the rapidly failing light it was difficult to see faces. The tall man's voice broke in on his ruminations.

'Yes, and you may keep the change. Have the kindness to indicate which street is George Street,' he said, in impeccable English.

The driver shrugged and pointed with his whip across the wide thoroughfare.

'Over yonder, 'tis one o' them alleyways wot runs down to the river. But 'ave a care, gennelmen, there's fog risin'

1

from the water on a night like this, an' rogues a' plenty jest waitin' their chance for thievin' an' willainy.'

Alarmed by his own imaginings, the driver glanced nervously over his shoulder, half raised his hand in salute and pulled quickly into the mainstream of traffic. The two men picked up their bags and advanced to the curb, where they paused and surveyed the teeming multitude of carriages and horses in some dismay.

'After you, my dear James, and step lively, there's a good fellow,' said the tall man, grinning at his companion.

'Not so, my friend, we go together or not at all. Remember how we confronted those footpads in Virginia when you were peddling the *Poor Richard Almanacs?* Watch for a lull and then shoulder to shoulder. Ready. Now, John.'

They plunged and dodged and darted and eventually arrived, winded, but unscathed, on the south side of the Strand.

'Which direction, left or right?' asked James.

'We don't want to go back to Charing Cross. We must be quite close, but it's hard to see in this dim light. I believe our jarvey was correct – there is a fog rising. See it swirling down this alley, or perhaps it is a street. Ah yes, here's a sign, Villiers Street. That strikes a chord. Let me think, I am sure I have seen books with that street on the title page.'

'John, for heaven's sake, man. Think about it some other time.'

The tall man thus addressed, sighed, smiled and pushed back his top hat to peer down the street.

'Patience, it will come to me. I am almost certain there dwells a member of the printing fraternity by name William Clowes. If we do not find George Street soon we will come back and enquire. I suggest that we walk in the direction of the City.'

They passed Buckingham Street and soon came to the next turning, which proved to be their destination. John consulted a slip of paper.

'Five doors down on the left-hand side. At the sign of the

Bell and Whistle. Do we count the house on the corner, I wonder?'

The street was quiet, the eerie yellow fog thickening as they approached the river. Inside the houses they could see the glow of candlelight and the mouth-watering smell of frying onions drifted up from one of the basement kitchens.

'Perhaps we have been too impetuous. We should have waited till morning,' said James, hesitating with his hand on the brass door knocker of the fifth house. The highly polished wolf's head stared at him unwinking. He drew back. 'The English are so punctilious in matters of social custom.'

'Nonsense. We're here now and we may never find it again or ourselves either, for that matter. Nothing ventured, you know, young James. I've never known you lacking in courage before.'

'"Tis different on one's own ground, in one's own country. I do not lack for confidence in any of our United States, but folks here can be hard to understand. They talk different and they think different.' He ended with a half-smile and a pronounced southern drawl.

John set down his bag, sat down on the third step and prepared to debate the point.

'You understand *me* well enough . . .' he began.

The door behind him swung open.

'Can I help you, sir.'

James jumped back down the steps as if stung, but his friend rose to his feet with leisurely grace, lifted his hat to the diminutive maid and glanced past her into the welcoming glow of a well-lit hall.

'Mr John Aylward and Mr James Ferguson to see Mr Farrell. We are newly arrived from America and bring letters of introduction. Is your master at home, young lady?'

The maid blushed at this unusual form of address, but replied politely,

'Step inside, sirs, if you please. Mr Farrell's in his office. If you'll follow me up the stairs I'll show you where you can wait while I enquire.' She led the way up the blue-carpeted stairway and along a passage. 'I won't be but a moment,'

3

said the girl, opening a door and gesturing for them to enter.

She disappeared, leaving them in a comfortably furnished antechamber. There was a small fire burning in the grate, spitting and hissing cheerfully in defiance of the grey chill without. There were books and journals in piles on every available surface and a window looking out on the cobbled street, which was now all but invisible in the misty twilight.

James stared down at the feeble gleam of light glinting on the pavement, while John warmed his hands by the fire. They waited in silence. Somewhere below a clock struck five. A door opened down the passage and they heard footsteps and a woman's voice saying teasingly,

'Dearest Papa, pray explain to me why only sad stories can be great literature. Does that mean that my taste in such matters is very low? I confess I have always preferred Shakespeare's comedies to his tragedies.'

An answering rumble pronounced genially, 'Of course your literary tastes are low, gel. You're a female and it can't be helped. Now run along, there's a good lass and improve your mind by reading to the men for an hour. It will speed up production if you distract them with the news of the day.'

'Strange logic, to improve one's work by distraction,' was the reply.

'Nevertheless, I have frequently remarked that the compositors are faster and more accurate when they operate automatically in setting up the type while their thoughts are occupied elsewhere.'

'Yes, Papa. However, do not forget my question . . . about sad stories, you know. It will return to haunt you at dinner time.'

'Do you wish me to send Hannah with a dish of tay?'

'If you please, Papa. Why, here she is. You're quite breathless, Hannah. What is to do?'

'Oh, ma'am, I've been lookin' for the master everywhere. There's two gentlemen waiting to see you, sir. From America.'

'Bless me, girl. From America, ye say.' His blue eyes

twinkled with amusement beneath thick brows. 'And do they have horns and tails, or are they as other men?'

Hannah giggled and her mistress protested, 'Hush Papa. They will hear you. Where have you put them, Hannah?'

'In the little front parlour, Miss Tamsyn. I mean Mrs Elsworth, ma'am.'

The three in the passageway turned simultaneously to observe the open door of the front parlour. Mrs Elsworth bit her lip.

'I shall leave you to your visitors, Papa. Some tea please, Hannah, in the workroom, and perhaps Mr Farrell would like some also.'

She paused, with one slender hand on the banister. 'I think today's *Post* is on the side table by the fireplace. Could you fetch it for me, too? Thank you, Hannah.'

With a mischievous smile at her father she ran lightly down the stair, her long dark curls bobbing and her skirts rustling in her haste. Mr Farrell squared his broad shoulders and gestured to the maid to precede him along the passage. He paused on the threshold and waited for her to announce his presence. The two gentlemen from America advanced to make their bows to the master printer, the one moving swiftly and impatiently, with an almost dancing step, while the other trod firmly and steadily. Mr Farrell did not consider himself a small man, by any means, yet he found he was obliged to look up to both men.

'Mr Farrell, forgive our intrusion at this late hour. We are newly arrived in London and are come but to pay our respects and to present our letters of introduction,' began the younger, lighter man, eagerly proffering a sealed package. A hand descended on his shoulder and he found himself set gently on one side.

'Peace, halfling,' John turned to Mr Farrell with a smile. 'Permit me, sir, to make known my good friend and fellow printer, Mr James Ferguson.' Solemnly Mr Farrell bowed in acknowledgment and James made haste to follow suit, his unruly fair hair falling forward to obscure the soft, brown eyes and long overshadowing lashes.

5

They straightened and John continued, 'And I am John Aylward, very much at your service. My kind benefactor, Mr William Pettigrew, has charged me with all manner of messages for you, as has another, one Adam Lindsay, who, I believe, may have written to you on my behalf.'

Mr Farrell stiffened and he gave John a keen, appraising glance, noting the well-defined jaw line, high cheekbones and long nose, with sensitive flared nostrils. The eyes were a cool grey and the hair an unremarkable mid-brown, though thick and springy in texture. His dark travelling clothes were of a cut and quality not usually worn by younger members of the printing fraternity and he held himself with an air of easy self-confidence and more than a hint of reserve.

'But perhaps you have had no word of our coming?'

The quiet prompting roused Mr Farrell and he hurried forward with outstretched hands, sweeping his guests ahead of him.

'Forgive me, sirs, 'tis the end of a long day. Yes, indeed I had word of your coming, though expressed in Adam Lindsay's own inimitable manner, which is to say hedged about with obscure legal jargon and much on the one hand and on t'other and the upshot was I did not expect ye until the new year. But you're most welcome. Sit ye down and we'll have some more coal on the fire. Hannah should be here in a moment with some tea, but I expect you'd like a drop o' something stronger. I never touch spirits during working hours; I find a clear head is best to check the type and set an example to the men, but no self-respecting man should be expected to assault his stomach with tea unvarnished, as it were, after a long journey.'

As he spoke he bustled about, shovelling coal from the well-filled scuttle onto the fire and poking it vigorously. Then he opened a corner cupboard and pulled out a decanter and two glasses, which he set on a small table at John's elbow, impatiently pushing aside a heap of newspapers, which fell on the floor and there remained until Hannah appeared to gather them up with much tongue-clucking and shaking of her head as she did so. She drew the curtains, lit some candles and poured the tea. Mr Farrell relaxed in his chair and stretched out his feet to the blaze, resting his heels on the fender.

'You didn't ought ter do that, sir,' said Hannah reprovingly, 'Likely you'll get chilblains and yer shoes 'll be so warped the cobbler won't be able ter mend 'em.'

Her master grunted, but did not move. The gentleman called Mr Ferguson grinned and Hannah sniffed loudly as she marched to the door.

Mr Farrell put the tips of his fingers together and surveyed his guests.

'Now, Mr Aylward, Mr Ferguson, how may I be of service to you?'

James looked to John to take the lead in this conversation, while he listened eagerly and nodded emphatically from time to time. He reminded Charles Farrell of his favourite dog, Gus, when a puppy.

John began, 'We have come to England hoping to learn all we can of the latest developments in the printing trade. I have also been accustomed to devote portions of my time to writing articles of news for various newspapers and journals and I have every expectation that my travels will prove fruitful as a fresh source of inspiration. Indeed, they have already done so, for I despatched a short piece earlier today on "First Impressions".' He gave a wry smile as Mr Farrell's mobile eyebrow flew up and added, 'I agree with you, sir, it is perhaps a little premature, but pray consider that the packet-boat will take at least a month to cross the Atlantic and the American appetite for tales of European travels is insatiable. The extra income can be put to good use in further travel or in the purchase of books, good quality paper, leather for bindings, a new case of type. Any number of things.' He spread his hands expansively. Mr Farrell nodded and turned to James.

'And you, Mr Ferguson, what can the Old World do for you?'

James ran his hand through his hair, his brow furrowed with the intensity of his reflections.

7

At length he pronounced, 'I would be immensely in your debt, sir, if you could direct me to a good tailor. Also I wish to obtain a gun with a percussion lock. I would value your opinion regarding gunmakers. Is Joseph Manton the best in town?'

Mr Farrell chuckled.

'My expertise does not normally lie in either direction, but it so happens that there have been several legal cases reported in *The Chronicle* recently concerning gunmakers who have infringed the patent for guns with percussion locks. Manton was one of the offenders, if I recall correctly. The patent is owned by Forsyth and Company and I would recommend that you seek them out. As for your other needs, I suspect my tailor may be a little long in the tooth for your taste, but we can make enquiries among my men. The younger fry keep abreast of the latest modes and ape the dandy set, but at my age comfort looms large in one's requirements and I have no desire to subject my internal organs to unnatural constriction according to the dictates of fashion. We are not all cast in the Byronic mould, though several of my lads think they are and have adopted a melancholy demeanour and an odd style of dress. But the noble lord brings poetry into their dull lives and so I do not object too strongly. Sometimes it is prudent to swim with the tide and Byron's popularity shows little sign of waning, despite his removal to the Continent, following his disgrace. I find his dissolute style of life uncongenial, but my daughter tells me that he is a genius and not subject to ordinary codes and morals. What think ye, gentlemen? Is his lordship much read in the United States?'

James opened his mouth to speak, but encountered a warning glance from his friend and subsided, a warm glow suffusing his countenance. John shook his head ruefully.

'You do not know what you are asking, Mr Farrell. James can recite *The Giaour* and *The Corsair* by heart. Lord Byron is directly responsible for his presence in England. His desire to see the country which nurtured his hero brooked no impediment. I cannot flatter myself that he came for the pleasure of my company, or even for the enrichment of his professional knowledge . . .'

Stung, James protested, "Twas I who told you about the steam printing press and insisted that you should see it in operation at *The Times* printing rooms.'

Mr Farrell beamed good naturedly upon them both.

'I surmise you two have been acquainted for some years?'

'Almost from the cradle, sir. John took me under his wing when I was first apprenticed to Master Pettigrew in 1810. I was fourteen that year and John was a journeyman way above me on the social scale. I was a country boy, unused to big city ways, but John took time to explain things to me and he protected me from the unthinking cruelty of the other lads until I overcame my longing for my home and learned to survive in Philadelphia.'

'Nonsense man. As I recollect you needed little help from me, though I never knew a youngster get into so many scrapes. Very hot-headed and easily provoked,' finished John, meeting his host's eye with a smile.

'I'd sooner have it so than have a lad sly and deceitful,' responded that gentleman tolerantly. He addressed himself to James. 'And, of course, that was many years ago. Now, sir, to change the subject somewhat, if you desire to visit Printing House Square I can arrange it. The editor, Thomas Barnes, is a friend of mine.'

James leaned forward in his chair and said, 'I would like it of all things. Tell me, sir, is it true, as they say, that it is four times faster than the hand press?'

'You mean the steam printing method. Very probably. It was installed by Barnes's predecessor, but he told me they are now able to print over one thousand copies of *The Times* in one hour.'

James whistled appreciatively and even his less impressionable friend looked amazed.

'That is indeed a vast improvement on any print production that I have encountered in our country. But how is the quality, is it possible to maintain it at such high speed?'

Delighted by their interest, Mr Farrell exerted himself to

explain the intricacies of the German invention, and produced copies of the newspaper that they might see for themselves the clear, even type. The talk became technical and an hour or more passed unnoticed by the three men, so intent were they on their discussion. John and James were peering at different type specimens through a magnifying glass and Mr Farrell was rubbing his incipient chilblains and beginning to think of his dinner, when Mrs Elsworth made a timely entrance.

'Ah, my dear, is it dinner time already?' he enquired, heaving himself to his feet.

The other two hastily followed suit and bowed when Mr Farrell presented them to the lady. She was tall and of statuesque proportions, generously endowed, but possessing slender, tapering hands and feet. She wore a black gown, partly hidden by a large fringed cashmere shawl. John found that her heavy dark curls were almost on a level with his chin when she advanced from her curtsey, hand outstretched.

'How do you do, Mr Aylward? I believe it is the custom in America to shake hands,' she said, smiling pleasantly.

'Yes, indeed, ma'am,' he replied, taking her hand, but holding her at arms' length, with no hint of an answering smile in his level gaze. Somewhat chilled by his reception of her friendly overture, she withdrew and turned to James. He did not disappoint her, but seized her hand and shook it warmly.

'By Jove, Mrs Elsworth, honoured to make your acquaintance, ma'am. May I ask where you heard about our American customs?'

'From a compatriot of yours, Mr Richard Rush.'

'The American envoy in London? We mean to call upon him. John knew him slightly when he resided in Washington.'

'He is a most charming man and quite young for a minister. I doubt if he has reached forty yet. I met him at a friend's house only last month and sat beside him at dinner.'

Mr Farrell broke in impatiently on these reminiscences.

'Tamsyn, I'm famished girl. Save these exchanges for a

better time. You'll join us for dinner, gentlemen. Come now, I'll not hear otherwise. There's plenty for all and 'tis the least I can do to make amends when I've kept ye here gossiping till this late hour.'

His hospitality brooked no protests and his daughter sped away to supervise the laying of two more places at table. The gentlemen followed more slowly.

As they descended the stair, John enquired casually, 'Will we be meeting Mr Elsworth at dinner?'

Mr Farrell looked puzzled for a moment and then shook his head,

'Why no, sir, I fear I did not make it plain. My daughter resides with me as my housekeeper and general factotum. Her husband died from wounds received at Waterloo. Tamsyn is a widow.'

2

The Next Morning

Tamsyn Elsworth was awakened early the next morning by a sharp nip on her ear, followed closely by a low rumble of satisfaction when she opened one eye and said, 'Sam, you beast, go away at once, sir.'

The large ginger tom treated this half-hearted protest with the contempt it deserved. He circled three times before settling comfortably on her chest; his green eyes met her blue ones and he twitched his whiskers to signify that he was ready to accept confidences. Tamsyn sighed and accepted the inevitable; she scratched his left ear. She told him he was incorrigible, but he did not believe her. She ruminated further, 'You're just like a man, filled with a sense of your own superiority and demanding for your comforts.'

Sam contrived to look indignant and smug at the same time. Tamsyn laughed and closed her eyes, allowing her thoughts to wander back to the previous evening. The presence of the two American gentlemen at the family dinner table had been oddly disturbing, yet stimulating. She had sat at the foot of the table, with her father at the head, Mr Aylward on her left and Mr Ferguson on her right. The talk had ranged widely; they had discussed the voyage but briefly and Tamsyn felt curiosity on a number of points. What had they eaten, how had they amused themselves, had they been sea-sick, had their fellow passengers been congenial? She had had no opportunity to enquire, as the conversation swiftly flowed to the importance of good relations between the two countries and all three gentlemen praised the efforts of the American envoy, Mr Rush, whose skilled diplomacy had done so much to counteract the ill feeling engendered by the unfortunate war a few years ago. Tamsyn had a vague recollection that the British had burned the White House in Washington, but that had been the year when she and Gilbert had been so happy in those last few months of peace in Europe, following their wedding in April 1814, and she had paid scant attention to the outside world. She remembered participating in the public festivities when the Allied Sovereigns of Russia and Prussia visited London that summer, but her own domestic pre-occupations had been so intense that she had quite failed to notice the thunderclouds approaching until Gil was summoned to rejoin his regiment before Waterloo. Her thoughts shied off at a tangent, as they frequently did when her mind wandered, unbidden, to the events of 1815.

The pain of her personal tragedy, the loss of Gilbert, had isolated her in the midst of the general rejoicing following the great victory over Napoleon and, she now realized, she had felt only half-alive ever since. For four years she had existed tranquilly enough; her mother had died several years ago and Tamsyn had slipped back into her rôle as mistress of the master printer's household as if she had never left it to marry Gil.

There was a light tap on the door and Hannah entered with her morning chocolate. Tamsyn sighed, stretched and sat up, displacing Sam, who jumped off the bed and stalked over to the window.

'Is it still foggy, Hannah?'

'No, ma'am, the sun is trying to break through and it's quite mild. Shall I bring your hot water now?'

'Thank you, no, I think I'll wait a little. Just pull the curtains and I'll ring when I'm ready.'

Hannah gave her mistress a curious glance at this departure from their daily routine. Usually Mrs Elsworth would be up promptly, dealing with her domestic duties, attending to her letters, assisting her father in the workroom and print shop or perhaps writing at the little bureau in her sitting room. What she wrote, Hannah was not quite sure, but she knew it was unwise to disturb her mistress at her composition.

'Will you be attending Mr Hempseed's lecture? Shall you be wearing your black bombazine?'

Tamsyn knitted her brow and answered, 'Good heavens, girl, how you vex me with all these questions. My eyes are scarce open and already you plague me for decisions.'

Taken aback, Hannah's eyes widened and her mouth dropped; Tamsyn's habitual good nature reasserted itself. She held out her hand to her maid.

'I beg your pardon, something I ate last night must have disagreed with me. Let me see, I'll wear my grey, with the wide lace cuffs and I will call on Lady Molesworthy. The cold collations which come after Mr Hempseed's lectures are delicious and her ladyship always fidgets and taps with her cane if he goes on too long.'

Hannah giggled and plumped up Tamsyn's pillow to indicate that she bore no grudge. Indeed, she had been in her mistress's service since Mrs Elsworth's marriage and there was a bond of affection between the two women. The mention of her ladyship's librarian reminded Hannah that she had seen the gentleman on the previous evening.

'He was here, Hannah? But why were we not informed?'

'You were at dinner, ma'am, and he insisted that I should not disturb you. He wanted Mr Farrell's advice about some bindings. He said it was not urgent.'

A vision of Oliver Hempseed, stiff and precise in all his movements, rose unbidden in Tamsyn's mind. She knew that he admired her, but was unable to give him any encouragement beyond the civility that politeness required. He had a keen intelligence and on occasion had been known to exhibit a certain dry wit, but Tamsyn found his manners lacking in both warmth and spontaneity. She remembered the light-hearted banter and fun she had shared with Gil

14

and shivered. It was difficult to avoid Mr Hempseed; in his official capacity he was a valued client of her father's and his position in the household of her godmother, Lady Molesworthy, meant that she saw him frequently when she visited in Portman Square.

'He left a message for you.' Hannah's voice broke in on her thoughts. 'He said to tell you Miss Gordon is home from Paris.'

'Alanna home. Oh, that's wonderful news. I did not expect her until the Spring.' Tamsyn sat up joyfully, then frowned. Hannah shook her head; surely her mistress was in a strange humour this morning, but she had done her best for poor Mr Hempseed. She picked up the empty cup and departed. Tamsyn pulled on a warm dressing gown and joined Sam on the window seat.

'Oh, Sam, my grey dress will look so dull beside Alanna's modish new wardrobe,' she mourned, pushing back the heavy curtain and gazing at the winter-bare branches of the old beech tree in the garden below. 'Of course, it does not matter, so long as I look neat and tidy and widowlike.' Another sigh. She rubbed her chin meditatively. It was odd that yesterday morning she had not cared a rush for her appearance and today she felt an immense dissatisfaction with the entire contents of her closet. Alanna must be consulted without delay. Tamsyn knew that her friend could be depended upon to have the very latest styles and colours at her fingertips. Tamsyn recognized that the Parisian modes would, in all probability, have to be modified for her English taste, but Alanna had a good eye for accessories and a touch of lace or ribbon, with a higher crown to a bonnet or a deeper flounce to a hem, could achieve remarkable transformations at modest cost. Tamsyn jumped up eagerly and rang for Hannah. Usually she made her own toilette, but now she wanted assistance to dress her hair.

'Pile it in a knot on the top and endeavour to tease some ringlets from these heavy curls,' she requested, flicking them disdainfully and smiling at Hannah in the looking-glass. The maid did her best to comply, twitching and pulling; her touch was far from gentle, but Tamsyn endured. To distract herself she thumbed through the ribbons in her dressing table drawer. They were nearly all black or white, very plain and proper; she tossed them aside impatiently and rummaged again. Hannah tugged hard.

'Ouch!'

'Do be still, ma'am. 'Tis difficult enough without your wriggling.' Tamsyn subsided and the work progressed. At last Hannah laid down the comb and held up the mirror for Tamsyn to see the full effect. They shook their heads. 'Your hair is so thick, Miss Tamsyn. It never will spring into those little corkscrews that you see in the fashion plates.'

'I know. You've done wonders, Hannah. See if you can find a blue ribbon somewhere in this box; a wide one to cover as many deficiencies as possible.' She relaxed on the stool. 'It does seem a long time since Miss Gordon left to be "polished", as my godmother put it. Do you recollect, did she depart in May or June? She is such a poor correspondent I feel as if we had been out of touch for years.'

Hannah nodded.

'She were always one for the active life, Miss Gordon. You didn't find her with her head stuck in some old book half the day.'

Tamsyn's eyes narrowed at her maid's indulgent tone.

'You would not be so tolerant if you had to rescue her from scrapes all the time,' she said tartly, 'and I do not have my head stuck in a book.'

Hannah raised her eyebrows, but forebore to comment. Instead, she threaded the blue ribbon through her mistress's curls and tied a deft bow.

'It fits, I mean, holds nicely, ma'am.'

Tamsyn's eyes twinkled.

'The cap fits, impertinent girl. At least it usually does, but today I do not wish to listen to Mr Hempseed talk about his books. I do not feel like a blue-stocking, not even light blue.'

'Blue is very becoming on you, Miss Tamsyn.' Hannah's sharp Cockney features softened; she hoped that her mistress was emerging at last from the private world into which she had retreated when Mr Gilbert died. She added, 'You could always make Miss Gordon your excuse not to attend the lecture. Lady Molesworthy must be delighted to have her granddaughter safely home again.'

Tamsyn grinned.

'Delight may not be her strongest emotion, but we shall see. Can you be ready to accompany me in half an hour?'

'Yes, ma'am,' said Hannah as she hurried to the door.

'Send Cook to me in the morning room,' Tamsyn called after her retreating back.

Tamsyn nibbled on some toast, gave her orders for the day and was ready to depart promptly at eleven o'clock. She felt in holiday spirits and decided to call at Hatchards bookshop on her way to Portman Square. Perhaps she would find the new edition of John Evelyn's *Memoirs* which she had ordered as a Christmas gift for her father. The object of her thoughts appeared in the hall as she was putting on her gloves.

'Good morning, Father, do you have any commissions for me?'

Mr Farrell heard the lilt in her voice and surveyed her shrewdly, noting the grey skirt below the three-quarter pelisse and the length of bright blue ribbon peeping out from under her bonnet. He had become so accustomed to seeing his daughter in black that he could not but be startled by this sudden change in apparel.

He said gruffly, 'And where might you be off to, young lady? I thought you were going to help me set the type for that treatise on Islamic philosophy.'

Tamsyn was stricken.

'Dearest Papa, I quite forgot. Hannah told me that Mr Hempseed brought news of Alanna's return to Portman Square and it is also the day for the monthly literary lecture. Can the treatise wait?'

'I suppose it will have to.' Mr Farrell relented. 'Give my best love to Alanna and tell her to come and see me soon.'

'Yes, Papa,' she said, as she pecked his cheek.

He smiled, and answered. 'You look well today, lass. I had thought to see you pale and tired after your late night. So

17

much animated discussion too; I had not realized you were so interested in the affairs of our erstwhile colonies.'

Tamsyn retorted loftily, 'My dear sir, those colonies have been an independent republic for some forty years or more. I think there is a great deal to be said for a written constitution and a truly equal form of democracy.'

'Indeed. How can slavery be accommodated with democracy and equality?'

'I don't know, but surely they will find a way. And at least they treat women very civilly. The way they deferred to my opinion was most flattering.'

'Most,' agreed Mr Farrell blandly, 'but America is a harsh country and I think you will find that women are free to work equally hard in it.'

Tamsyn laughed and tapped her foot.

'I refuse to argue with you, Papa. Here is Hannah with the hackney.' She turned on the doorstep and enquired casually, 'After I left last night, did you make any arrangement to see Mr Ferguson and er, Mr Aylward again?'

'Well now, let me see, I have a notion I might have done. They need an introduction to Barnes, if they are not too busy gadding about seeing the sights. You suggested enough places of interest to keep them going from here to kingdom come. I thought your wits had gone a-begging when you mentioned tea gardens in the middle of December.'

Tamsyn blushed and started to run down the steps.

Her father's voice boomed, 'I expect them to wait upon me later today. What d'ye say to a little theatre party for Christmas; would that be a hospitable gesture to our American printing brethren?'

Although she had not set foot in a theatre since her widowhood, Tamsyn heard herself saying, 'What a good idea. I should like it of all things.'

Not giving herself time to change her mind, she waved and jumped into the carriage. She decided to go directly to her godmother's house and call at the bookseller's on her way home.

*   *   *

18

Mr Farrell closed his front door and strolled through the workroom to his inner office, humming a saucy little air as he went. His men grinned at one another, but he appeared not to notice as he took the Islamic manuscript from the shelf and bent his head to his task. The connecting door remained open and peace reigned; but from time to time Mr Farrell would sing another verse of the catchy song.

Meanwhile, as she had hoped, Tamsyn arrived early for Mr Hempseed's book talk. She told Hannah to await her in the servants' hall and requested Josselin, her ladyship's butler, to show her to the library.

'Is Miss Gordon at home, Josselin?' she enquired, almost trotting to keep up with the man's stately, yet rapid motion, as they crossed a small courtyard. Dead leaves rustled, but the fountain was still and silent, waiting for spring. The butler held open a long, glass door.

'Well, Mrs Elsworth, I believe I may safely say, ma'am, that she will be at home for you. She was still abed half an hour ago, and Fanny just took up her breakfast.' Josselin beamed at Tamsyn with the privileged familiarity of one who had known her since childhood. He had kept a jar of lollipops in his pantry especially for her. Later, she and Alanna, several years her junior, had made many attempts to imitate Josselin's sonorous vowel tones, particularly the long 'O', as they crunched their lollipops on the nursery window seat. She remembered this now with some shame as she waited for him to fasten the door; he had aged very little since she had first known him, perhaps a few more wrinkles, a touch of grey at the temples. For a moment she could almost fancy herself a little girl again.

'Dear Josselin', she laid her hand on his arm and smiled at him conspiratorially. 'Pray discover if she will receive me. I will make my apologies to Mr Hempseed and await you in the morning room. Where is my godmother?'

'In her room, ma'am. She will be down at any moment.'

As always, he succumbed to the beseeching expression in her deep blue eyes, understanding full well the enormity of her decision to skip the morning lecture, which she had attended with faithful regularity every month for the past two years. Her devotion to the gathering had given rise to some speculation in the servants' hall, but Josselin did not believe a word of it. He felt sure that dry stick, Hempseed, would be unable to engage Mrs Elsworth's affections, not after Mr Gilbert. However, he had had the occasional twinge of doubt, which he stoutly suppressed, so he now scurried eagerly away to deliver his message, certain that Miss Alanna would be able to give her thoughts a new turn.

Left alone, Tamsyn drew a deep breath, lifted her chin and entered the domain of Oliver Hempseed. It was a handsome, high-ceilinged room, filled with alcoves all lined with book-shelves. A faint musty smell pervaded the atmosphere despite the best efforts of Lady Molesworthy's maids to keep it at bay with beeswax polish and strategically placed bowls of *pot-pourri*. Tamsyn edged past the chairs, which were set ready in several neat rows, facing a tall bookstand, which was used by the speaker for his notes. Beyond the furthest alcove was a door, which led to the librarian's inner sanctum. She approached with some trepidation and met Mr Hemp-seed emerging from his study with a pile of books under his arm and a glass of water in his hand. He peered near-sightedly at Tamsyn and saw a blur of grey and blue, which he did not at once associate with the widow.

'Good morning, ma'am,' he said abruptly, each syllable clipped as if he begrudged it. Everything about him was well-cut; his clothes, his features and his accent. His receding hairline brought into prominence the fine bones, but made him look older than was probably the case.

Tamsyn stepped back, so that the light from the long window fell full on her face.

She said, 'Good day, Mr Hempseed. I hope I find you well.'

On hearing her voice, his expression was transformed.

'My dear Mrs Elsworth, forgive me,' he hastened to set down the books and water. Eagerly he took her hand to lead her to her accustomed chair near the bookstand, where he could gauge her reactions to his *bons mots*. With a new awareness, Tamsyn realized how, imperceptibly, his manner had become quite possessive. Belatedly she reproached herself for allowing this state of affairs to develop unchecked.

'You are early today,' he remarked when she remained silent. He hung over her, one hand resting casually on the back of her chair. She felt a tingle of apprehension and tilted her head to glance at him sideways; she caught him watching her with a look of unguarded ardour, which caused her to jump up and move away, pulling a book at random from the shelves.

'Yes, I am a little early. I hoped for a private word, I mean, I wished to speak with you before your lecture.'

She was annoyed to find herself trembling. He was behind her, so close that she could smell the fresh scent of lemon soap. Tamsyn bent her head and turned the pages blindly. Mr Hempseed took the book from her nerveless fingers and turned it the right way up. He stood back and perched on the edge of a table.

'Yes?' he prompted.

This produced the desired effect. Feeling foolish, Tamsyn met his eyes resolutely.

'I came to thank you for your message last night,' she began, 'I wish that you had come in and met our guests.'

'I regret, I was otherwise engaged. 'Twas merely a passing call. Two gentlemen from America, I understand?' He regarded her narrowly over the top of his spectacles.

'Yes, indeed. We had a most interesting conversation about printing and publishing in America and about the political situation and social life. It all sounded most appealing, quite free from so many of our conventional restraints.' Tamsyn sighed wistfully.

'In my experience such naivety goes hand in hand with a lack of civilization and culture,' observed Mr Hempseed drily.

'You and my father share a number of similar prejudices, I think.' Tamsyn shook her head and laughed.

21

Mr Hempseed said, 'In my case it is a prejudice born of some practical knowledge. You may not know that I made an extended tour of the United States several years ago.' His companion's eyes widened in a gratifying fashion. He smiled. It was an engaging smile, one which he rarely used. He added, 'If you wish, I will be happy to tell you about it one day, but now I must prepare for my lecture.'

Recalled to her real mission, Tamsyn straightened.

'I should like it of all things,' she said graciously, 'And you must meet Mr Ferguson and Mr Aylward. I have promised to do my best to think of entertainments for them.'

'I shall be pleased to act in that capacity,' responded the librarian. There was a little bustle by the door. He resumed, 'Well, Mrs Elsworth, I am going to talk about female novelists today and their tendency to use ten words where one will do. I hope it will amuse you.'

'It will not amuse *me*. I do not care to hear my sex maligned by a gentleman, however learned he may be,' interjected a sharp voice at Tamsyn's elbow. They turned to find a little, old lady, heavily rouged and wearing a turban of alarming proportions. Lady Molesworthy tapped her gold-tipped cane imperatively.

'Godmama,' Tamsyn curtsied and kissed the lady, taking care not to displace the artfully placed beauty patches, 'How well you look.'

'Nonsense, child.' Lady Molesworthy was not displeased. She surveyed Tamsyn through her lorgnette. 'You've cast off your weeds, I see. High time, in my opinion. That blue becomes you. Black makes people invisible. That minx, Alanna, has brought back trunkloads of fripperies from the Continent. Scarcely decent, some of 'em, but she has enough and to spare. Get her to give ye some.'

'I *should* like to see them and Alanna, too, of course,' Tamsyn hesitated. Lady Molesworthy came to her rescue.

'Well, why are you hanging about here, dancing attendance on all these old crows? Mr Hempseed will excuse you, not that it's any of his affair. Away with you, before my granddaughter comes in search of you and disturbs our earnest deliberations.'

Her ladyship waved her cane in the direction of the door, just as Josselin ushered in a bevy of ladies bearing the unmistakeable stamp of the blue-stocking.

Lady Lucinda Molesworthy poked her librarian in the chest. 'Well sir, are you ready?'

Mr Hempseed bowed impassively. Tamsyn fled, wondering, not for the first time, why a man of his deep learning and impeccable taste submitted to the patronage of that small tyrant, her godmother.

3

The Widow and her Friend

Garments of every colour and description covered every available surface; Tamsyn paused on the threshold of Miss Gordon's chamber and surveyed the chaotic scene with a mixture of amusement and envy. On the far side of the room a maid was scurrying to and fro, moving articles from one pile and placing them on another. It seemed a hopeless task. Tamsyn closed the door with a click. She approached the vast bed, which appeared to contain a more solid and compact heap than those strewn elsewhere.

'My dear, have you been robbed?' she enquired softly.

The heap sighed, grunted and bounced out from beneath the cover in a froth of ribbons and lace. Miss Gordon's fair features came uppermost, framed in a fetching nightcap with a large pink bow tied securely under her small round chin. Enormous guileless eyes, blue as the heavens on a sunny day, met Tamsyn's own.

'Tammy,' she said.

Tamsyn winced.

'Don't you dare call me that, Alanna Gordon, or I shall never speak to you in friendship again.'

Giggling, Alanna jumped off the bed and flung her arms about her visitor.

'Dearest, how I have missed you and your commonsense. I wish you could have come with me. I vow I have not opened

24

a book in six months; the exertion of reading the French newspapers was almost too much for me, but one must keep informed of the latest *on dits.*' She bit the tip of one rosy finger reflectively and confided, 'French gentlemen are so passionate about politics. It can be very tedious.'

'But surely they did not talk of politics all the time?' queried Tamsyn with a smile.

Alanna perched on the bed and pulled the coverlet round her shoulders. Tamsyn drew up a chair close by.

Miss Gordon addressed her maid.

'Fanny, you may leave that and go and have your dinner. But first bring me the two boxes I told you to keep separate from the rest. Do you know where they are?'

'Yes, miss, I think so,' came the muffled response, as the obliging maid plunged into a billowing sea of shawls and wraps. She emerged red-faced, but triumphant, and staggered over to the two young ladies with the unwieldy oval boxes held in a firm clasp. She set them down, her worn, capable hands making light of the load.

'Thank you, Fanny. What should I do without you?' said Alanna, 'Fanny is very happy to have her feet back on good English soil once more, Mrs Elsworth, with good English fare on her plate.'

'Aye, that I am, ma'am,' Fanny corroborated, 'A body can starve in double quick time livin' at the mercy o' they Frenchies. Why, 'twas a spoonful o' this and a taste o' that, *soupçon* they called it, with the plates whisked away and the meat gone and replaced by lettuce leaves smothered in oil before you could say Jack Robinson.' She shuddered.

Alanna nodded solemnly and said. 'You see we had to come home before Fanny withered away to a mere bag of bones. She was so good and waited up for me till all hours with her poor stomach quite hollow; she did not even care for the wine. Well, one night we were both in low spirits and I decided that the only cure would be a true Christmas dinner in Portman Square. That night I dreamed of Josselin bringing in the plum pudding, which I have always loathed, and I realized that the situation was even more serious than

25

I had supposed. The very next day I sent Fanny to purchase our tickets and here we are.'

'Homesickness manifests itself in strange forms,' observed Tamsyn, her eyes twinkling. 'But I am truly glad to have you back. It has been all work and no play since you left and now I need your help to entertain two gentlemen . . .'

She paused and was not disappointed in the effect these few words had on her audience. Alanna snapped her fingers and gestured towards the door; Fanny obeyed the unspoken command and departed, her lips puckered in a decided pout. Her mistress giggled.

'Poor thing, she's torn between curiosity and hunger,' she said as the door closed. Then she leaned forward and patted Tamsyn's hand encouragingly. 'Two gentlemen, my dear, why two? Do tell. You know, I am entirely at your disposal.'

Alanna watched closely as Tamsyn gathered her thoughts. The young ladies knew one another well and Alanna was intrigued by the fact that her normally calm and reserved friend was undeniably flustered. Her colour was high, her breathing quick and shallow.

'Oh Alanna, I feel so foolish. I have not felt this way since Gil and I were betrothed and after he died I had no interest in other men until . . .'

'Until . . . ,' Miss Gordon prompted.

'Last night. Two gentlemen came to call upon Papa. It was late and he invited them to stay for dinner.'

'Yes, yes. Don't keep me in suspense.'

'Be patient,' Tamsyn was beginning to enjoy herself. 'They were from America.'

This produced an impression, but perhaps not the one she desired.

'America! *Quelle horreur!* Were they big and hairy and quite untamed?' Alanna wrinkled her nose.

'Not at all! I had not thought to find you so narrowly prejudiced. They were very tall, 'tis true, but well-groomed, well-spoken and well-informed.'

'I see. They must be paragons indeed.'

'My dear, don't be provoking. Mr Aylward and Mr Ferguson are gentlemen printers from Philadelphia. Mr Aylward also writes articles and I suspect he may have some private means for they are staying at the Clarendon in Bond Street and he spoke of purchasing large quantities of printing supplies, including the presses.'

'And you wish me to present them to Grandmother?'

Alanna strove valiantly to overcome her inbred distaste for the taint of connections with trade. Her expression betrayed her.

'Yes,' said Tamsyn firmly, 'I assure you they are quite presentable and I suspect my godmother will find them a refreshing change. Remember, Alanna, America is a democratic country and the people believe in equality.'

'So do the French, but they are civilized about it,' muttered the younger lady.

'Quite a recent development, I believe,' retorted Tamsyn. She changed her tack. 'Do not let us quarrel. I know you despise trade, but indeed the strength of our nation depends upon it. One day America will be a great nation and we should try and make her citizens feel welcome here. They work hard, Alanna; they do not have time to spare for many cultural refinements, but they are aware of their deficiencies in this respect, so Mr Ferguson said, and one day they will have leisure to cultivate the arts and other civilized pursuits.' She paused and added, 'I have, perhaps, expressed myself ill, but I have a liking for the gentlemen and cannot bear to have you condemn them unseen. After all, my own dear Papa is also a printer and I am proud that he considers me sufficiently skilled to be able to help him in his work. By the by, he sent his best love to you.'

Alanna jumped up impulsively and gave her friend a quick, warm embrace.

'My dear, you do right to chide me. I think I must have been too much polished in Paris. I am become pompous, stuffy and heartless. Forgive me and pray give Uncle Charles a kiss from me and tell him that I shall wait upon him soon in my most fetching new bonnet. It has long curling feathers which tickle my nose and make me sneeze, but . . .'

'But you look ravishing in it and it makes a most gratifying impact upon the sterner sex,' Tamsyn finished for her.

Alanna nodded and they both laughed, happy to be in harmony once more.

'I have a gift for you, which I hope you will like. Uncle Charles must be relieved that you have put off your weeds at last. I know he detests black for he told me so just before I left for the Continent. I quite agree with him and I vow I shall have hysterics if anyone at court dies and we are all plunged into mourning. It would be too bad, for I recently purchased a charming red velvet evening gown, trimmed with lace from Valenciennes, which will be perfect for a special Christmas party. I will show you in a moment, but first tell me, what manner of man is he, this Mr Ferguson?'

Tamsyn put her head on one side and considered.

'He is the perfect romantic hero,' she said at last, 'He is clean, but casual in his dress. His hair a trifle long, his eyes large and soulful . . .'

'Stop, he is not the one,' interrupted Alanna.

Tamsyn was not to be diverted.

'He can recite Lord Byron's poems by the hour and he listens with the greatest respect to every word I utter.'

'Very flattering, but scarcely challenging.'

'Indeed, I liked him exceedingly and I thought it a most encouraging sign that his lordship's works have been received with such acclaim in the United States.'

'George's poems are much too long and filled with obscure references. For myself, I infinitely prefer a simple Gothic tale or a little essay in the *Ladies' Museum*, which does not take all day to read. I am convinced that most of the young ladies who fall into raptures over the latest Cantos have not read above half of them and understood less. He is fashionable, that is all.'

'You are severe. He would be quite crushed could he but hear your strictures. No one would ever know from your literary tastes that you were related to his lordship. I think he is a genius.'

'I know you do. Nevertheless, one poet or poetry reader in the family is quite enough to overcome. Besides, he is almost certainly unaware of my existence; the connection is very slight.'

'A touch of pique?' Tamsyn teased.

'Not the least in the world,' responded Miss Gordon loftily.

'Good. Now that is settled, pray tell – what do you have for me? I hope it is something pretty to wear or something amusing to read.'

Alanna smiled mischievously and pulled the two boxes which Fanny had left on the floor up on to the bed. She gestured to her friend.

'Open them and see.'

Tamsyn's eager fingers removed the lid of the smaller box and gently parted the layers of tissue.

'Ohh,' she breathed.

'Try it on,' urged Alanna, 'I had to guess, but I think it will fit. I hope so. Your hair is so thick and I did not know you had taken to piling it on top in that new way.'

'Only today. I will wear it down again if necessary.'

Tamsyn lifted out the most exquisite bonnet she had ever possessed with reverent touch. It was an enchanting confection lined with pink silk and topped with Provence roses.

'Most of the bonnets in Paris are of chenille stuff this season and you will notice that it is deeper in front than those worn last year. I chose the roses and I'm so glad I did. Mademoiselle Louise insisted that pomegranate flowers are the most popular, but I thought they looked ugly.'

'Your taste is impeccable. It is perfect. Thank you so very much.'

Tamsyn carried her gift over to the looking glass and put it on. Alanna tweaked the bow and set one of the roses straight. She nodded, satisfied with her choice.

'And now, the other box.'

Alanna was a generous young lady. It gave her great pleasure to watch as Tamsyn slowly withdrew a dinner dress in

29

deep rose-coloured China crepe. The gown was made long in the waist and full in the back, confined by a sash. The sleeves were fastened up in the ancient Grecian style on the shoulder and the hem was caught up in small flounces embroidered in flowers of various silks. Tamsyn's eyes sparkled; she gazed at her friend speechlessly.

'You like it? It will fit, never fear. I asked Hannah for your measurements. We shall have to find a suitable occasion for you to wear it.'

Tamsyn found her voice.

'Alanna, it is a dream gown. I shall feel like a princess in a fairy tale and it comes so opportunely for the festive season. I'm convinced there is nothing to equal it in the whole of London. Heartfelt thanks, my dear, I am quite overcome. But you are so kind, I do not like to take advantage of your good nature. Can I not reimburse . . . ?'

Miss Gordon broke in hastily, 'Certainly not. 'Tis I who am in your debt many times over; you have always been there when I needed you, you gave me a family and companionship when I came to Portman Square a lonely little orphan. Do you recall when we first met? I was beginning to recover from that terrible typhus fever which killed my parents and my little brother, Jeremy. I was in very low spirits and Grandmama was at her wit's end, so she sent for your mother. Dear Aunt Sarah, she came at once and brought you.'

'And I brought you the black kitten in a basket.'

'Horatio. What a fighter he was, but very affectionate.'

'So long ago. Soon after Trafalgar. And don't forget, Alanna, that my family benefited too. Mama was so happy to be reconciled with Lady Lucinda.'

'I always wondered why they were estranged, but feared to ask.'

'Oh, her ladyship did not approve of my Papa. She felt that the daughter of her old schoolfriend had married beneath her, but she did relent somewhat when I was born and consented to be my godmother. I believe it was Papa's suggestion and Mama swallowed her pride for my sake. However, there was almost no social intercourse between us, just gifts for my birthday. Then you came upon the scene and Lady Lucinda felt helpless when you were so ill. To her great credit she put your needs first and summoned Mama. Afterwards she met Papa and succumbed to his charm and nowadays she rarely makes a decision of importance without consulting him.'

'It was fortunate for everybody that we liked one another,' observed Alanna thoughtfully. 'But tell me, Tamsyn, did Grandmama consult Uncle Charles before bundling me off to stay with the Ellincourts in Paris?'

'She may have done. Why do you ask?'

'I'm not sure. I don't deny that a little finishing was in order, but on reflection it seemed to me that I had been hustled out of the country before Robert Hawksmore returned from his tour of classical antiquities. So dull, why go to look at old Greek ruins when one can go to Paris?'

'Perhaps the late wars gave some gentlemen a feeling of ambivalence towards French culture and society,' suggested Tamsyn drily.

'But that is over and done with now – and you are about to wear a Parisian gown yourself, I hope.' Alanna hesitated before adding, 'Oh, I don't mean to wound you, how could I forget Gilbert?'

Tamsyn met her eyes steadily.

'Don't reproach yourself. It is wrong to live always in the past. Gil would have been the first to say so. I know it in my mind, but in practice it is hard to let go, even of painful memories. But let us think of you. Why should her ladyship have wished to avoid a meeting between you and Sir Robert last summer?'

Alanna shrugged.

'She thought I was too young and silly for a man of his years and experience. She wishes for a match. She sees me as mistress of Oak Place in the county of Berkshire.'

'And you?'

'I'm not eager to bury myself in the country. I would like

31

to have one full season. Grandmama had me whisked away so soon after my presentation at court that I felt resentful. She treated me like a child that could not be depended upon to behave sensibly.'

Tamsyn smiled and said comfortingly, 'Well, I think you are a very modish young lady now. I can't think why I did not hear of this before. I remember I had a bad cold and missed your come-out ball, but Sir Robert was not present, in any event?'

'No, of course not. He was in Greece, or Italy.'

'How old is he?'

'About thirty, I believe, perhaps a trifle younger. He fought at Waterloo. I met him just before he left on his tour. He told me he knew he was rather old to be going on a tour, but he wished to make up for all the experiences he missed during the wars. He wanted to travel in a leisurely way, through peaceful countryside, with no hint of a battle-field anywhere in sight, so he said.'

'Europe is so full of battlefields he must have been obliged to go by a very circuitous route. Did you like him?'

Alanna clasped her hands in her lap and frowned in an effort of concentration.

'I met him only twice and it was a year and a half ago, in the summer of 1818. I was both repelled and attracted. He seemed to be filled with restless energy. He came to call upon Grandmama when we stayed in Windsor. I think his father was an old beau and she had known Robert as a boy. Then Robert went off and fought in the Peninsula and she did not see him again for many years. Apparently they met at some grand dinner for the allied Sovereigns in 1814 and got along famously. I daresay you would like him – he collects books as well as antique coins and *objets d'art*. He has cold grey-green eyes that look through you, quite tall, with undistinguished features, but nevertheless a presence. My grandmother thinks that we would complement one another and he is heir to a valuable estate.'

Privately Tamsyn thought her ladyship had made a mistake in stating her wishes so plainly.

32

Aloud she said, 'I wonder if he knew Gil. They must have been of an age.'

Alanna shook her head.

'I don't think so. I did mention his name. When I met Robert I did not realize what was in Grandmama's mind. It became evident the night before I left for France, when she had taken a little too much wine.'

'Why did you not tell me of him before?'

'I thought little of him. I was only seventeen, not even out. Besides, it may all be Grandmama's fanciful imagination.'

'And where is Sir Robert now?'

'In London. Grandmama looked in this morning on her way downstairs and told me he had left his card and will call upon us later in the week.'

Tamsyn stood up.

'My dear, I feel in my bones that this is going to be an exciting month. I have not told you half my news, but it will keep. Can I have your promise to join us for a theatre party which my father is arranging? With supper afterwards. I have not been to the theatre in so long, and I do enjoy almost any performance, my critical sense deserts me the moment I enter Drury Lane. A pantomime would be entertaining, nothing too serious.'

Alanna walked with Tamsyn to the door. They paused.

'Thank you. I will be delighted to come. My engagement book is quite empty at present.'

'Not for long, when news gets out that the elegant Miss Gordon is back in town. I will send word of our plans very soon, so that you may keep the date free. By the by, it is possible that Mr Ferguson and Mr Aylward may join our party,' She finished casually.

'I thought as much. *A bientôt, ma chérie.*'

They kissed affectionately and parted, Tamsyn promising to send Hannah to fetch her gift boxes. This caused a slight delay and Tamsyn and her maid escaped only one step ahead of the blue-stocking brigade. They were hard on their heels as Josselin closed the front door and Tamsyn heard Lady

Lucinda's ringing tones echoing through the hall, declaring, '. . . in that case, my dear Esmeralda, strong morality seeks to compensate for intellectual feebleness. I have to tell you, the two are quite incompatible.'

4

Encounter in a Bookshop

'I think it will be best if you wait here, Hannah,' said Tamsyn, as the carriage drew up outside Hatchards bookshop in Piccadilly. 'It is too cold for you to sit outside on the servants' benches and too crowded to bring those big boxes inside. I will only stay a moment.'

Hannah nodded and sank back contentedly in her corner, grateful that she did not have to descend in the keen wind. Tamsyn clutched her bonnet and hurried across the pavement to the shop door. Inside she found the usual group of gentlemen clustered by the fireplace, reading the daily papers and discussing the news in stentorian tones.

'They'll all be moving back for luncheon at Albany soon, Mrs Elsworth,' whispered a voice at her elbow.

Tamsyn smiled and shook her head.

'Sometimes I think your shop is nothing but a fashionable rendezvous, Mr Hatchard,' she teased, following him to the inner recesses of the establishment, where the shelves were lined with new books, bound in leather, tooled and edged in gold. She sniffed appreciatively. 'All fresh, not even a little bit musty. I hope all your books go to good homes.'

John Hatchard's eyes twinkled.

'So do I, m'dear, and by that I mean homes where they will be fingered and read, not left to languish with uncut

35

pages, which I fear is the fate of many books bought with decorative rather than literary intent.'

'I like to think that every book will have at least one owner who will truly appreciate it,' said Tamsyn, 'But I assure you I am here with literary intent. Did you succeed in persuading Mr Colburn to let you have an advance copy of John Evelyn for me? He is such a kind man and a very good printer and I feel guilty for not going to him directly, but . . .'

She hesitated and Mr Hatchard finished for her, 'But he is a great gossip and might let slip to your father that he had seen you.'

She nodded and he patted her shoulder with the familiarity of an old friend.

'Your secret is safe. I sent young Humphrey round to Conduit Street to pick up the volumes with some other items yesterday morning. I told Henry Colburn merely that I wished to do a favour for a very special young lady. Fortunately, he is a romantic soul and did not question me further.'

'I am in your debt. A thousand thanks. Papa will be so happy. I feel so fortunate to have spent most of my life among book people. It does not seem to matter which branch of the book world they are in, printing, publishing, selling . . . even writers, journalists, librarians, I have met very few whom I did not like. In general, I find they are considerate, thoughtful, intelligent people – like you, dear Mr Hatchard.'

The influential bookseller, patronized by no less a royal personage than Queen Charlotte, reddened and cleared his throat. To hide his confusion, he bowed.

'Such a compliment, coming from you, ma'am, does me great honour, for you are uniquely placed moving at ease both in fashionable circles and among the book trade fraternity. And as a writer yourself . . .'

'Hush, Mr Hatchard, if you please. A few articles and poems in ladies' magazines do not entitle me to call myself a writer. But perhaps when my children's tales are published, I shall feel more professional. I put in some good strong morals to make up for my weak drawings – but I wish it could have been the other way around.'

'As your publisher, I feel confident that you have the blend exactly as it should be. Your sketches are charming and the humorous nonsensical behaviour of the animals will be more palatable to the young than many other juvenile works that I could name. The engraver has almost finished his stag for the title page and then when you give me the final two or three tales we can go to press early in the new year.'

'I will be as quick as I can, but there may be a little delay. My friend, Miss Gordon, has just returned from Paris and my father needs my help to entertain two American gentlemen. I love to write, but it is a true test of my ingenuity to produce moral tales without a single instance of death or permanent suffering among the animal characters.' Tamsyn frowned at the very thought and then added cheerfully, 'But I hope you noticed that I did throw in two drownings at the canal lock and a maiming while playing with fire in the blacksmith's forge.'

Mr Hatchard regarded Tamsyn shrewdly.

'I did indeed take note of these calamities and I surmise you were in quite a different humour on the day you wrote that story to the one you are in today. But come with me and we will ask Humphrey Wilmot where he has put Mr Evelyn.'

They found Mr Wilmot in the reading-room at the rear of the shop intently poring over a fore-edge painting with another gentleman. It was Mr John Aylward.

'Ah, Humphrey, there you are,' Mr Hatchard hailed him. He turned to Mr Aylward. 'Excuse me, sir, I fear I must borrow this young man for a few minutes.'

Mr Aylward raised his eyebrows, but observing Tamsyn in the wake of the bookseller, he said courteously. 'To serve a lady, but of course. Good afternoon, Mrs Elsworth.'

Mr Hatchard looked from one to the other in surprise and Tamsyn made haste to perform the introduction. John Aylward smiled, a smile of genuine warmth.

'My dear sir,' he exclaimed, 'Your name is a household word in Philadelphia, and especially in my family. When our book orders arrive from your subscription department my mother's household is quiet and contented for days. My sister, Susannah, says it is a box of delights.'

Mr Hatchard beamed but, remembering his duty, bustled away bearing the hapless Humphrey, an awkward youth, all elbows and knees, in tow. Mr Aylward and Mrs Elsworth watched the proprietor's elegant grey back and neat closely-cropped head disappear through the opening which led into the shop.

'I thought he would be older . . .' began John.

'What a beautiful fore-edge painting,' remarked Tamsyn at the same moment. They both stopped.

'I believe Mr Hatchard is about fifty. He and my father have been friends since before I was born.'

'Thank you for the excellent dinner last night. I always feel that fore-edge paintings are an expensive and wasteful indulgence since most of the time they are hidden on the shelf. It would be better to decorate the spine.'

They stopped again. Tamsyn kept her eyes fixed on the fanned-out edge of the book, which the American held casually but firmly between strong fingers. It was a heavy book and the painting was a delicate pastoral scene of a picnic with a lady in the costume of a century earlier, sitting in a swing.

'Is it a French book?' she asked at length. 'The painting looks like Fragonard or Watteau.'

'Does it?' He straightened the book and the painting disappeared, to be replaced by the usual gilt edge. He opened it and shook his head.

'Not French, rather English or Scottish, I would guess, but a cunning technique.'

'A thing of beauty is a joy for ever,' said Tamsyn, gently touching the book with her finger.

'How true.'

Puzzled by his quizzical tone, Tamsyn looked up and found him regarding her with a very direct and intent expression. Unwilling to admit that she was disconcerted, she raised her chin.

'I am glad you enjoyed your dinner last night. My father enjoyed your company and that of Mr Ferguson very much. I wonder where Mr Hatchard can be, I left my maid waiting in the carriage and she will be hungry for her dinner and vexed with me.'

As if to emphasize her point, Tamyn's stomach gave a hollow rumble. Tamsyn gave Mr Aylward one fleeting glance, and saw him bite his lip, in distaste no doubt. She fled to the door with a muttered word of farewell, clinging to the tattered shreds of her dignity. It was as well for her peace of mind that she did not see the American gentleman bent double with uncontrollable laughter the second after she had quitted the room.

Mr Hatchard met her in the shop and triumphantly pressed into her hands a weighty package tied up with brown string.

He hesitated, delaying her, blithely oblivious to her toe-tapping, glove-fidgeting hints.

'How thoughtless of me, perhaps you wished to examine your purchase? It looks very fine . . . and a most interesting man. My one criticism would be that it is a trifle over-embellished, but I quibble, my dear Mrs Elsworth. It is in truth a handsome production of which Mr Colburn may justly be proud. Worth every penny of five pounds fifteen shillings and sixpence. Were you aware that John Evelyn . . . ?'

Perceiving that he was about to launch into a lengthy disquisition, Tamsyn broke in hastily, 'Forgive me, sir. I fear I cannot stay longer. Hannah is waiting and I know I can depend on your judgement in the matter of the Evelyn volumes. I will examine them later when I am at leisure. I am truly grateful to you for obtaining them for me. Could you do me one more kindness and charge them to my account?'

Mr Hatchard waved her away.

'Of course, of course. Pray let me know how your papa gets on with the great diarist,' he said affably, ushering her once more past the gentlemen and their newspapers. 'I must

return to Mr Aylward. I like to keep abreast of their requirements in the New World. Dear me, I almost said the colonies.
Now that will never do. Don't forget those tales you promised
me. I know what you ladies are like when you start stirring
puddings and other Christmas junketings.'

With this final admonishment he handed her into the
carriage, leaving her a prey to the mixed emotions of indig-
nation, relief and amusement.

On re-entering his premises, Mr Hatchard found his
American customer standing a little apart from the group
of fireplace philosophers. He was ostensibly leafing through
a copy of *Blackwood's Magazine*, but from his attentive attitude, head to one side, lips curling grimly, John Hatchard
surmised that he was lending at least half an ear to the
animated discussion of the group. A portly man, with a florid
countenance and fearsome beak of a nose, was holding the
floor.

'And in my view, republicanism is responsible for all the
evils that one finds in America today, notably immorality,
lack of religion and illiteracy.'

'Well, there I must take issue with you Reddingley,' interposed a soft-spoken, mild-eyed little man, who yet commanded their respectful attention. 'You refer, I imagine to
that scurrilous set of articles in *Blackwood's* a few months
ago, which totally misinterpreted Fearon's book and perhaps
Bristed's also, although I confess I have not read it. I consider writing in that vein to be both spiteful and harmful.
America is a young, but growing country. Surely we can be
magnanimous – in our own interests, as well as theirs. Young
countries are like young people, sometimes boastful or over-
sensitive, but eager to learn and in maturity grateful to those
who have lent a helping hand. I believe it is the responsibility, mission if you will, of a civilized country to share its
culture and traditions with new and developing societies.'

The man called Reddingley snorted and stabbed with his
finger certain lines in a journal which he flourished before
the company.

'Indeed, you are entitled to your opinion, Drayton, but I

refuse to budge one iota. Listen to this, sir, "there is nothing to awaken fancy in that land of dull realities". Not very fertile soil, I fear, for culture and tradition.'

Mr Hatchard glanced apprehensively at John Aylward's impassive visage and stepped forward as if to intervene.

A firm hand descended on his arm and Mr Aylward said quietly, 'Pray do not distress yourself on my account. I have heard such talk before and it will not be settled in a moment. Instead, if you can spare me a little of your time, I would be glad if you could assist me in the selection of some books to send to Philadelphia. Is there anything new by the author of *Waverley*? My sister dotes on his tales . . . and I require some children's books for my mother to give as prizes to the pupils in a charity school in which she takes an interest. She asked particularly that some should be for amusement as well as instruction.'

Mr Hatchard was diverted, as John had intended that he should be; they moved across the room and began to browse amid the well-stocked shelves, conversing amiably as they searched.

'Forgive me, I do not recall the name Aylward on our subscription list,' Mr Hatchard said casually.

'We're probably listed as Windlesham. We answer to both names in the United States – but here I am known as Aylward.' John met the gentleman's eye steadily.

'Oh, of course, sir,' said Mr Hatchard, the soul of discretion. He turned back to the shelves and located a work of possible interest; he remarked over his shoulder, as he stood on a set of library steps and reached precariously, 'There is indeed a new book coming by the author of *Waverley*.'

'Allow me,' John suggested, removing the two volumes without difficulty. Mr Hatchard smiled and sat down on the top step, watching his customer shrewdly as he skimmed the pages and added the books to his pile. The American was quick and decisive, but his taste was excellent. He seemed absorbed, but yet he asked, 'And what book is that, pray?'

'It is an historical romance entitled *Ivanhoe*. Unfortunately,

I do not have a copy at my disposal, although I have a number on order. The publication date is fixed for the end of the month, but I can add your name to the list, if you wish?'

'Please do. Have you any idea of the author's identity?'

Mr Hatchard assumed a cautious expression and answered. 'The world favours Mr Scott, but there are a number of contenders for the honour. I reserve my judgement.'

'How very prudent. Now, advise me. What is suitable reading fare for little girls? The same as for little boys?'

'Oh, by no means, sir,' Mr Hatchard was shocked, 'You mentioned charity pupils, I think, not young ladies of refinement?' He pondered, chin in hand.

'What difference does it make?' queried John, impatiently, 'Given the opportunity, I imagine any young reader can enjoy Perrault's *Fairy Tales* or Mrs Edgeworth's tales.'

Mr Hatchard perceived that despite his gentlemanly appearance and English accent, Mr Aylward harboured republican notions. It also seemed that he would not tolerate fools gladly; Mr Hatchard hastily adjusted his ideas.

'You are familiar, I expect sir, with the productions from John Harris's publishing establishment? There is a new illustrated ABC book from him, called *Nursery Novelties for Little Masters and Misses* or some such title, which I can recommend without reservation. I myself am venturing in the children's book preserve, but I regret that Mrs Elsworth's tales are not yet available.'

John raised his head and regarded Mr Hatchard with a probing eye.

'Elsworth, you mean Edgeworth?'

Mr Hatchard realized too late that he had perhaps betrayed a confidence. However, he was a Christian man and believed in telling the truth.

'No, I mean Mrs Elsworth. She has a considerable reputation as a writer of articles for the ladies' magazines, and er, poems too, of course, and she has almost completed a little collection of animal tales. I expect to publish them in the spring.'

John forebore to question him further. He placed a weighty tome of sermons on top of the heap with a gesture of finality and said casually,

'Well, perhaps you will reserve a copy for me. And now, I suspect I have taken advantage of your kindness and your time. I will take my leave.'

'You wish me to ship your purchases to the Filbert Street address, Mr Aylward?'

'If you please.'

John was tempted to shake Mr Hatchard's hand, but realized that this informal gesture would make the conventional shop owner distinctly uncomfortable. He contented himself with a stiff bow and the two men parted on cordial terms.

John Aylward continued on his way to the London Coffee House on Ludgate Hill where he found James Ferguson in deep talk with several other American travelers. They lingered over a late luncheon and then called once more, by appointment, on Charles Farrell. Mr Aylward half-hoped to see the tantalizing Mrs Elsworth again, but she did not appear and having dealt with their business, the two Americans departed for their hotel and Mr Farrell ate dinner alone with his daughter.

'Well, Papa, did you get the type set for the treatise?' Tamsyn asked, as they began their soup.

'Yes, I did, at some cost to my eyesight. It was one of the most difficult manuscripts that I have ever tackled. I'm mighty glad to be rid of it at last. Young Stephen helped me – he's coming along well, that lad.'

'Hum, I'm sure he is,' she nodded and gazed into space, her spoon suspended in mid-air.

'And how was Hempseed's talk? Diverting, illuminating, tedious?'

'Oh, yes, of course. I mean I expect it was, it must have been, but I don't really know, I didn't go,' she stopped.

The soup plates were removed and Mr Farrell tried again.

'You saw Alanna instead, I take it?'

With an effort Tamsyn pulled her wandering wits together.
'Forgive me, Papa, it has been an eventful day. Alanna
sends you love and kisses and promises to come and see you
very soon in her most stylish Parisian bonnet.'

Mr Farrell beamed. He cherished a soft spot for Miss
Gordon, who was able to twist him around her little finger
without the slightest trouble; Tamsyn had often envied her
this faculty. She occupied the remainder of the meal with
an account of her visit to Lady Molesworthy's household, a
somewhat edited version, suitable for parental ears.

Her father listened attentively and, just as Tamsyn was
preparing to leave him to his port, he startled her by asking,
'And what were you doing at Hatchards over-priced
emporium?'

Tamsyn slowly lifted her napkin to her lips and trying
in vain to emulate Alanna's favourite expression of bland
innocence, she responded, 'I suppose one may have some
secrets at this time of year. Did Hannah tell you she had to
wait for me?'

Mr Farrell measured his glass with care, sipped the deep
amber liquid with relish and regarded his daughter with a
teasing smile.

'No, my child, do not blame the maid. 'Twas Mr John
Aylward who let fall that he had met with you there. Now,
pray leave me in peace. I'll be with you shortly.'

Taken aback by this unexpected revelation, Tamsyn made
a small curtsey to hide her confusion and retreated to the
drawing room. Mr Farrell liked to maintain a certain level
of style and elegance in his private domestic apartments,
although he and his daughter lived above the business premises. Charles Farrell was a hospitable man and when his wife
was alive they had entertained frequently both eminent City
families and among Mrs Farrell's more literary circle, with
a smattering of friends and relatives from the country gentry.
After the deaths of Sarah Farrell and Tamsyn's husband,
Gilbert, the little household in George Street had sunk into
gloom and despondency under the burden of grief. Mr

44

Farrell recovered first; it was not possible for a man of his sociable temperament to remain long in seclusion. He mourned deeply and then turned once more to the task of living; he was seen again in his accustomed haunts and was able to offer support to Tamsyn in her time of sorrow. Perhaps the double loss which she suffered, her mother and her husband, made Tamsyn less resilient. She had taken longer to heal but, she realized now, as she sank down in her mother's faded, brocade-covered chair, that the process of recovery was almost complete. She closed her eyes and relaxed, rubbing her fingers gently on the arm of the chair; the fire crackled and the coal slipped, sending out a warm glow. She dozed and awoke with a jump to find her father replenishing the fire and the coffee set ready on the table. She sat up and reached for the pot.

'I didn't hear Hannah come in,' she said, smiling as she handed Mr Farrell his cup. He helped himself to sugar with a generous wielding of the tongs.

''Tis a pity to have a fine new frock and nowhere to go,' he stirred the sugar meditatively, making a vigorous tinkling sound so that Tamsyn feared for the fine Limoges china. Mr Farrell did not care for the current vogue in French goods and fashions, the result of years of deprivation during the wars.

'I hope you will like it, Papa. I will wear it for you on Christmas Day.'

'French, I suppose?'

'Of course, Papa, Alanna had it made for me by her own modiste in Paris.'

Mr Farrell shook his head and said decisively, 'I think you should wear it to the play. It will be wasted on an old curmudgeon like me.'

'The Play! I had forgotten. Don't tease me, when do we go? Did you mention it to er, the American gentlemen? I have Alanna's promise to accompany us.' Tamsyn was all eagerness, her eyes a deep blue-violet in the candlelight.

Mr Farrell savoured the success of his strategem; he liked

to give pleasure and it was high time, in his opinion, that the young widow indulged in a little frivolity.

'It was not easy to get tickets, but I had a stroke of good fortune. I walked over with our two Americans to *The Times* offices to introduce them to Thomas Barnes and in the course of conversation it transpired that Barnes has reserved a box at Drury Lane for the Christmas season and he offered to place it at our disposal for the first night of a new pantomime called *Jack and the Beanstalk*. I did not ask him, 'twas his suggestion. A kindly gesture, don't ye think?'

'But that's wonderful,' cried Tamsyn, 'Dearest Papa, I'm so happy.'

'Hold hard, my girl, how do ye know the gentlemen were free?'

Tamsyn's mouth fell open in dismay; her father gave a rumbling laugh.

'Nay, nay, I do but tease you. They expressed themselves delighted to bear us company. You'd better send a note to Alanna to keep the night of the twenty-eighth of December free. Do you think her high and mighty ladyship might care to join us?'

Tamsyn blinked at the prospect and pulled a pin from her topknot; her curls came tumbling down in dark profusion.

'Fiddle-de-dee,' she said, 'I think it would be a good idea to invite her; she's lonely and likes to be included, but she may not come. She seldom goes to the play.'

'Likes the sound of her own voice too much to listen to others,' suggested Mr Farrell drily. He grinned. 'I can understand that.'

Tamsyn pricked her finger with the hairpin.

'Ouch! Did Mr Aylward say anything more about Hatchards?'

'Not a great deal, but I gather he and John Hatchard got along famously and he bought a quantity of books. A man of some sense, but his world is not our world . . .' He paused and then said abruptly, 'He asked after your writing. I told him he should apply to you, but that I doubted he would glean much since you are always very close about your work until it is published. Now, go to bed, Mrs Elsworth, your hair is down and your finger dripping blood. It's been a long day and you are in sore need of rest and refurbishment.'

At the door he hesitated and said, 'Lord knows, I want you to be happy, lass, but don't lose your heart to a foreigner. English roses don't transplant easily – and young Stephen has a way to go before he'll be your equal in setting type.'

Tamsyn tiptoed to kiss his stubbled cheek.

'Don't be so foolish, Papa. What can you be thinking of? I met John Aylward for the first time yesterday.'

But Charles Farrell, wise in the ways of women, was not to be mislead. He watched his daughter climb the stair, candle held high.

'Stars in the eyes, absentmindedness, all the signs,' he muttered, as he damped down the fire and quietly made his way to bed.

5

A Striking Resemblance

A few days before Christmas, Tamsyn and her father were
bidden by Lady Lucinda to attend a small evening party in
Portman Square. The guest of honour was to be Sir Robert
Hawksmore, newly returned from a tour of the eastern Medi-
terranean.

Tamsyn had passed the preceding week in a flurry of
seasonal preparations. When her mother was alive the Far-
rells had always held a supper dance for the workmen in
the print shop, their wives and sweethearts and a few guests
from the printing fraternity on Christmas Eve and this year
Mr Farrell had decided to reinstitute the custom. Consequently, Tamsyn had been preoccupied for days in helping
the cook with the baking, doing marketing with Hannah
and in between times, writing seasonal notes and messages
to friends and relatives at a distance. The notes for her last
two animal tales lay neglected in her bureau drawer; there
would be time enough for those after the holiday season,
she consoled herself on the night of Lady Lucinda's party
as she rummaged in the drawer for a length of string which
was needed in the kitchen, the usual supply having been
exhausted by the unprecedented demand generated by Mrs
Jennings, the cook.

'No, Sam, I'm sorry, I don't have time to play,' she said,
giving the cat's head a quick rub when he jumped up beside

her on the desk and extended a tentative paw to pat the string.

'Come along, boy. We'll see if we can find you some scraps.'

Tamsyn hurried downstairs, with Sam in close attendance. She found Mrs Jennings with her feet up by the fire, enjoying a well-deserved cup of tea. With the usual feline instinct for comfort and self-gratification, Sam leaped on to her lap and began to purr.

'Mrs Jennings, please be an angel and find Sam some little bits of pastry. See, I have stolen his string to tie up your puddings.'

Tamsyn laid the string on the large, well-scrubbed table and smiled at the older woman, who nodded placidly.

'Yes, Miss Tamsyn, mum, don't you worry about Sam. He won't starve, he's a good mouser, I'll give 'im that, but 'ee knows I allus keeps some choice morsels on the top shelf in the larder. You run now, miss. Hannah went up to your room with the elderberry lotion ten minutes ago.'

Tamsyn stretched out her hands, surveying them ruefully.

'I doubt if all the elderberry lotion in London can make any difference in time for the party tonight.'

'Don't you fret, mum, 'tis a concoction which I made up from a recipe wot's bin 'anded down in my family for generations. I mixed in some ground fumitory, which is healin'. Yer 'ands will be soft 'n white again in no time, and them fine ladies at the party will never guess at all the 'ard work you've bin doin'.'

'Well then, my faith is in you, Mrs Jennings. Thank you. Goodnight and you too, Sam.'

Tamsyn sped upstairs and found Hannah waiting to transform her from kitchen maid to young lady going to a party.

'I feel like Cinderella,' said Tamsyn, some three quarters of an hour later, as she stood before the looking glass, while Hannah stepped back and regarded her handiwork with approval. 'You must tell Mrs Jennings her lotion is nothing short of miraculous – even the inkstains have disappeared.'

'It's a pity you couldn't wear your new gown from Paris,

Miss Tamsyn, but white satin suits you. I 'opes you have a nice evening.'

'Thank you, Hannah. Could you hand me my gloves and my shawl. I will wear my new gown for the theatre party next week. That will give you plenty of time to make the adjustment on the hem. I rather dread this evening, it's so long since I went much in society.'

She shivered, then, catching sight of the little maid's concerned face, she stooped and gave her a quick embrace. A moment later, she was gone, leaving Hannah to have her supper and a good gossip with Mrs Jennings by the kitchen fire.

Mrs Elsworth allowed no sign of inner trepidation to appear on her face, when she entered the library of Lady Molesworthy on her father's arm at a little after nine o'clock. Her ladyship rustled forward to greet them. She wore a gown of deep tawny-orange taffeta, enhanced by a dazzling array of chains and gems which hung from every available space and paradoxically made her appear both tiny and formidable at the same time. She raised her lorgnette and dropped her cane. With admirable promptness Charles Farrell bent and retrieved it. Lady Lucinda tapped him on the shoulder with a regal gesture that made Tamsyn think of Good Queen Bess.

'Charles, how gallant. You are a noble soul quite wasted on this prosaic age. 'Tis good of you to venture from your fireside on such a cold night and Tamsyn too. Good evening, my dear, you will find some members of our literary circle here this evening and we're gathered in the library because Sir Robert has brought some bits of pottery and sculpture for us to examine. Not really my line of country, give me a good book any day, eh Charles? But it doesn't do for us all to be interested in the same things. Ah, Mr Hempseed, there you are. Be so good as to show Mrs Elsworth Sir Robert's gleanings from antiquity. You come and sit with me, Charles, I'll introduce you to Robert by and by when the crush has subsided. I see that Esmeralda Lovett has him cornered at present, but I'm confident he is more than equal to the occasion. Alanna will be down directly. Have you seen her since her return from the Continent? A marked improvement, I think you'll find.'

Mr Farrell was borne inexorably away, leaving Tamsyn no choice but to accompany Oliver Hempseed to a large table covered with a large quantity of unidentifiable items, mostly broken fragments of heads and feet. Tamsyn's gaze wandered idly over the collection and came to rest on the center-piece, a well-preserved section of an ancient Greek male torso. Tamsyn raised her eyes quickly and met the quizzical smile of a pair of grey-green eyes watching her from across the table. She stared hard at the gentleman, swayed a little and clutched the table for support; on first glance he was almost the exact likeness of Mr John Aylward.

Mr Hempseed observed her distress and attributed it to the very natural embarrassment which any young lady might be expected to feel on her first encounter with the lack of modesty which had been customary in classical times. He had felt all along that the statue should have been less prominently displayed in mixed company, but Lady Molesworthy had overruled him, saying firmly that she had not invited any silly milk-and-water misses to her party and that her blue-stocking ladies were quite familiar with the fashions prevalent in fifth-century Athens. The librarian, greatly daring, put his arm about Tamsyn's waist and cried,

'Make way, if you please, Mrs Elsworth is feeling faint.'

Tamsyn stiffened.

'I beg you, sir, no fuss. See. I'm quite recovered.' She pulled away from him, aware of a sea of curious eyes watching her around the table.

The room felt hot; dimly she heard a deep voice saying, 'Sit here, ma'am. Give us a little space. Fetch some water, Hempseed, show a little initiative, man. Does anyone have some smelling salts? Thank you, Miss Lovett. Now leave us in peace for a few moments and I assure you this lady will feel much more the thing.' A fan was plied energetically and the sal volatile was passed close to her reluctant nose.

Tamsyn sniffed and opened her eyes to meet those of the unknown gentleman. They were sitting in an alcove near Mr Hempseed's sanctum and the rest of the company was kept at bay by the gentleman's broad back. Tamsyn's eyes widened as she absorbed the details of his appearance. He was tall, with a nose to rival Wellington's own, hair darker than Mr Aylward's, she now observed, but thick and springy. The most remarkable feature was the chin, jutting and firm, an exact replica of the American's. She sneezed. The gentleman put the stopper back in the bottle and placed the fan in her lap. Tamsyn clutched it and sat up.

'Forgive me, sir. We have not been introduced. I am Tamsyn Elsworth.'

'Robert Hawksmore, at your service.' He regarded her searchingly, brows drawn together. At length he said abruptly, 'Ye don't look like a woman who gets the vapours from exposure to statues, nude or otherwise. What's the matter? Stays too tight?'

Tamsyn laughed and shook her head.

'I don't think so, though I confess I haven't worn this dress since Waterloo,' she paused.

'Well, I shouldn't wear it again. White ain't your colour, Miss Elsworth!'

Tamsyn lifted her chin and retorted, 'I'm Mrs Elsworth, Sir Robert and white makes a pleasant change from black.'

His eyes narrowed.

'There was an Elsworth with the Duke at Waterloo. Any relation?'

'My husband, Gilbert, was one of his aides. Not a regular one, you understand, but after so many fell. Gil fell too. We brought him home, but an infection set in after he lost his leg. He died that autumn.'

Sir Robert nodded.

'I remember him. Slight acquaintance only. Understood he was a brave officer, but bookish too. Unusual that. We had some talk the night before the battle at the Duchess of Richmond's ball. She held it in the coachhouse. Can't think why we all went, she was an ill-tempered woman, but His

Grace had a liking for her. You were not there, I think?'

'No, but if I had been I should not have expected you to recall, among so many and the battle must have blurred the impression of previous events,' said Tamsyn gently.

'I should have remembered,' he spoke positively. 'Strange, but all the events of that time are indelibly inscribed in my memory. Your husband and I talked of book collecting and he gave me the names of several rare booksellers in Brussels. Unfortunately, I did not have time to seek them out. He also recommended a printer and binder in London. Said he was some relation.'

'I expect he meant my father, Charles Farrell. His work is all around you, Sir Robert. My godmother, Lady Lucinda, is constantly giving him commissions.'

Sir Robert smiled, a smile of peculiar charm, which again reminded Tamsyn fleetingly of John Aylward.

'Then, Mrs Elsworth, we are remotely connected, for my aunt Angelica married Gerard Molesworthy, who was Lady Lucinda's brother-in-law? Do I have that right? Yes, I think so. Therefore, I must be related, at least in spirit, to any god-daughter of Lady Lucinda's. Don't you agree?'

Tamsyn laughed at his logic, but sobered as he took her hand and said, 'Good, your colour has come back. Before we rejoin the party may I have your permission to call upon you soon? This is the first sensible conversation I have had since I returned to this town of fribbles and fops. Forgive my remarks about your gown, clumsy of me.'

'But true. Please do call, Sir Robert. And now, I fear I have monopolized you for far too long. You are the guest of honour, sir.'

Lady Lucinda, who had just become aware that Sir Robert was not mingling with the company as it was his duty to do, began to bear down upon them, but a diversion was created simultaneously by the entrance of Alanna, enchanting in a gown of pale pink, with rosebuds in her hair, and Josselin who announced sonorously that refreshments were laid out in the Drawing Room.

A general shuffle through the great double doors commenced and Sir Robert whispered in Tamsyn's ear, 'And I still do not know why the sight of me, or my statue, caused you to be overcome. Do you care to enlighten me?'

Mrs Elsworth edged past the table of antiquities, smiled mischievously over her shoulder and replied, 'No, Sir Robert, I wish to preserve the element of mystery, at least for the present. But I do thank you for your timely aid. I will give you a hint. Let us say that I felt the way one does when a ghost walks over one's grave.'

The library was almost deserted, but Sir Robert showed a disposition to linger. Tamsyn made a quick, decisive curtsey and offered her hand, which he promptly kissed. A loud throat clearing and the sharp tapping of a cane heralded the return of Lady Lucinda.

Belatedly Tamsyn recalled that Sir Robert was destined for Alanna and, not wishing to incur her ladyship's displeasure, she moved hurriedly towards the door, saying, 'So foolish of me to feel faint. It must have been the heat. Pray give me Miss Lovett's smelling bottle. I would like to thank her, most efficacious.'

Lady Molesworthy appeared, chin out-thrust, and glanced suspiciously from one to the other. Sir Robert raised a sardonic eyebrow but made no comment and Tamsyn, to her annoyance, felt her colour rising. Knowing of old her godmother's sharp tongue, she feared the worst and was not disappointed.

'I was not aware that you two were so well-acquainted,' her ladyship remarked coolly.

In other circumstances Tamsyn would have admired the way in which Lady Lucinda compensated for the smallness of her stature by the dignity of her bearing; she felt guilty although she knew herself to be innocent.

Sir Robert, apparently, was made of sterner stuff. He may not have been accustomed to being bullied by little old ladies, but he knew how to deal with them.

'Your ladyship supposes incorrectly. Mrs Elsworth and I are not well-acquainted, but 'tis my earnest desire that that may soon be remedied. However, I was acquainted with

Mrs Elsworth's husband and that circumstance has allowed us to er, penetrate to a deeper level of understanding than is usual on a first meeting. I trust your ladyship has no objection?'

Tamsyn wished that the ground would open and swallow her up. Lady Molesworthy, while not going quite that far, perceived that she had been a little overzealous in her eagerness to protect Alanna's interests; and besides, she was really very fond of Tamsyn. She raised her lorgnette and met Sir Robert's flinty grey gaze, which held an expression of unyielding determination. Lady Lucinda's hand trembled and she turned to Tamsyn for support.

'This man would have frightened me out of my wits when I was your age. I should give him a wide berth, if I were you, my dear.'

Tamsyn smiled in relief that the storm had passed and slipped forward to take her ladyship's elbow, saying, 'You are quite right, Godmama. I shall avoid him for the rest of the evening.'

True to her word, Tamsyn did her best to keep at a distance from Sir Robert, though she noticed that he was often within earshot and several times she caught him watching her across the room. This was disconcerting and she redoubled her efforts to concentrate on Mr Hempseed's intelligent remarks as to the propriety of removing antique works of art from their original sites.

'In my view, classical sculptures should be viewed in their proper setting,' he finished, reaching for his glass and turning courteously to Tamsyn for her opinion.

'That is all very well if one can visit the proper setting, but the difficulties and hazards of travel do not always make that very practicable, Mr Hempseed,' she observed. 'For my part, I am most grateful to men like Sir William Hamilton and Lord Elgin, who have shared their treasures with the public in the British Museum. However, it is a problem, I grant you. One would not wish the great monuments of Greece and Rome to be completely plundered in order to furnish the museums of the world.'

She bit a sandwich meditatively and turned the full force of her deep blue eyes on the hapless librarian, who coughed and spilled some wine. While he mopped himself up, Tamsyn allowed her glance to wander round the room, noting idly the trailing Christmas greens and the two tall Christmas candles on the sideboard. What was the matter with her, tonight? Why was she teasing poor Mr Hempseed? It was undeniably invigorating to test her powers, but she must not indulge in deliberate flirtation. It seemed so long since she had flexed those particular wings. She caught Sir Robert's shrewd eye, put up her chin and inclined her head, before turning back to her companion contritely.

'Tell me, Mr Hempseed, do they have any museums with classical pieces in America? Do they have any museums at all? I was most intrigued when you mentioned the other day that you have visited that country. Did you travel widely?' She heard her own voice, rattling on, but part of her mind was elsewhere, brooding on the burning topic of why Sir Robert's mention of 'stays' had produced no flicker of embarrassment in her bosom. Would she have felt the same had John Aylward asked the question? She did not think so. Why were the two men so alike and yet so different? She said at random, 'And what did you think of Philadelphia, sir?'

'Quite an old city, by American standards, but clean and neat. Orderly and still with a strong Quaker influence. Dr Franklin lived there for many years. I was pleased to find that the Library Company which he founded was flourishing. Many of the main streets were named after trees – odd the things one remembers.'

Tamsyn set down her glass.

'Yes indeed, but one forgets so much too. I had forgotten that Benjamin Franklin lived there. You did refer to the printer, I presume?'

'Yes, but he was much more. Did you ever read his autobiography, Mrs Elsworth?'

'Hum, no. I beg your pardon, what else did he do?'

Mr Hempseed launched into a lengthy sketch of the great

American's life. Tamsyn pondered, why did Sir Robert make her feel like a sensible woman, while Mr Aylward reduced her to a silly missish state, where she felt barely out of the schoolroom. And why, indeed, did she care about the emotions aroused by these two men, both of whom were almost total strangers to her? She sighed.

'I fear I bore you, Mrs Elsworth,' said Oliver Hempseed quietly.

'Oh no, sir. I'm just a little tired tonight. So many things to do just before Christmas. You should write a book about your experiences in America – such reminiscences are much in demand, so Mr Hatchard tells me. Will you be celebrating the holiday with family or friends, Mr Hempseed?' Tamsyn looked directly at the man beside her and observed that he had taken unusual care with his appearance tonight. His brown coat was well-brushed and a white waistcoat and intricately folded neck-cloth enhanced the general air of elegance which he projected.

'I have lost touch with my family and my friends are here,' he replied, polishing his spectacles. He peered at her with a certain myopic intensity.

She jumped up, saying lightly, 'Then you must come to our party on Friday night, Mr Hempseed. It will be good for you to get out of your library for a little while. But you must promise me you will not take refuge in a corner with Mr Barnes and Mr Harris. There will be dancing and games, and cards, of course. Come at eight, if you please.'

Relieved to have escaped, Mrs Elsworth threaded her way across the room, in search of her father and Alanna. She was detained frequently to exchange seasonal greetings with members of the literary society and she paused for a few moments to thank Miss Lovett for the loan of her smelling salts. She liked the lady who was very proud of her patrician features, noble brow, strongly curving nose and receding chin. Esmeralda Lovett was of indeterminate age, but very decided opinions and she did not allow Lucinda Molesworthy to browbeat her. They exchanged a few words on the subject of the rival merits of Greek versus Roman sculpture. It was a favourite topic which Miss Lovett and Lady Molesworthy had debated many times, Miss Lovett stoutly defending the Roman style (she had once visited Rome in her youth and the experience had left a permanent mark), while her ladyship preferred (on the basis of no experience whatsoever) the 'purity and simplicity' of the Greeks. Tamsyn said tactfully that she thought there was a great deal to be said in favour of togas.

Sir Robert, who chanced to overhear this remark, murmured as she passed by, 'Do you think it would improve my statue if I draped him in a toga?'

Tamsyn refused to be drawn. She smiled but shook her head and Sir Robert fell into step beside her. He was still at her side when she arrived at the sofa where her father was sitting, enjoying a comfortable coze with Alanna. Mr Farrell glanced up and saw them.

He regarded Sir Robert with unfeigned astonishment, but before he could speak Alanna cried, 'My dear, where have you been this age? I was telling Uncle Charles that I have been home nearly two weeks and you have only spent one afternoon with me. Always excuses, "I must go marketing, I must write letters, I'm needed at home". And Sir Robert, forgive me, have you met Mrs Elsworth's father? This is our guest of honour, Uncle Charles, Sir Robert Hawksmore. Sir Robert, may I introduce Mr Charles Farrell?'

The two men regarded one another in silence for a moment. Then Mr Farrell heaved himself to his feet and bowed. Sir Robert responded gravely.

These formalities completed, he flicked an imaginary speck of fluff from his sleeve and remarked, 'I'm a trifle puzzled, Mr Farrell, I must confess. When your daughter first saw me she nearly swooned and when you saw me you looked as if I could have knocked you down with a feather. No doubt there is a rational explanation?'

The older man nodded and said calmly, 'The explanation is perfectly simple, Sir Robert. You bear a striking resemblance to another gentleman of our acquaintance.'

'Indeed? I was not aware that I had a double, you interest

58

me extremely. Why have I not met this gentleman, I wonder?'

Mr Farrell hesitated.

At length he said, 'It is unlikely that you would move in the same circles. The gentleman is one of the printing fraternity, newly arrived from America.'

Sir Robert frowned, but said dismissively, 'An odd coincidence certainly, but probably no more. Perhaps you could furnish me with his name and I will seek him out. I may have some distant cousins in the New World. What is his name?'

'John Aylward,' answered Mr Farrell. Sir Robert showed no sign of recognition.

'Windlesham was our family name. But he may be a distant connection. I will enquire.' He turned to Alanna, who was not best pleased to be ignored, and said, with a hint of malice, 'Forgive me, m'dear, I have neglected to tell you how charmingly you look tonight. Such neglect must be rare in your experience. Do try and persuade Mrs Elsworth to wear pink, I have already suggested that white drains her natural colour.'

'And makes me look quite hagged. Yes, I know, thank you very much, Sir Robert.'

Tamsyn spoke humorously and turned to her father, who appeared inclined to huff and puff about a fellow who set himself up like Beau Brummell to be an arbiter of ladies' fashions. She sat down beside Mr Farrell and said soothingly 'Alanna has given me a beautiful gown of deep pink from Paris, Sir Robert, but I did not wear it tonight because it needed some minor alteration.' She smiled apologetically at her friend. 'But Papa, Sir Robert was acquainted with Gil. They met in Brussels and Gil recommended you as the best printer and binder in all London. Sir Robert is a collector of rare books in addition to his other interests.'

This information created a diversion and the two men began to converse amiably about Sir Robert's recent acquisitions. Tamsyn relaxed and was able to pull Alanna aside for a private word, under cover of a general movement to depart.

They stood together in the hallway and Tamsyn said quickly, 'I'm sorry to have missed seeing you when you called on Papa, but I do have work I must do, Alanna. I'm not a lady of leisure . . .'

'Like me, you would say,' Alanna finished for her. She smiled and gave her a peck on the cheek. 'I understand, my dear, but I shall expect to see your new frock at the play next week. Uncle Charles has persuaded Grandmama to join the party, though she may not stay for supper afterwards. Is not that wonderful?'

Tamsyn nodded, but her mind was elsewhere.

'How do you find Sir Robert? I'm dying of curiosity?'

Alanna wrinkled her nose and pursed her lips.

'He reminds me of some Gothic tale, Tammy. So stern and unbending and always talking of his old marbles. He makes me shiver and I hear myself saying all kinds of stupid and frivolous things, which I don't mean, in my nervousness.'

Tamsyn was surprised.

'It's not like you to be nervous. I always admire your social poise.'

Alanna squeezed her hand.

'I expect it's because Grandmama is always throwing out hints. It's difficult to behave normally. But he spoke differently to you, more respectfully. I have never seen him appear so, so human. Perhaps you should marry him.'

They giggled, but Tamsyn shook her head.

The last of the party began to drift into the hall, Sir Robert and Mr Farrell last of all, with Lady Lucinda between them. 'Goodnights' and 'Merry Christmases' were exchanged, with many thanks for a delightful evening.

Tamsyn and her father sank back in Lady Molesworthy's luxurious carriage with contented sighs.

Tamsyn said, 'Should we have told Sir Robert about Mr Aylward, Papa?'

In the darkness, her father chuckled.

'A striking resemblance, Tamysn. It could not remain a secret for long, even if it were desirable, but it surely will set the cat among the pigeons and no mistake.'

'What can you mean, Papa? Do you know something of this relationship which you have not told me?'

'Perhaps, but it's none of our affair.'

Tamsyn leaned forward impatiently.

'We have already meddled, although quite innocently – at least on my part. Papa, I beg you, tell me the whole.'

Mr Farrell patted her hand and said provokingly, 'What curious creatures women do be.' Then he relented, settled himself back in his corner and said cautiously, 'Now, this must go no further, at present.' Tamsyn promised eagerly and he went on, 'John Aylward is the heir to Oak Place. If he can prove his credentials satisfactorily, he will disinherit Sir Robert Hawksmore. What do you say to that, eh, my child?'

6

Christmas Festivities

On Christmas Eve, at about nine o'clock in the evening, Mr Aylward and Mr Ferguson presented themselves once more at the door of Mr Farrell's establishment in George Street. They were obliged to ply the wolf's head knocker several times before they could make themselves heard. A young man in his shirtsleeves with a half empty glass in his hand, opened the door wide. They stepped inside and were greeted by a blast of warm air and the aromatic scents of the season, bayberry candles, oak and apple woodsmoke and the elusive, but pungent spices of the Wassail bowl.

'Welcome, sirs, welcome,' said the young man with slightly tipsy dignity, 'Pray let me take your coats, for Hannah is dancing with the Master and Mrs Elsworth is helping Cook set up the supper tables in Mr Farrell's study. One moment, if you please.' He disappeared down the dimly-lit passage, bearing their outer garments, but returned speedily and ushered them before him with an engaging grin, 'Age before beauty, or so my mother taught me. I'm Stephen de Lacey, Mr Farrell's assistant.'

The two Americans responded with brief introductions as they entered the spacious workroom, transformed tonight into a large hall, brightly lit with candles and decked with greenery, including the many-berried holly and a large bunch of mistletoe, which had been hung strategically near the main entrance. A line of tall windows which ran down the left of the room had been covered with skilful paintings representing the twelve days of Christmas and at the far end an enormous log blazed in the fireplace. The work tables had been pushed back against the walls, to clear a space for dancing and a lively country dance was in progress as the three men edged their way to the right, squeezing through the throng of chattering onlookers until they reached Stephen's goal, the table whereon reposed the Wassail bowl. Their glasses filled, James at once plunged into an exhaustive enquiry concerning London tailors. Mr de Lacey's replies proving most helpful, the talk turned to deeper subjects such as horseflesh (about which Stephen knew little), guns and gunmakers (where he did rather better) and the rival merits of republican and monarchist states (where they agreed, most amiably, to disagree). It was apparent to John that the sharp, stocky Englishman and the tall, dreamy American had much in common, not only professionally, and would soon become fast friends. He sipped the warm, sweet liquid and allowed his attention to wander. The dance had ended and the fiddlers were taking some refreshment. The floor cleared briefly as the groups reformed and John was amused to see Sam, the kitchen cat, stretched at his ease in front of the fire with all four paws extended, quite oblivious to the noise and confusion around him.

Tamsyn, emerging from the supper room with a plateful of mince pies, caught sight of Mr Aylward in this unguarded moment. He raised his eyes and saw her, dressed in a seasonal gown of plaid taffeta, half hidden by a large white apron. They smiled and Tamsyn approached, proffering the pastries.

'Good Evening, Mr Aylward. Cats are an example to us all, are they not? So placid and contented, dear Sam, except when he is hunting, of course. He is an accomplished mouser, I regret to say.'

John munched his pie meditatively.

'Surely it should be a matter for congratulation, rather than regret?'

63

Tamsyn set down the plate and shook her head.

'Well, yes and no. I am quite fond of mice and have used them in several stories. I do not care to see their heads bitten off like lollipops and crunched up with quite unnecessary relish.'

John brushed crumbs from his elegant white waistcoat and Tamsyn recalled belatedly that mice were scarcely a fit topic for a Christmas feast. Her mind leapt to the interesting information which her father had imparted concerning the heir to Oak Place. She had had little time to ponder the implications of this revelation, but it now occurred to her that Oliver Hempseed had been invited to their party and he would undoubtedly remark the likeness between Sir Robert and Mr Aylward. She had been sworn to secrecy, but did this include John Aylward himself? she wondered. It was indeed no affair of hers, except insofar as it affected her friend, Alanna, whose betrothal to Sir Robert Hawksmore was all but announced; And what of Lady Molesworthy? She was a distant connection of Sir Robert's. Was she aware of the existence of a rival claimant? It was odd, now that she thought of it, that Sir Robert had not yet claimed his inheritance. However, he had been abroad when old Sir Jeremy Windlesham died some months ago. She could not remember exactly when he had died, but it had been well-reported in the Society columns. She supposed it took time to wind up the affairs of a large estate. It was all most intriguing. She regarded Mr Aylward covertly out of the corner of her eye and found him watching her steadily.

She said at random, 'Are you observing us closely, sir, so that you may write an article on quaint Christmas customs in England? It must be hard to be away from home at the holiday season. Do you eat mince pies in America?'

'Yes to all three questions, Mrs Elsworth, although you slant your enquiries a little unkindly. James and I are most grateful for your father's and your hospitality and would not think of abusing it by describing your living traditions as quaint. Mince pies and most of the other delicacies of the English table are well-known in Philadelphia, I assure you.

I do miss my family very much at this time of year. My mother and my sisters and their families will gather at our home on Filbert Street and they will observe the season much as you do, I imagine, with feasting and churchgoing and visiting with friends. I do intend to write an article on the kindness shown by many when one is away from home at Christmastime. It will not contain a single carping or critical note, I promise you.'

'Then no one will read it, sir,' Tamsyn rejoined sharply, for she felt the implied rebuke more than she cared to admit. Mr Aylward's face fell and she stretched out her hand, saying impulsively, 'Forgive me, of course they will read it. We are so ignorant here of American ways and that can make us cruel. But I must not monopolize you. I see Papa over there trying to catch your eye. He's standing under the third day of Christmas with Mr Harris and Mr Hatchard. Supper will be ready soon.'

'Those Christmas paintings are remarkable, very effective,' said John. 'Where did you obtain them? I should like to send a set to my mother.'

Recognizing this as an olive branch, Tamsyn blushed and responded,

'I painted them. At least the design was mine and some of the apprentices helped me colour them. Perhaps I can do another set for your mother, if you really think she would like them.'

'Of all things. I know you are busy, but pray do not go before you promise me a dance. After supper, very well. I shall look forward to it. Your servant, ma'am.'

He executed a low bow with something of a flourish and threaded his way across the floor. Tamsyn watched him go with a half smile. She saw him greeted by her father and his cronies before she turned away with a sigh and re-entered the supper room to resume her duties as hostess.

She cast an expert eye over the groaning board, moved the ham a fraction to the right, picked up the crumbs which had been dropped by a young guest who could not wait to eat until the appointed hour and gave Hannah a nod of approval. The maid, still flushed from her exertions on the dance floor, had donned a voluminous apron to protect her Sunday best frock and stood ready with the taper to light the Christmas candles which had been placed at either end of the sideboard, to illuminate the plum puddings and pastries, apples and oranges, nuts and raisins and all manner of sweetmeats. The candles were lit with some ceremony and Mr Farrell wished his men and their families the peaceful, hopeful blessings of the season. Everyone began to converge in the relatively small space afforded by their host's inner sanctum. Tamsyn slipped out by the back door, which led past stockrooms and store cupboards and then divided, one passage leading to the kitchen and other domestic offices, while the second curved under the stairs and rejoined the entrance hall. This part of the building was old, worn and stone-flagged. She paused to catch her breath; it was cool and quiet, the noise from the merrymakers muffled by the thick walls. Suddenly a door opened and there came a rush of feet from the direction of the kitchen. She pressed against the stairwell to avoid being trampled by Stephen and James Ferguson, one bearing a tray of jam tarts and the other a large jug of cider.

Catching sight of her in the nick of time Stephen exclaimed, greatly daring, 'Come and enjoy the party, Mrs Elsworth. You've worked so hard and I know for a fact you haven't danced all evening. James and I will lend Mrs Jennings and Hannah a hand.'

'But Mr Ferguson is a guest,' protested Tamsyn weakly.

'Do please call me James, Mrs Elsworth. I like to help, it makes me feel at home, pray don't forbid it,' begged the young American with such a comically imploring expression that Tamsyn threw up her hands in despair.

'Oh very well, if you insist. Don't forget to eat something yourselves.'

'Never fear, we have first pick of the larder. What Cook's eye doesn't see . . .' They grinned and went on their way.

'Thank you Stephen, thank you James,' she called after them. They waved and disappeared.

66

With renewed strength, Tamsyn ran up the back stairs to her room to bathe her face and tidy her hair. For once her unruly curls obeyed, she applied a touch of scent behind her ears, removed a smudge of dirt from her cheek and, gazing earnestly in her looking-glass, pronounced herself tolerably satisfied with her appearance; not that anyone would notice a respectable widow, but for her own self-esteem it was necessary to be neat and clean. She wondered if the taffeta gown had been a mistake; without the apron it glowed brilliantly red and green. She shook her head, too late now to change it. The party would be over while she dithered in her chamber. She slipped her fan over her wrist and hurried to snuff the candle.

Sitting on the lowest step, Tamsyn found Oliver Hempseed, dressed all in black like the spectre at the feast, with an empty plate and glass beside him. Her heart sank, for he was quite alone. She inched past him, with a word of greeting. On hearing her voice, he jumped to his feet, and addressed her with unwonted animation.

'Ah, there you are at last, my dear Mrs Elsworth. I feared that perhaps some mishap had overtaken you or that the joyfulness of the season had proved too much for your gentle spirit to bear. I have looked everywhere for you.'

Tamsyn was rather inclined to resent his proprietorial tone.

She said distantly, 'Mr Hempseed, I am quite well. Was there something particular which you wished to say to me?'

Aware that he had presumed too far, he made haste to mend matters.

'Yes, indeed, ma'am. I noticed during my circumambulation of the dance floor, that there was a certain gentleman in converse with your father. At first I thought it was Sir Robert Hawksmore, but then I realized this was not so, although the resemblance is most marked. Can you enlighten me as to his identity, Mrs Elsworth?'

He rubbed his thick-lensed spectacles on his sleeve before replacing them. He bent his head, giving Tamsyn the uncomfortable sensation that a bird of prey was hanging over her.

She said, 'He is one of the American gentlemen whom I mentioned to you the other day. You recall he was at dinner with us the day Miss Gordon returned home? His name is John Aylward and I believe he may be related to Sir Robert, though distantly.'

'Indeed. Do they know one another? Have they met, I wonder?'

Tamsyn was a little surprised by his persistent curiosity, but she replied, 'I do not know. I was myself taken aback by the resemblance when I met Sir Robert at my Godmother's, and Papa noticed it too. Sir Robert told us that he had relatives in America and mentioned that he would seek out Mr Aylward, but I do not know if he has done so.'

'They are very alike,' mused Mr Hempseed, 'Sir Robert is older, of course, and has a more sallow complexion. I should guess he is an inch or two shorter, but they might pass for brothers easily.'

By this time they had moved and were standing in the doorway. From this vantage point they had a clear view of John Aylward, who was perched on a pile of trays of type, with a plate on his knee and Mr Rudolph Ackermann, the well-known printseller and publisher at his side.

As they watched, Mr Farrell appeared and hailed his old friend, 'Ah, there you are Ackermann, my dear fellow. Hannah is setting up a couple of card tables for us in Tamsyn's sitting room above stairs. When supper is over we will leave these young people to frolic to their heart's content, while we broach a bottle or two in peace and comfort. I'm glad ye two have met. You know, Mr Aylward, that Mr Ackermann is almost my neighbour for his shop is on the Strand, less than five minutes' walk from door to door?'

John smiled and nodded, but his reply was inaudible to the watchers by the door, for the fiddlers were striking up again, and there came a scraping of chairs and general movement, as the company moved aside to make space for the dancers.

Mr Ackermann and Mr Farrell came towards Tamsyn and her companion. She greeted the famous printseller affectionately.

He beamed at her and said, 'I am disappointed, my dear, that you have still not persuaded your father to have gas lighting. Such a marvellous utility, it cannot be equalled for fine work. But I must not keep you when you will want to be dancing. My friend Charles has promised me a fine port in honour of the season. Happy Christmas, and to you also, Mr Hempseed.'

The would-be card-players retired upstairs.

Her ladyship's librarian muttered in Tamsyn's ear, 'Demmed foreigner. I can't understand why your father invites him.'

Tamsyn drew herself up haughtily.

'It is not for you or I to question my father's wishes, sir. As it happens, Mr Ackermann has long been my kind mentor when it comes to drawing and colouring. I am much attached to him and quite at a loss to comprehend your prejudice. Can it be that you are envious of his success, perhaps? Does your intolerance extend to Americans also? I think it might be unwise for me to introduce you to them.'

'It was an ill-judged remark. I beg you will overlook it, Mrs Elsworth. I fear my experiences on the Continent, during and after the French wars have clouded my mind. Will you be so good as to forgive me? I rarely generalize in such a foolish way. I meant no offence.'

Tamsyn gave him a warm smile, so friendly that John Aylward, observing her from afar, wished it had been directed at him.

'Poor Mr Hempseed. How scarred we all are by those dreadful years. We will think no more about it. Come now and eat a little more. It will cheer you and I am famished, for I have had not a mouthful as yet and I cannot dance on an empty stomach.'

'You mean to dance?' He looked shocked.

Tamsyn said firmly, 'Yes I do. Being miserable will not bring Gil back and I know, for he told me so before he died, that he would wish me to enjoy my life and go about in society. I think I am ready to do that again now.'

They found the supper room almost empty and the dishes likewise. However, they foraged enough remnants to make quite a substantial repast. While they ate they talked of Christmas customs. Mr Hempseed proved knowledgeable, as always. Tamsyn relaxed and listened and nibbled contentedly.

When her companion paused to sip some wine, she said, 'Father was saying earlier that he remembers my grandfather would have no nourishment but a dish of frumenty on Christmas Eve.'

'What was that?'

'I believe it was composed of wheat cakes boiled in milk, with rich spices added, but I do not know which spices. It somehow makes me think of Mr Woodhouse in that novel by Miss Austen, although I doubt if his supper dish would have contained any spices, rich or otherwise. But I suppose you have not read *Emma*, Mr Hempseed?'

'You suppose correctly. I read very few novels. I prefer to read about real people in works of biography and history.'

Tamsyn laughed.

'My dear sir, people in novels are real people in disguise. Sometimes the disguise is quite thin. You must remember the scandal when Lady Caroline Lamb published that *roman à clef* about Lord Byron. *Glenarvon*, yes?' She tilted her head enquiringly.

He frowned.

'Whatever one may think privately of Lord Byron, one must not forget that he is a cousin of Miss Gordon's,' he said primly.

'And as such above reproach? Alanna would be the first to disagree with you. We both thought Lady Caroline caught his character very well. It is not necessary to approve of the man in order to admire his poetry. And his lordship does have a wicked sense of humour. That line about Coleridge in *Don Juan*, how does it go?

'Explaining metaphysics to the nation, I wish he would explain his explanation.'

'It's in the dedication,' said a new voice behind them. 'James, I forgot that Lord Byron is your hero. May I present Mr James Ferguson from Philadelphia; Mr Oliver Hempseed, librarian to Lady Molesworthy.' They bowed.

'I have found that to talk of poetry usually frightens the gentlemen away,' continued Tamsyn, glancing mischievously from one to another. 'My dear godmother says, however, it is the mission of the literary lady to elevate and refine men's thoughts and tastes.'

'But not on Christmas Eve,' interposed John. Tamsyn jumped and whirled round to find him leaning against the sideboard, engaged in cracking a walnut. 'I think it is time for our dance, Mrs Elsworth.'

The wretched creature, how long had he been standing there, she wondered.

Aloud she said, 'Yes, of course. But may I first make you known to Mr Hempseed, who is a good friend and mine of information on books old and rare. My Godmother, Lady Molesworthy's collection, is unrivalled in certain spheres, thanks to his good offices.'

Mr Hempseed preened a little and said, 'You do me too much honour, dear lady. I am delighted to make your acquaintance, sir. Mrs Elsworth has mentioned two gentlemen from America in our recent conversations. I much benefited from your country's hospitality when I visited several cities a few years ago.'

'Before or after the war?' asked John, humorously lifting his eyebrow. Oliver Hempseed smiled slightly in return.

'I went to execute some commissions for my employer in 1816. I was able to be of service to some acquaintances in the book trade, but your compatriots' kindness and generosity far outweighed my trifling assistance.'

'The inhabitants of the book world cross frontiers with ease,' nodded John.

He turned to Tamsyn, but before he could speak, Mr

Hempseed observed, 'True, indeed. Pray pardon my frankness, but had I not known, I should have taken you for an Englishman, Mr Aylward.'

John regarded him keenly.

'Is that intended for a compliment, sir? I shall certainly take it as such. May I ask why?'

'You bear a remarkable resemblance to Sir Robert Hawksmore of Oak Place,' Mr Hempseed said bluntly.

Tamsyn held her breath. Mr Aylward's reaction was disappointing.

'So Mr Farrell informed me. I have not met Sir Robert, but it is quite probable. We are first cousins. I was not born in England, but I have English blood, like many in my country. Shall we dance, Mrs Elsworth?'

James, kind-hearted and sensitive to atmosphere, spoke hastily, 'My family came from Scotland, near a place called Perth, I understand, but several generations ago. Are you a Londoner, Mr Hempseed?'

John bore Tamsyn inexorably away.

As they waited for the movement in progress to finish, she murmured, 'How good-natured of James.'

'He's a good friend,' agreed John, 'even though the young scamp has a privilege denied me.'

Tamsyn wrinkled her nose and opened her eyes wide behind her fan. The room had grown very warm.

'And what is that?'

'You call him by his Christian name.'

'Ah, but he helped us in the kitchen. One must earn such privileges, sir.'

The dancers were reforming for a country dance. The hour was well-advanced, but the couples appeared fresh and eager for more, as Tamsyn and her tall partner took their places in the line. She felt very conspicuous and knew a momentary qualm about her ability to execute the steps. Many a curious glance came their way, but they were welcomed among the workmen and their wives and sweethearts with quiet goodwill.

As they waited their turn, she said, 'I hope I don't disgrace you. I haven't danced in four years.'

A twinkle glinted in his grey eyes and his long, thin nose quivered responsively.

'Allow yourself to be guided by me. I will not lead you astray,' he said and, suiting the word to the deed, he took her hand and led her confidently down the length of the line.

As the dance progressed, Tamsyn's assurance increased and she looked about her, observing with amusement the way in which the line weaved to avoid the two large printing presses, so that the couple at the head of the set were frequently obliged to halt under the mistletoe. All the lower berries were soon plucked as those men fortunate enough (or cunning enough) to stand directly beneath the kissing bunch made haste to claim their traditional reward.

Seeing that Mr Aylward had followed her gaze, she said, hoping to divert him, 'It is very cramped in the workroom, I'm afraid. My father is considering moving to larger premises south of the river, but we are much attached to it here, where we know everybody, and I have lived here all my life, apart from my marriage. I think Papa cannot bring himself to take the plunge, although he knows we need more space to house new equipment. That is why he has hesitated to install gas lighting.'

They were separated by the figure of the dance.

When they came together again, she asked, 'Do you think you will like England, Mr Aylward?'

'Why not? I like you,' he responded with alarming promptness.

'Thank you, but that is not very logical . . . ,' she began.

'There are certain situations in which logic does not apply. Stand still, one moment, Mrs Elsworth, if you please.'

Wondering if she had a fly in her hair or a lash near her eye, she waited expectantly, lips slightly parted. With unhurried ease, John reached up and removed the highest white berry from the bunch. In one swift action, he took her hand, placed the berry in her palm, used his other hand to steady her and kissed her full and firmly on the mouth. For one timeless second, she gazed into his eyes while the room spun and receded.

Then he released her and said, grinning, 'Happy Christmas, ma'am. Now tell me, has this forward American earned the right to call you Tamsyn?'

7

The Prologue and the Play

This was not a moment to be missish. It was Christmas and everyone was laughing and clapping, except Oliver Hempseed, who was watching the proceedings with a very stern frown indeed. To her dismay, Tamsyn's eyes filled with tears; observing this phenomenon, John took her elbow and guided her to a shadowy corner where the candles had guttered low in their sockets. She sniffed and smiled at him mistily.

'So foolish, forgive me. It's been so long – not since Gil died . . .' she faltered.

He nodded and said, softly, 'But may I hope it was not an unpleasant experience. You are not offended?'

More moved than she cared to admit by his earnestness, she met his gaze levelly and conceded, 'No, no, Mr Aylward. 'Twas really not unpleasant at all.'

His intent expression relaxed.

'John,' he insisted, 'My name is John. I make you free of it.'

Tamsyn bowed her head.

'Very well, since you are so far away from home, it shall be as you wish – John.'

He pursed his lips and furrowed his brow in mock dissatisfaction. He looked much younger and more approachable.

'Can it not be for myself alone, with no condition?' he pleaded.

Tamsyn had quite forgotten her earlier grief, as perhaps Mr Aylward had intended. She giggled happily. It was amazing to feel so at ease on such a brief acquaintance; it must be the magic of the season or the fact that American manners differed from the polite conventions which normally pertained in England in several important particulars, notably the speed in which a friendship between the sexes should be allowed to advance. She was tempted to apply a little English reserve, but it did not seem appropriate. With the familiarity of many years, she gave a jump and settled herself comfortably on the pile of type-holder trays under the window. This meant that she could look down on John's head as he leaned against the trays. She swung her feet gently and surveyed the room, while she pondered her reply. She meditated so long, that her partner spoke first.

'You are very agile, Mrs Elsworth. I fear I have been too presumptuous. Do you seek to escape from me in your lofty perch?'

She felt a trifle breathless, no doubt because of her recent exertions.

She responded evenly, 'I am unused to flattery, sir, but I do not dislike it, nor do I seek to escape it. I merely sought a respite.'

Mr Aylward appeared to give this speech his solemn attention, but when he looked up Tamsyn perceived that his eyes were brimming with amusement. She fixed her gaze on his strong jaw; she thought it would be formidable, when clenched.

'My dear girl, flattery has never been my strong suit. Actions speak louder than words, I believe.'

So saying he reached up, encircled her waist with his hands and set her on the ground, all in one swift movement.

'What are you going to do with me?' she gasped.

'Dance with you. We will talk another day. Come, Tamsyn.'

Obedient to the pressure of his hand, she accompanied him on to the floor, where they trod a stately, intricate

cotillion, followed by a lively Scottish reel. Then she performed a waltz with James. This was a novel experience for
Mrs Elsworth, but young Mr Ferguson danced with grace
and skill, which obliged his partner to do likewise. However,
when the music ended, Tamsyn was not reluctant to pause
and rest, while James went in search of some lemonade.
Then she danced with Stephen and with James again. The
freedom of movement was exhilarating and her happiness
was infectious. The company kept the musicians hard at
work far into the night and Tamsyn did not notice that
Oliver Hempseed had slipped away until general fatigue at
last overcame everyone; they gathered by the fire, where the
yule log still blazed merrily and sipped a nightcap of mulled
ale.

Tamsyn voiced her thought aloud to John, who was seated
beside her on one of the compositor's three-legged stools.

'That gentleman regards you with a proprietary air. Am I
poaching on Mr Hempseed's preserve?' John asked, regarding her keenly.

James had taken up a guitar and was strumming idly, his
shoulders leaning against the mantlepiece. A lock of hair
covered one eye. He began to sing the old air: 'What Child
is This?' to the tune of 'Greensleeves' in a pleasant baritone
and gradually his audience joined in or hummed along,
according to their inclination.

Tamsyn replied quietly, 'I have known Oliver Hempseed
for several years. He is a very intelligent man and I hold
him in great esteem . . .'

John glanced down at the top of her head, noting the
dishevelled curls and clasped hands; his face softened, he
bent down and whispered in her ear, 'Good.'

Startled she exclaimed, 'Why?'

'My dear lady, it should be obvious to the meanest intelligence that if, in all that time, he has progressed no further
than "esteem" then any overtures on his part are doomed
to failure. James sings rather well, don't you think? How
about you, does your singing voice match your lovely
speech?'

Tamsyn wrinkled her nose and laughed, saying emphatically, 'No sir, it does not. At least, I should say I cannot hold a tune in my head and only trust myself to sing in church, when accompanied by other, finer ears and voices.'

James's voice soared clear and true, 'The King of kings salvation brings; Let loving hearts enthrone Him' and his audience joined in the final refrain.

Tamsyn thought of the scene with a warm glow the next morning, as she sat beside her father in their pew in St Dunstan in the West. Once again she sang some of the old carols, which had been sung only a few hours earlier with Mr Farrell's employees and friends – for the gentlemen, hearing the Christmas music, had abandoned their card game and joined the group by the fire. Father and daughter smiled at one another and sang 'I saw three ships' and 'While shepherds watched' with enthusiasm, if a trifle flat, and listened tolerantly to an overlong sermon, which strayed many times from the joyful text of the day.

Tamsyn began to feel tired and her attention wandered. She felt happy and at peace in the old Fleet Street church, where the *New Testament* translator, Tyndale, the poet Donne and the writer, Izaac Walton, had also worshipped. She thought how much she loved London, especially the City, and how she would miss it if she were ever obliged to move. She remembered James saying, the first night when they had stayed for dinner, that 'In a frontier society we all learn to use weapons, and John fought in the war.' Mr Aylward had intervened to protest that she would think they lived in a wilderness, and James had retorted that, compared to London, they did. She sighed, but was painfully recalled to an awareness of her surroundings, by a sharp dig from Mr Farrell's forefinger. She stood up, received their vicar's blessing and edged her way slowly down the aisle in her father's wake, exchanging seasonal greetings with her neighbours as she went. They emerged to find grey skies and a chilly breeze, which discouraged much lingering in the churchyard.

Tamsyn was content to spend the rest of the day quietly.

She and her father consumed a traditional Christmas dinner and exchanged their gifts. She received a large Norwich shawl, woven in wool and silk in a rich array of colours, with a deep red border. It was pressed immediately into service over her flimsy muslin dress and she pronounced it quite perfect. Mr Farrell beamed, for he liked his generosity to be appreciated and, reaching down on the far side of his chair, he produced another package, secured with a big blue bow. This he also bestowed on his delighted daughter. As requested, she unwrapped it with great care to reveal a delicate, hand-tinted original print from Mr Ackermann's Repository of the Arts, depicting a cobbled street, and people of all shapes and sizes, browsing in trays of books and peering in the bookseller's window. It was a wintry scene in soft browns, greys, blues and greens, with leaves swirling in the gutter and the sparkle of raindrops on the roof tiles, but the men and women were intent on their books and appeared immune to their surroundings.

Tamsyn jumped up and kissed her father on the top of his head.

'How well you know my taste, Papa. I shall treasure it always. Now, it is your turn.'

Tamsyn had bought some wool and had persuaded Mrs Jennings to knit some mittens, for her father liked to wear them in the print room to keep rheumatism at bay and, although willing, she knew herself to be incapable of knitting any garment that any normally-shaped human being would be able to wear. Mrs Jennings's efforts being approved, she then laid John Evelyn's *Memoirs* on his knee, replenished the fire and tactfully left Mr Farrell to read or doze, as he felt inclined.

After so much rich food, she felt a great longing for some fresh air. She decided not to disturb the servants, who were eating a late dinner after labouring all morning to remove the vestiges of last night's party. Quietly, she slipped on her oldest and warmest pelisse, and her well-worn Witchoura mantle, which had a long cape and was fur-trimmed. Tamsyn then tied her bonnet, tucked her key in her muff and walked briskly down towards the river. The sky was grey and lowering and there were few people about. Tamsyn stood for a few moments at the top of the York Building's Stairs. The tide was high, so the mud was not visible and she revelled, as always, in the sight of the shipping, both large and small, which strained and creaked at its moorings, while the keen wind whipped the waves that lapped hungrily at the bottom of the steps. She walked along as far as the Black Lion Stairs and then turned back, for the light was beginning to fade and she did not wish to cause concern. She saw a cat chasing a rat, but no other sign of life. Much refreshed, she returned home before anyone had missed her.

As she laid aside her mantle and prepared to join her father for tea, Hannah tapped on her door and appeared, carrying a posy of hot-house roses.

Tamsyn received them with surprise.

'Who can be sending me a nosegay?'

'I couldn't say, miss. A boy bought them a few minutes ago. 'Tis very dear to buy flowers in the wintertime.'

'They must be from Alanna, of course, or my Godmother. They have many exotic blooms in the conservatory in Portman Square.'

She sniffed the flowers and spied a card, hidden in the silver filigree holder. Water dripped unnoticed on her gown. She examined the seal, which bore an uncanny resemblance to a bird of prey, and read the short missive.

My dear Mrs Elsworth,

On my way to call upon you, I chanced to catch sight of you, windswept and deep in thought, on the river steps. I dared not venture to intrude upon your reverie, but I make bold to offer this small seasonal token and trust that you will find it an acceptable pomander for your visit to the play on Tuesday. Until then I remain, your humble servant and admirer, R. H.

She crumpled the note and exclaimed, 'The man must be mad.'

She tossed the paper in the fireplace and gave Hannah the flowers to put in a more suitable receptacle.

'Tea, Hannah, if you please, and quickly. Where did I put my new shawl? It was so clever of Papa to choose dark red. Did he perhaps have a little help?'

The maid grinned and Tamsyn gave her a warm embrace, before seeking her father, whom she found wide awake and disposed for conversation. It was a relief to turn her thoughts to John Evelyn, whose Diary, she learned, was filled with descriptions of great spectacles, grand processions, delicious fruit and jewels. He recorded all things sumptuous and ornate, but was remarkably reticent concerning his private life.

'So much pomp, but I would prefer to know what his wife was like and if she shared his views,' she commented, when Mr Farrell finished reading aloud a lengthy description of the death and character of King Charles II.

'He was no domestic gossip,' he agreed. 'But what say you to a game of backgammon,? If memory serves, I was roundly trounced last time and I cannot rest until I am revenged.'

Accordingly, they played with great concentration and exchanged little small talk for the remainder of the evening. Mr Farrell triumphed and went to bed happily; Tamsyn followed and also slept soundly, grateful for the tranquillity and security which her father's home provided.

By Tuesday, the day appointed for the visit to the Theatre Royal, Tamsyn had quite recovered her equilibrium after the intriguing developments of the past week, but she felt hot and cold with excitement as she donned her Parisian rose-coloured gown and sat passively while Hannah fastened the Grecian clasps on the shoulders and arranged her hair in a becoming cluster of curls and rosebuds. She hesitated but a moment before rejecting Sir Robert's floral pomander, in favour of her ivory fan, Gil's gift on their betrothal. Thus fortified, she joined her father, who was waiting impatiently in Lady Molesworthy's second carriage, lent for the occasion, and they drove in state to Drury Lane. The traffic was heavy and Mr Farrell was tempted to jump down and walk, but he forebore in consideration of Tamsyn's delicately shod feet. Notwithstanding the throng, they arrived in good time and were half-way up the right side of the double staircase, when Lady Molesworthy and her party entered the vestibule below. Her ladyship was accompanied by quite a retinue, including Alanna, Miss Lovett, Sir Robert, Oliver Hempseed, her maid and two footmen. She was attired from head to toe in her favourite imperial purple and was clearly enjoying herself tremendously. She peered about her and addressed Miss Lovett in an audible whisper, which reverberated around the domed Corinthian rotunda.

'I cannot agree with you, Esmeralda. Her conversation is insipid and her dress ill-chosen. Always has been and always will be.'

Everyone looked about them, trying to guess the object of these strictures, and a titter of laughter echoed up and down the staircase. Quite oblivious, Lady Lucinda perched on the clasped hands of her two stalwart footmen and was carried up the grand stair, her maid following with her cane, reticule and other indispensable appendages.

The whole party foregathered in Mr Farrell's box, where they found Mr Aylward and Mr Ferguson before them. Introductions were performed hastily, as the curtain was about to rise and, to her chagrin, Tamsyn missed the meeting between Sir Robert and his American cousin. She was obliged to take her place among the ladies at the front of the box, while the gentlemen settled themselves in the semi-darkness behind them.

'Who wrote *The Dramatist?*' whispered Alanna in her ear. 'Is it someone you know?'

Tamsyn shook her head and scanned her playbill.

'Oh, it was Frederic Reynolds. You probably won't recall a play of his, which was performed a few years ago, where a live dog saved a child from drowning by leaping from a rock and plunging into real water. I forget what it was called.'

Alanna nodded.

'I remember the dog, but had forgot the playwright. Is this to be a comedy or a tragedy?'

'A comedy, or so I infer from the names of the characters, Ennui, Vapid and the like. Now pray hush, my dear, 'tis years since I have seen a play and a pantomime and I intend to enjoy them to the full.'

'What a quaint notion. Nobody comes to the theatre to see the play,' Alanna retorted, but she spoke to empty air, for her friend's attention was riveted on the stage.

Alanna gave half an ear to the actors, and leaned forward to look around the audience. There was scarcely a seat unfilled in the building. Several of her acquaintance bowed to the beautiful Miss Gordon; satisfied she sat back and glanced at her Grandmother and Miss Lovett, who were laughing heartily at some witticism made by their host; Mr Farrell had seated himself strategically between the two older ladies and was devoting himself to their entertainment. Miss Lovett was quite bright eyed and flushed; Alanna wondered at the eccentricities of the generation which had been young in the last century. It was undeniable, however, that no gentleman was honouring her with special attention. Sir Robert and Mr Aylward were both watching Tamsyn with the absorbed concentration which that young lady was giving to the antics of Lord Scratch, the newly-made peer; even Oliver Hempseed had eyes for no one but her friend. Piqued, Miss Gordon shifted her chair slightly, dropped her opera glasses, and adroitly caught Mr Ferguson's gaze. She contrived a penitent, beguiling smile. James was hooked at once and retrieved the glasses with alacrity. He hitched his seat closer to Alanna's and began to converse easily and amusingly. An hour passed; Sir Robert suggested that Mr Aylward might care to join him to blow a cloud. With a quiet word to their host, the two men withdrew and did not reappear until five minutes before the intermission.

Tamsyn, whose attention had at last become detached from the interminable convolutions of the plot, watched the cousins with curiosity as the whole party partook of refreshments in the supper room. She thought Mr Aylward appeared amiable and relaxed, while there was a certain discernible tension in Sir Robert's expression. Others had now the opportunity, in the bright light, to observe the uncanny resemblance between the two men. The undercurrents which Tamsyn felt made her uneasy, but her Godmother knew no such qualms. She addressed her host, while tapping the tall American on the arm with her lorgnette to obtain his notice.

'Charles Farrell, you're a dark horse. Why did you not tell me these two men were as like as two peas in a pod? Tell me your name again, sir'

'I am John Aylward, ma'am,' he responded, with more than a hint of reserve in his tone, as he looked down his long nose at Lady Molesworthy.

Her ladyship flashed him a shrewd glance.

'Just so. Good patriotic Americans do not believe in titles, do they, Mr Aylward?'

'We believe that titles should be earned by merit – your ladyship.'

The assembled company held its breath, but Lady Lucinda gave a cackle of laughter.

'Very wise, Mr – Aylward; pray come over here to the sofa, my shoes are pinching me and I wish to talk to you.'

She leaned heavily on his arm as he escorted her to her chosen alcove, a little apart from the rest. There was a general sigh of relief. Everyone began to speak together, politely ignoring the subject which was uppermost in their minds.

Mr Hempseed quoted to Miss Lovett the famous line from Lord Byron, referring to the degradation of the drama:

While Reynolds vents his 'dammes, poohs, and zounds'
And common-place and common sense confounds.

'Indeed, the quotation is apt, but I did not know it. I confess to a weakness for Reynold's plays from my youth; it has given me immense pleasure to see *The Dramatist* again,' she responded stoutly.

Meanwhile, Alanna was much intrigued by James Ferguson. It was her first exposure to an American of her own age and, once she had succeeded in overcoming the awe which he clearly felt in the presence of a young lady of fashion, newly returned from the Continent, they got along famously. James had recalled that Mrs Elsworth's friend was related to the great poet. When he mentioned his idol's name, Alanna bestowed on him a look of withering scorn.

'He is a man of mediocre talent and no morals and I am thankful that the connection is but a distant one,' she said firmly.

Caught between a rock and a hard place, James faltered, but stood his ground. He began an impassioned defence of his hero and soon they were squabbling as if they had known one another from the cradle.

Tamsyn, who had been watching them, turned away with a smile and almost bumped into Sir Robert.

'May I compliment you on your gown, Mrs Elsworth. That shade of rose is exactly right, impeccable; a vast improvement on the one you wore in Portman Square.'

Tamsyn raised her eyebrows.

'I regret the rosebud trifle which I sent you did not find favour. I recognize the fan from our first meeting at Lady Molesworthy's – an old friend, perhaps?'

Tamsyn retorted, 'I must thank you for the flowers, Sir Robert, but I think the holder was too valuable a gift to send to a slight acquaintance. It would have been more appropriate to send it to another lady who, I believe, has a prior claim on your attentions. Also I do not care to be spied upon when I take a walk.'

Sir Robert did not pretend to misunderstand her; he drew her to one side, for the bell was ringing for the next act and people were beginning to drift back to their seats. He said, 'My dear lady, 'tis a pity that you have only a modest widow's portion, but there it is. I make it my business to find out such matters.' Tamsyn made a movement of disgust, but he continued with sublime disregard for her feelings, 'And Miss Gordon is a young lady who understands the obligations

85

that are due to her position and will abide by the rules of society.'

Tamsyn murmured indignantly, 'You suggest I should betray my friend for some discreet dalliance? – you misread my character, sir.'

Sir Robert smiled crookedly. He looked very handsome and Tamsyn felt quite weak at the knees.

'Think about it, many a *ménage à trois* has worked very well. Alanna is fond of you and I respect your keen intelligence. Such an arrangement would be to everyone's advantage.'

'Not mine,' said Tamsyn through gritted teeth. Quite unperturbed he bowed and left. 'Insufferable arrogance!' She unfurled her fan and plied it vigorously.

The last stragglers were returning to their box.

'Tamsyn, hurry along gel, or you'll miss the pantomime. I believe 'tis *Jack and the Beanstalk*. I know you always had an affection for the tale.'

'Did I Papa, I wonder why'.

Gratefully, she took her father's arm and returned to her seat. Sensibly, she determined not to allow Sir Robert's strange proposition to spoil her enjoyment of the entertainment. She closed her fan with a snap, put up her chin and gave her full attention to the stage. Not one glance did she vouchsafe in Sir Robert Hawksmore's direction for the remainder of the evening.

8

Anticlimax

It was, indeed, difficult to know where to look during the performance of the pantomime, which departed quite far from the original fairy story and lasted much too long, in Tamsyn's opinion. She observed, with sympathetic amusement, that James was much shocked by the coarseness of the dialogue and crude vulgarity of the gestures. He was not at all mollified when Alanna informed him that she had seen far worse in Paris.

After Jack had climbed the beanstalk for the third time, Tamsyn had a strong sense of *déjà vu* and began to wish that the giant would catch him and punish him for his greed. It was very warm and noisy, as the audience participation from the pit and the gallery reached a crescendo. Tamsyn smothered a yawn, just as Lady Molesworthy gave a loud snore. Glancing in her ladyship's direction, she noticed that her father and Miss Lovett were enjoying a whispered, but quite animated, conversation and her thoughts went off at a new tangent. This was a budding friendship which she felt should be encouraged for their mutual benefit; she hoped her godmother would not awake too soon.

'Fee-fi-fo-fum, I smell the blood of an Englishman,' roared the Giant, and the audience roared with him, to warn Jack, who was in some danger of being caught in a compromising situation with his hostess, the giant's wife.

Tamsyn's mind wandered; she thought of Sir Robert's proposal to make her his mistress. Had he discussed the idea with Alanna?; he had seemed very confident of her consent. Her own acquaintance with him was slight; the more she pondered, the more irritated she became by his arrogance and lack of appreciation of all finer feelings. She feared very much for the prospects of her friend's future happiness.

'Tamsyn.'

John's voice made her jump; she half-turned and remarked with satisfaction that Sir Robert had overheard Mr Aylward's use of her Christian name.

She smiled and said sweetly, 'Yes, John?'

'I was just thinking, yours is an unusual name. What is its origin?'

Unaware that it was John's laudable desire to distract her attention from the stage at a particularly embarrassing moment, she replied, 'I can't recall the exact meaning. I know it is a Cornish name and it has been given in my mother's family for at least two hundred years. The masculine form is Thomas.'

'My name is a feminine form of Alan,' broke in Miss Gordon, 'Mr Hempseed looked it up for me in the library. Do you recollect the meaning, sir?'

Thus appealed to, Mr Hempseed, who had been listening to the conversation with interest, took off his spectacles and polished them with a black flannel pen wiper, which happened to be in his pocket.

'Yours is an Irish Gaelic name, I believe, Miss Gordon and if memory serves it means "fair or comely".'

He replaced his spectacles with care; the lenses were now much smudged with grains of powdered ink but Mr Hampseed appeared not to notice.

James said gallantly, 'Very apt, Miss Gordon. 'Tis a pity more names do not fit their owners, but I suppose it is not possible for parents to know how their infants will turn out,' he concluded fair-mindedly.

'Many people don't think about it at all. They choose family names to give pleasure or win favours. I have always been grateful that I was not called Agatha, which means "the good" or even worse, Agnes, like a school-friend of mine. She was anything but "gentle" and "meek". However, she did inherit a handsome string of pearls from her great aunt Agnes, so that was some compensation.'

Alanna grinned.

The proceedings on the stage were now drawing to a close; the young ladies, whose ears and eyes had been adroitly diverted at the danger point, were permitted to watch Jack cut down the beanstalk with his axe so that the giant could tumble, most convincingly to his death, giving a blood-curdling cry as he fell. This left Jack in triumphant possession of the golden hen. The sale of the golden eggs enabled Jack and his mother to become very rich and he married a great princess and they lived happily ever after. The clowns capered, the harlequin moped and the unpredictable audience in the gallery clapped and cheered with genuine appreciation. Lady Lucinda awoke.

'I hope you enjoyed your evening, Lucinda?' said Mr Farrell, as her ladyship's maid came forward to swathe her mistress in wraps and shawls.

'Very much, I thank you, Charles, but I'm unused to these late hours. Don't suffocate me, gel, stop fussing. I abhor zeal unsupported by intellect.' she tottered to the back of the box, followed by her long-suffering, but devoted, servant.

The rest of the party moved slowly in her wake.

John muttered to Tamsyn, 'Zeal unsupported by intellect. I must remember that. Lady Molesworthy has a way with words.'

Tamsyn whispered back, 'Her bark is worse than her bite. Evans has been with her for years and is quite immune to her sarcasm.'

The cold night air swirled about them as they descended the stairs and they did not linger in the foyer. Brief thanks and promises to call soon and the company dispersed into the moonlight to seek the comfort of their beds with all deliberate speed.

*   *   *

The night at the theatre had unfortunate repercussions for several members of the party who caught severe colds despite all their precautions. Mr Farrell and his daughter both succumbed to the ailment and soon after they were struck down, word came that Lady Lucinda was also confined with a feverish chill. Tamsyn greeted the new year of 1820 not with champagne, but with a cup of beef tea. However, this was an advance on the thin gruel which had been her portion for the past several days and she hoped that it marked a turning point in her convalescence.

Late on Saturday afternoon, Tamsyn ventured downstairs for the first time since the night of the play. She peeped in to her father's study and found a domestic scene which delighted her eye. Mr Farrell was seated in his leather wing-backed chair, with his feet steaming in a mustard bath, while Miss Lovett sat upright on a very hard chair and a bright fire burned between them. Miss Lovett was reading aloud from John Evelyn's *Memoirs*. Not wishing to interrupt, Tamsyn retreated quietly to her own sitting room and poked the fire, which obstinately refused to burn with any enthusiasm.

She determined not to give way to an attack of the megrims and seating herself at her desk, she took a fresh sheet of paper and composed a moral tale designed to placate the strictest critic and to depress the liveliest child. She wrote for an hour and a half with scarcely a pause, then sat back and pushed the papers away, chewing the end of her pencil meditatively. Her eye fell on the miniature of Gil which she kept on the little shelf above her writing table. She picked it up and carried it over to the fire; she crouched huddled on a stool and examined the face of the man she had once loved with all her heart. She could not remember the sound of his voice; she sniffed dolefully, feeling at a very low ebb in her spirits.

'May I come in, Cinderella?' John Aylward spoke from the doorway.

Taken by surprise, Tamsyn took one look at the tall, living and breathing American, and burst into a flood of tears, still clutching Gil's portrait in her hand.

'My dear girl, what is the matter?'

He strode forward and knelt down beside her, enfolding her in a comforting embrace. She wept unrestrainedly for some minutes, but at last the sobbing ceased, except for an occasional cough or splutter. She tried to push him away.

'You will catch my kolb,' she gulped thickly.

He laughed, but did not release her.

'I will risk it,' he said. They sat quietly until Tamsyn began to shiver. He glanced about angrily. 'Why are you sitting here with this apology for a fire?'

'The servants don't know I am here. I expect Hannah thinks I am still in bed.'

John fetched a shawl which Tamsyn had dropped by her desk, wrapped her in it and placed her bodily in her chair; then he applied himself to the fire and soon coaxed a flicker of flame from the recalcitrant coals.

'We shall be cosy in no time. Would you care for some tea?'

Tamsyn went to nod, but sneezed instead; she fumbled for her handkerchief, and dropped the miniature. John picked it up and took it with him as he went to pull the bell. Hannah appeared, and began to apologize for her apparent neglect of her mistress. John cut her short with a cold air of command and sent her running for the doctor's tonic. She returned with the medicine and a little later with wine and soup. When all was arranged to Mr Aylward's satisfaction, he sat down and sipped his wine, while Tamsyn ate the broth.

'You were very hard on her,' she commented, 'She has been run off her feet with two invalids to care for . . .'

'I realize that. I was a trifle harsh. My concern for you must be my excuse, but I will find an opportunity to mollify her. I came but to wish you and your father a Happy New Year. I had no idea you were ill until young Stephen let me in. Hannah, no doubt, would have shown me the door, but he merely pointed up the stair and said Mr Farrell was in his study. When I looked in . . .'

'You saw Miss Lovett.'

91

They smiled at one another in silent understanding.

'I was about to slip away,' continued John, 'when I heard you cough and so I ventured to intrude. Now that you are comfortable, I will not stay long. I know you must feel unequal to much conversation. Shall I emulate Miss Lovett and offer to read to you? I have brought you a New Year's gift, which I hope you will accept with my thanks for your kind hospitality to a stranger.'

He reached down beside his chair, retrieved a parcel, neatly wrapped in brown paper, and laid it on Tamsyn's lap, in place of her empty soup bowl.

The parcel was heavy; she looked at him in eager enquiry, as she untied the string. Inside she found *Ivanhoe; A Romance* by the author of *Waverley* in three leather-bound volumes. On the flyleaf of the first volume John had written. 'To T. E. from J. A. January 1st, 1820'.

'Oh, how did you get it so soon? I thought the first printing was sold out', she breathed, tracing the gold-tooled design with her forefinger. 'Thank you so much, Mr Aylward, I am most grateful. I am tempted to be ill a little longer, so that I can spend my days and nights in reading without fear of interruption.'

Content with the success of his offering, John rose to take his leave.

'Let us say, I am deeply in Mr Hatchard's debt and some poor soul on his subscription list will have to wait for the second printing. I shall expect a full review when next we meet. Where would you like me to put your miniature? May I ask if it depicts your husband?'

Tamsyn nodded.

'Yes, it was a good likeness of Gil, although something is not quite right and I cannot recollect what it was – perhaps the eyes are too dark. His eyes always sparkled with life.'

John put the frame on the desk.

'Do you still miss him?' he asked and then added quickly, 'No, pray do not feel obliged to answer that question. It was impertinent of me. Good evening, ma'am and pray accept my best wishes for your speedy recovery.'

He turned on his heel, but stopped at the sound of his name. Tamsyn held out her hand. Their eyes met.

'Dear John,' she said, 'I am weak and exhausted and when you came I was feeling sad and yes, I do miss Gil, but I want you to know that your visit has made me feel better and when I have read *Ivanhoe* I shall be quite restored. Goodnight – and thank you.'

Mr Aylward kissed her hand and departed without another word and Tamsyn read her novel far into the night.

In early January the weather turned bitterly cold, with sleet and snow to add to the general misery. Tamsyn's cough settled on her chest and she stayed close to home. She passed the days in writing a few more tales for her book and in reading *Ivanhoe*, which she found an ideal escape from her present woes. She offered to help her father work on the Arabic tome, but he told her bluntly to keep above stair and not spread her cold around the workroom. He, himself, was much better and Stephen, who made no attempt to understand the language, was doing a fine, accurate job as his assistant. Feeling superfluous, but too weak to argue, Tamsyn retreated. The days dragged by and she read until her head ached and her eyes crossed. She was deep in her mediaeval epic when word came that the old king was sick and like to die at Windsor. She spared him a pitying thought, but looked forward to the reign of George IV with little enthusiasm; the self-indulgent and extravagant Prince Regent was not beloved by his people and few felt any pride in their monarch-to-be or his much abused but badly behaved consort. Yet, for all their faults, it was impossible to imagine England without the royal family.

Tamsyn felt restless and decided to paint an illustration for the story which she had just finished. It was about a young squire who became so engrossed in the side-stalls and circus tricks on a feast day, that he forgot to help his knight prepare for the tournament. As a consequence one of the knight's knee straps broke at a vital moment, his opponent's lance pierced beneath his arm and one of the great flowers of chivalry perished. Unwilling to tackle the difficult problems of horse and armour, Tamsyn sensibly chose to picture the boy watching the clowns perform. She had already outlined the sketch and was beginning to colour the clowns' costumes, when Alanna swirled into the room. Before Tamsyn could rise, she had advanced, gripped her friend's shoulders with both hands, laid a cold, fresh cheek against Tamsyn's hot one and announced,

'It is perfect. How clever of you to contrive the expression of wickedness and innocence on the clown's face – just like the one who was so outrageous the other night. I saw it all, despite Mr Ferguson's best endeavours. My dear, how are you? Grandmama said to give you her best love and to tell you that although her life was not in danger, she was nonetheless exceedingly unwell, which is quite true and my excuse for not having been to see you sooner.'

Miss Gordon looked enchanting, shining-haired and bright-eyed. She tossed aside her enormous sable muff and fur-lined cloak, while a waft of subtle perfume which could only be French, penetrated even Tamsyn's cold-dulled senses as she allowed herself to be pulled over to the fire.

'You shouldn't be here now. Are you not afraid of the infection?' she muttered ungraciously, blowing her nose.

Alanna eyed her friend shrewdly as she shook out her skirts and stretched out her hands to the blaze.

'No, dearest, for I have spent the past two weeks in the sickroom reading to her ladyship and ministering to her whims. She was fretful, just like you, but I escaped the contagion, as you see. Here are some grapes for you, I told Grandmama she would have an upset stomach if she ate any more.'

'I beg your pardon, Alanna, 'twas no way to greet a friend. What can I do to make amends?'

'Let us have some tea and toast. We can make it here by the fire if you ask for a fork. Have you heard about the poor king? Of course, I am sorry that he is so old and mad, it must be quite terrible for him in that draughty old castle, but I do feel it was careless of him to lose the American colonies and I must say his children do him no credit, particularly Prinny. Did I tell you how hard he pinched me last time I went to dinner at Carlton House? I was black and blue for a month. Grandmama has a soft spot for him, but I think he is a disgusting old man. And the worst of it is, when the king dies, as he may do any day, we shall all be plunged into mourning and my Parisian gowns will be quite outmoded, or at least commonplace, by next season. It is too bad.'

Tamsyn laughed.

'Well, mourning will not be any hardship to me. Most of my gowns are black or grey, but I do offer you my commiserations, I can quite understand how very tiresome it will be for you to put by all those delicious French confections.'

'I would not mind wearing it for someone I really cared for; but court mourning goes on so long. If he dies tomorrow, we will be fortunate to be permitted to wear lavender by Easter. Ah, here is Hannah with our tea. Let us talk of something more cheerful.'

'Tell me, what have you been reading to my Godmother? I have been perusing the most marvellous tale by the author of *Waverley*. I am sure the author is Mr Scott. No one else can write half so well in a historical vein.'

'*Ivanhoe*. Oh, how I long to hear your opinion. I have had nothing so amusing. Mostly articles from old copies of the *Ladies' Monthly Museum*. Mrs Hannah More was the favourite object of censure. We did not feel equal to Dr Johnson or any other gentlemen for that matter.'

They made and munched buttered toast and discussed *Ivanhoe* happily for some time; a large pile of toast accumulated and disappeared.

Replete at last, Alanna daintily licked the tips of her fingers and said, 'Well, I will try it, although three volumes is a daunting prospect, if only to prove to James Ferguson that I do read literature. However, I confess that I prefer life, unlike your admirer, Mr Hempseed, who takes refuge from life in literature.'

Tamsyn responded good-humouredly, 'Oliver Hempseed

95

is not my admirer and I doubt very much if he would count romantic adventure tales, no matter how authentic the background, as literature. But James may be more easily impressed.'

Alanna sniffed and rattled her teaspoon.

'I do detest Mr Hempseed's habit of assuming that one knows things of which one is ignorant; with Grandmama confined to her room, I have been obliged to partake of several meals *à deux* with our learned librarian.' She mimicked his dry tones with wicked accuracy. '"You are, of course, aware Miss Gordon that the Byzantines, not Charlemagne, were the true heirs of the Roman Empire. Mr Gibbon has done the Eastern Empire a grave injustice, I fear . . ."'

They giggled.

At length Alanna said plaintively, 'Even Miss Lovett has abandoned us.'

'I know. She's been here; Papa thinks she is an angel.'

'Possibly,' agreed Alanna. 'She's poor as a church-mouse, but very proud. Mr Hempseed has to look to his laurels when she bends her powerful mind to Byzantine problems.'

'I wonder if she understands Arabic,' mused Tamsyn.

'Very likely; her father was a great linguist – and a great tyrant. She's been much happier since he died last year.'

'How did she meet Lady Lucinda?'

'Oh, years ago, when Grandmama first moved to Portman Square, soon after it was built. Mrs Montague, one of those blue-stocking salon ladies, also lived in Portman Square and they both attended the meetings.'

'How interesting. Did you know that Lady Montfort, the writer of Gothic novels, also lives in the square?'

'Yes, but I've never met her. Hester Vane spends most of her time in Sussex these days. Speaking of meetings, I will tell you a secret. I looked so blooming when I came in because I had not come directly from the sickroom. I have been skating on the Serpentine . . .' She paused for effect and Tamsyn said wistfully, 'How delightful, but why is it a secret?'

'I went without Grandmama's knowledge; I felt so cooped up. Fanny was with me so it was quite proper. I met Mr Ferguson and Mr Aylward and we had a wonderful game of "tag". They are both accomplished skaters. Oh, and Mr Aylward asked after you most particularly and they both send their best wishes.'

'Thank you. Which reminds me, I have not asked what opinion you formed of the two American gentlemen the night of the play?'

'Mr Aylward is a little too much like Sir Robert for my taste, but James Ferguson amuses me – he interprets my slightest remark quite literally. He makes me feel very worldly and sophisticated. However, I have not told you the half. We had just executed a very creditable spin when James caught me, and when we stopped whirling the first face that came into focus was that of Hawksmore himself, looking very much like the bird, his namesake. My dear, he fixed me with a most riveting stare – I vow I began to tremble. Fortunately, he was distracted by Mr Aylward. They acknowledged one another with polite hostility on Sir Robert's part and studied indifference on Mr Aylward's.' She shivered at the memory. 'I hope he does not tell Grandmama.'

Tamsyn observed her with concern, but said comfortingly, 'Stuff and nonsense. You have done nothing improper. But, Alanna, forgive me, I do not mean to pry, but does Sir Robert have any right to regard you with a proprietary air?'

Alanna nodded.

'He has proposed and I have accepted him. It will be a marriage of convenience, of course. I saw him speak to you at the play; I thought he must have told you of our arrangement.'

Tamsyn reached out and took her friend's hands.

She said grimly, 'He asked me to be his mistress in a *ménage à trois*, but Alanna, that cannot be what you want? It is certainly against all my inclination; I much prefer my independence, and I would not hurt you in such a way for the world.'

Miss Gordon's beautiful blue eyes filled with tears.

'Tammy dearest, I need you desperately. Sir Robert treats me like a spoilt child, like a doll without feelings. How can I live alone with him?'

Tamsyn shook her gently.

'Think again, I beseech you. Lady Lucinda would never force you to wed a man you find abhorrent.'

Alanna stood up with an air of dignified finality.

'I have given my word. Grandmama can be implacable and she has set her heart on seeing me mistress of Oak Place, partly because she has been fond of Robert since he was a boy and also because the Molesworthy estates, which I shall inherit and of which Grandmama is a trustee, march side by side with the Windlesham lands. After all, one man is much like another. I expect we shall contrive well enough, as well as most people and when Robert is away, collecting more old ruins, you will come and stay. Promise me, Tamsyn.'

Uncertain of her ground, Tamsyn said nothing regarding John Aylward's possible claim to the Windlesham land.

Privately resolving to make enquiries at an early opportunity, she said, 'Very well, darling, if you wish it. Have you set a date for the wedding?'

Alanna dabbed her eyes with a minute lace handkerchief.

'Some time in the late spring. Help me with these fastenings, there's a dear. Now, make haste and get well. Don't come down, stay here by the fire. Goodbye, I will call again soon.'

'Goodbye, my best love to her ladyship; and thank you for coming, you have quite taken my mind off my troubles.'

A quick, affectionate embrace and Miss Gordon was gone, leaving her friend to brood by the fire, with Sam, the cat, on her lap. Sam was a very good listener and a comforting presence in times of distress; there were occasions, Tamsyn felt, when the company of animals was infinitely preferable to that of humans.

9

Charitable Endeavours

'Listen to this, my dear,' said Mr Farrell, one morning in late January, as he and Tamsyn took breakfast together, 'There is a report here that very considerable damage has been done among the shipping in the river, by the floating ice. I myself saw two brigs and a schooner driven by the tide towards London Bridge, and the mast of one of them was carried away owing to the impetuosity of the current.'

'How dreadful. Would you care for some more bacon, Papa? The newspapers do seem to revel in bad news; it makes me feel quite depressed to read them. Is there anything else I should know about?' She sat back and sipped her tea, waiting patiently while her father scanned the small print.

'Huh!' he ejaculated presently, 'our plan to succour the paupers in the City is mentioned with commendation. There are some paragraphs about the general distress and the large numbers of persons wandering destitute in the streets, without food and shelter and, it is quite true, many of whom have seen better days. Then the article says "Some gentlemen, whose names will ever be dear to humanity"' (well, never mind about that), but it goes on: '"waited upon the Lord Mayor on the 14th, ... and Mr Hick, of Cheapside, humanely offered a large warehouse for the temporary use of the poor sufferers. The Lord Mayor was in the Chair, and a subscription, amounting to 800 pounds, was made by about

300 gentlemen present. The warehouse was immediately prepared as a refuge and one part was appropriated to the use of women; another to the men. The room was well warmed and ventilated, and clean straw provided for each. Every individual had on entering at night, a comfortable meal, and another in the morning before they departed, as they were not allowed to remain during the day. It is calculated that temporary relief has already been afforded to some 2,000 persons and further subscriptions have been raised to help support this truly-benevolent asylum." '

'But where do these poor souls go during the day?' asked Tamsyn, much touched by this affecting account.

'They seek work or beg or pick pockets, I suppose.' responded Mr Farrell prosaically. 'Some more bacon, please, Tamsyn, and then I must get to work. The inclemency of the weather has caused much sickness among the men and we are in arrears in several quarters, including the invitations for Lady Molesworthy's Valentine Ball and some dance programmes. And how are you feeling, my dear, Do you have any engagements today?'

'I am feeling much better, thank you, and ready for a little activity. I would like to help those poor people in the warehouse.'

'I have subscribed quite liberally, there is no need . . .'

'You misunderstand me, Papa, I do not mean money. I thought perhaps I could help prepare the meals, or serve them. Hannah could come with me to Mr Hick's warehouse on London Wall, if you give us directions.'

Mr Farrell regarded his daughter with a mixture of pride and exasperation.

'There's no denying they need every hand they can get, but you must promise me to be home by six o'clock and to avoid anyone who looks sickly. You must not take any unnecessary risks.'

Tamsyn smiled.

'The change will do me good. Can I do anything for you this morning, Papa? I wonder – if the king dies – will Lady

Molesworthy need her invitations? Alanna will be most put out if her Ball is cancelled.'

'From all I hear, it is doubtful if his Majesty will last the month. I was in company yesterday forenoon with Charles Knight, who is a young, but very able man. He is editor of the *Windsor and Eton Express* and keeps well-abreast of the situation at the castle. Knight is acquainted with William Clowes, the printer, and Clowes introduced us when I chanced to look in to his military bookshop at Charing Cross with our two American friends. I would say it is exceedingly unlikely that anyone will be holding balls in February.'

Mr Farrell munched his bacon with gloomy satisfaction.

Tamsyn said abstractedly, 'Poor man, but it will be a merciful release for him. Mr Aylward and Mr Ferguson are well, I trust?'

Her father pushed back his plate, wiped his mouth and stood up, brushing crumbs from his ample waistcoat.

'Quite well, I believe,' he observed, eyes twinkling beneath his shaggy brows. 'John Aylward did mention that he intended to call upon you today. It slipped my mind until this moment. Now, my girl, can you spare an hour to read to the men after the noonday meal when they are always drowsy? Clowes was talking of setting up a benevolent fund for his workmen. It's not a bad idea and I intend to enquire further into his scheme. Incentives and a cheerful workplace produce more willing employees. It is the old story of the carrot and the stick.'

'You have always been very good to your men.' Tamsyn jumped up and kissed her father affectionately, 'They work fewer hours and are better paid than is usual in the publishing world.'

'It is quality, not quantity that counts,' said Mr Farrell, not displeased by the praise. He liked his good deeds to be recognized.

As he made for the door, paper in hand, Tamsyn called after him, 'Dear sir, did Mr Aylward give any indication when he might appear?'

Hand on the doorknob, Mr Farrell paused and answered,

'Three, four, teatime,' he said vaguely. 'I will not be joining you. I have promised to escort Miss Lovett to view the Burlington Arcade.'

Tamsyn began, 'But, Papa, you detest shopping . . .' She stopped and bit her lip and added, 'Most of the boutiques sell quite useless articles and they are very dear. What are you looking for?'

'We are looking for a little frivolity, a commodity which has been sadly lacking in Miss Lovett's life,' he said gruffly, 'and she has heard that there is one place which specializes in collars for puppy dogs. She wants one for her spaniel, Mischief.'

He departed with dignity. Tamsyn glanced at the clock and realized that she must bustle if she were to perform her household duties, read to the men and be ready to entertain her visitor by mid-afternoon. She rang the bell for Hannah to clear the table and plunged into a whirlwind of activity.

Fortunately, Mr Aylward did not come until nearly a quarter to four. He found Tamsyn giving final instructions for two large baskets of food to be packed and ready to accompany her to Mr Hick's warehouse.

'We must leave at four-thirty,' John heard her say to Mrs Jennings. 'See that there are plenty of meat- and potato-pies and make sure there are two large aprons, one for Hannah and one for me, if you please. Oh John,' she exclaimed, catching sight of the newcomer, 'how nice to see you. Do go up to my sitting room, I'll be with you in a moment. Now, Mrs Jennings, have you any suggestions. Is there anything I have forgotten?'

Mr Aylward proceeded upstairs obediently. He was uncertain whether to be flattered at being treated so informally, or to be affronted at being so summarily dismissed. In his, fairly wide, experience with young ladies, he was accustomed in his dealings to be the centre of attention and his vanity was piqued; previously, only his sisters had dared to disregard him with careless good nature. He decided not to sit down, but went to stand stiffly by the window.

His hostess found him in this position when she entered quietly.

Recognizing his displeasure by the rigidity of his back and other subtle signs, she drew a deep breath and advanced, saying apologetically, 'My dear sir, do come and sit down. Pray forgive me for keeping you waiting,' she smiled disarmingly and fluttered her long lashes. John consented to be mollified and withdrew from the window. Tamsyn chattered on, 'I have been longing to discuss *Ivanhoe* with you, but I fear I cannot do it justice today, as I have to go out in a little while. My father omitted to tell me you were coming until this morning and I have a prior engagement.'

At these words, John, who had been in the act of seating himself, stood up again. He frowned and his nostrils flared, giving him the appearance of a highly-bred horse. Tamsyn half expected him to paw the ground.

'I see that I have come at an inconvenient time. I will delay you no longer, now that I am reassured as to your health and well-being.'

A mischievous mood seized Mrs Elsworth; she found that she was by no means averse to teasing a man who was being so pompous and stuffy.

She said airily, 'Oh, I can spare a few minutes yet. I must ask you, there is one aspect of the novel which has puzzled me very much. Have you read it, sir?'

John nodded and perched uncomfortably on the edge of his chair; he had not seen Tamsyn in this playful humour before and determined to proceed warily.

Tamsyn gazed at her companion, her expression one of bland innocence.

'How can it be possible,' she mused, 'to love two women at the same time? I find it incredible that Ivanhoe can have been attracted to both the Saxon princess, Rowena, and to Rebecca, the daughter of Israel. The two were so very different, in looks and temperaments.'

'I can only surmise that their very differences appealed to contrasting aspects of the valiant Knight's character, but I confess I have not given the matter much thought. I was more intrigued by the blunt, rough honesty of Cedric the Saxon and the savage brutality and unrelenting ferocity of Front-de-Boeuf.'

'I expect you thought the description of the tournament was admirable also?' prompted Tamsyn.

'Why certainly, it is most authentically conceived.'

Tamsyn sighed.

'Gentlemen always respond to scenes of violence, either real or imaginary; but *Ivanhoe* is so much more . . .'

John interrupted, 'Before you wax eloquent, Mrs Elsworth, may I say that I much enjoyed all aspects of the novel and I particularly admired Rebecca's passive fortitude – I found it very "womanly".'

Tamsyn pouted; John's grey eyes glinted with amusement, he had succeeded in provoking his hostess. She took refuge in contrition.

'My remark about violence was simply a statement of fact, it was not intended to imply criticism. I only wanted to tease you a little, because I felt awkward after our last meeting when I behaved so foolishly. My illness must be my excuse. I really wish to convey my thanks – I cannot tell you how much pleasure these volumes have given me.'

It was John's turn to be dismayed.

'I have thought a great deal about our meeting. Good lord, woman, how can you be such a ninny, such a goose.' He jumped up, paced the room, and with his back to her, he said evenly, 'You must know that I love you.'

Stunned by the unexpectedness of his declaration, Tamsyn could think of nothing to say. She gripped her hands together and sought vainly for some light, bantering rejoinder. She felt very much the pain of her prolonged hesitation. Suddenly, John caught her chin in a strong clasp and forced her to look up.

She saw the tenderness in his eyes, although he spoke fiercely, 'I have been too abrupt, too precipitate, but I was so sure . . . Can you not care for me at all, my dearest, or does the shadow of Gil lie between us? Perhaps it is not possible for one woman to love two men, even if one of them is dead?'

Tamsyn found her voice.

'It is not possible in so short a time, to fall in love. I value our friendship, but you will be returning to America soon, I presume, and I . . . I like my independence.' He looked so crest-fallen that she added gently,' John, reflect – it is less than two months since we first met. Matrimony is such a big step . . .'

She would have said more, but they were interrupted by Hannah, who entered wearing a cloak and carrying another over her arm.

At the sight of Mr Aylward, she stopped, 'Excuse me, Miss Tamsyn, I did not know Mr Aylward was here. You told me to be ready to go to the shelter with you at four-thirty.'

Tamsyn stood up.

'Yes, indeed, I'm just coming, Hannah. Please get Stephen to help you find a carriage and put the baskets in it. Leave my cloak there and my boots. Thank you.'

Hannah withdrew and John knelt to help Tamsyn fasten her boots.

His head bowed, he said, 'I haven't performed this service for a lady since my sister Susannah married James's brother, William Ferguson. I give you fair warning, I have not relinquished all hope, but we will let the matter rest for now. Tell me, what is this shelter your maid spoke of?'

Tamsyn resisted the urge to touch his thick, springy hair with her fingertips.

'It is a source of food and refuge for the homeless people in the City. My father was one of the gentlemen who was instrumental in causing the shelter to be set up.' She shook out her skirts and picked up her cloak. 'I would have liked to take some little toys for the children, but I haven't been out. Perhaps next time.'

'Penny whistles would be popular,' suggested John.

Tamsyn said doubtfully, 'Possibly, but do you think so much noise in a confined space is really a good idea?'

John shook his head and they smiled at one another.

John followed Tamsyn down the stairs; she paused by the mirror to adjust her hood, while he put on his coat, hat and gloves.

'I think I will come with you,' said Mr Aylward as the door opened to reveal Hannah waiting patiently for her mistress. It was a cold, windy day, but snow lay on the ground, hiding the dirt and suppressing the smells of the metropolis.

'How beautiful it is,' Tamsyn sniffed the keen air appreciatively, 'We would be happy to have your company, sir, but our way lies up Cheapside and beyond. Your hotel is in the opposite direction.'

He handed her into the hackney and climbed in after her, observing, 'It will soon be dark and the roads are treacherous with hidden ice. You may need assistance. Are you warm enough? Ah, good girl, Hannah, a hot brick and a thick rug should keep your mistress – and yourself – from suffering unduly on this errand of mercy. I wonder, Mrs Elsworth, that your father permitted you to undertake such a project so soon after your illness.'

Tamsyn gazed out of the window at the streets which were faintly illuminated by the dim rays of a watery sun.

She said firmly, 'You forget, I think, that I am responsible for my own actions. Being a widow gives one privileges and greater freedom than that accorded to an unmarried lady. Please do not concern yourself – I shall be much better for the stimulation of exercise and a change of scene. The traffic will ease when we get beyond St Paul's Churchyard. After Cheapside we will go up Wood Street, which is a major thoroughfare. Our destination lies on London Wall. My father told me that you met Mr Clowes yesterday. I have always been very fond of him; I hope you liked him?'

Tacitly John accepted the reproof and the talk turned to impersonal subjects. Tamsyn learned that Mr Clowes was much interested in harnessing the power of the steam machine to increase book production, while at the same time, reducing the price of books.

'He is a true philanthropist and wants to make books available for the mass of the people. Of course, the contents of the books would have to be designed to appeal to a wide readership. Mr Knight of Windsor has some interesting ideas on subject matter. I hope to pursue the topic further by visiting him when I go to view Oak Place, which is also in Berkshire. By the by Mr Clowes let fall one intriguing piece of gossip; it appears that Mr Knight's father was a natural son of Frederick Louis, Prince of Wales, eldest son of George II and father of George III, and a Miss Knight. It follows that Charles Knight the elder is a half-brother of your esteemed Sovereign, at present expiring at Windsor.'

Tamsyn nodded. 'Yes, I have heard that before. I see no reason to doubt the veracity of the report. Mr Clowes told me that the King was a frequent visitor to Mr Knight's book-shop in Castle Street, but that was many years ago, before his illness. I wish the American Colonies still belonged to England – then they would not seem so far away,' she explained illogically.

With unnerving swiftness, John seized on this crumb of hope.

'Hannah, put your fingers in your ears,' he commanded. The maid giggled and obeyed, but managed to listen avidly, nonetheless. 'Now, Tamsyn, kindly explain that last remark. Am I to understand that you would marry me if America could be brought closer to England in some way?'

Grateful for the all encompassing twilight gloom of the carriage, Tamsyn murmured, 'I don't know; but I do know the distance is insuperable. I know nothing about your family or your life; and my father is here, my friends are here and I like London and my life in general. Ah, here we are, at last. These baskets are heavy. Perhaps if Hannah and I carry one between us . . . ?'

Temporarily resigned, John helped mistress and maid to descend. He extracted both hampers with some difficulty, while the women waited. Then he paid the driver and told him to return in about an hour.

The frozen snow crunched beneath their feet and they could smell chestnuts roasting in a brazier. The vendor called out to attract their attention, but they ignored him.

'You jest lead the way, mum, I'll be right behind ye,' drawled John. Hannah grinned, but Tamsyn swept regally up the steps and entered the warehouse, where she reeled from the multitude of sounds and smells which assailed her senses. Gathering her forces, she wended her way across the floor, with her small retinue trailing in her wake.

John said to Hannah, 'I fear I must regret some hasty words last time we spoke. My concern for Mrs Elsworth's health must be my excuse. Please accept my apologies.'

'That's all right, sir, no offence taken. It was just one of those days when the fires burn sluggish.'

John set down the baskets where Tamsyn indicated, and fumbled in his pocket to find a coin, which he pressed into Hannah's unwilling palm. She gasped.

'A sovereign! No need for that, sir.'

'I think there is; now let's forget the matter.'

They stood in a small group, trying to get their bearings. The place seemed to be orderly and well-run, but it was very hot and crowded. On one side of the large brick building people were queueing at a long table, which held several steaming caudrons, giving off a mixture of appetizing aromas. Roaring fires burned in enormous hearths at either end of the large room; there were wooden steps to an upper storey and several young boys were performing acrobatic feats on the rail. Those who had already obtained their meals were sitting in groups on bundles of straw and sacking, their tongues loosened by the warm viands. A few had wrapped themselves in blankets and turned their backs on the world.

Hannah wrinkled her fastidious little nose and said, 'We should have brought soap and scrubbing brushes, if you ask me, miss.'

'Hush, they will hear you,' said her mistress repressively. She stood on tiptoe and exclaimed, 'Good Heavens, there is Lady Molesworthy behind that enormous tureen. I might have guessed she would have a finger in this pie.'

They approached the soup table; her ladyship caught sight of them and waved an enamel ladle.

'Put the baskets in the kitchen, if you please, Alanna will show you where to find things. We need every pair of hands.'

She turned briskly to serve the next person in line, but before anyone could move, the woman who was holding out her plate pointed a finger at John, shrieked, 'Vile Seducer!' in a piercing wail and collapsed in a dead faint on the floor, amid the splintered fragments of china.

Everyone gathered round, all speaking at once. One rough-looking man, with a black eye and intimidating mien, doubled his fists in a most menacing gesture. Lady Lucinda, with great presence of mind, banged her ladle on the cauldron, summoned her footman to carry the still unconscious woman to the back kitchen and addressed the milling throng.

'Be calm, good people. Starvation has caused the poor woman to confuse this gentleman with another. May I introduce to you Mr John Aylward, newly arrived from America. Now, I am going to see what I can do for this afflicted soul, but there is food and plenty, so eat your fill and rest yourselves. I will let you know how it all falls out.'

Very deliberately she took John's arm, obliging him to accompany her.

As they went she said cheerfully, 'I forget if I told you, John, that Mr Franklin was once quite a beau of mine. Such a charming man, but with an eye for the ladies. His achievements must be household legends in Philadelphia?'

'Why yes, ma'am, I myself peddled *Poor Richard's Almanac* one long hot summer, on a walking tour of the State of Virginia.'

'Indeed, how very interesting. You will scarcely credit this, but I have always longed to visit Williamsburg . . .'

Conversing animatedly, they disappeared from view and the inhabitants of the shelter returned to their former occupations, whispering among themselves, but no longer hostile.

John smiled down at Lady Lucinda and patted her hand.

'I thank your ladyship for your protection. They were ready to tear me limb from limb.'

They found the woman conscious and sipping water, with Tamsyn and Alanna by her side and Hannah replacing the stopper in a bottle of smelling salts. John fetched a chair and Lady Lucinda sat down. The woman watched him, studying his countenance with a puzzled frown.

'You are not Robert,' she said at length, 'I see that now.'

John shook his head gravely, Alanna gasped and Lady Molesworthy said, 'This gentleman is Mr John Aylward, cousin to Sir Robert Hawksmore. What is your name?'

At the sound of the name 'Hawksmore' the woman blenched.

Her eyes dark and shadowed with hunger and fear, she hissed, 'Curses on his name and on his house.' She sighed and seemed to crumple, her lustreless black hair fell forward, as she bowed her head. Her bones were small and delicate and it was obvious that she had once been beautiful. She spoke well, but with a pronounced French accent. They waited quietly and after a little she resumed. 'My name is Gabrielle St Marque and I come from a respectable family of lacemakers near Bruges. Robert came to us wounded, after the great battle. I regret, madame, it is not fit for the young ladies' ears, but in a nutshell when he left I was *enceinte*, with child, you would say, and when he discovered, my father, he disowned me. I came to England and wrote to Robert, but he ignored my letters. *En fin*, what would you?' She shrugged, an expressive world-weary gesture, 'I became a courtesan, but times are hard and now I am destitute and can no longer support my child. She must be cared for by the parish.'

'Is she here with you?' asked Tamsyn, much moved by this pathetic tale. Alanna said nothing, but shivered uncontrollably.

Observing this, her ladyship, who had been listening with an air of judicial scepticism, said decisively, 'Well, we will see what is to be done tomorrow. Mademoiselle, I suggest that you return to Portman Square with myself and Miss Gordon. Where is your child?'

'She lives in the country, madame, near Windsor. It was

not possible that she should share my life in London, so I found a family to look after her and I visit when I can.'

'But Oak Place . . .' began Alanna.

Mademoiselle St Marque gave Alanna a curious glance, then nodded, 'As you say, Oak Place is also near Windsor. I hoped that if Robert saw his daughter . . .' She smiled, but the smile did not reach her eyes. It was not a pleasant sight to see. She turned to Lady Molesworthy. 'I thank you for your kind offer of hospitality. I do not like to trespass, but I fear I 'ave leetle alternative.'

The matter being settled, Lady Molesworthy sent word to the inhabitants of the shelter, as she had promised, that the woman was better and would be cared for. The whole party then departed by the back door, a rather subdued group, with several members a prey to conflicting emotions. They found her ladyship's carriage at the end of the alley. Tamsyn and Hannah accepted the offer of a ride, but John declined, saying he had already engaged a hackney. He took his leave and the ladies trundled home in virtual silence, each a captive of her own thoughts.

10

Undercurrents

Contrary to her expectations, Tamsyn awoke feeling more lively and alert than she had for several weeks. By ten o'clock she had bathed, breakfasted and dispatched her most pressing domestic duties. Miss Lovett arrived opportunely and offered to read aloud to the men in the print shop, so that Tamsyn would be free to put the finishing touches to her manuscript before delivering it to Mr Hatchard on her way to Mr Hempseed's usual monthly literary lecture.

'Pray make my excuses to Mr Hempseed and tell Lucinda that I have been unavoidably detained on a mission of great importance.'

The two ladies smiled at one another conspiratorially and Tamsyn stooped to give Miss Lovett an embrace of genuine warmth.

'You are a treasure. I cannot imagine how Papa and I would have fared without your kind, but unobtrusive assistance this past month.'

Miss Lovett's rouged cheeks reddened even more and her faded hazel eyes brightened.

'I am happy to have been able to ease your burdens a little, my dear. Also, one likes to be needed – I have felt so useless since my father died. Dare I confess that even the tribulations of the later Roman Empresses were beginning to lose their savour, but Charles has changed many of my preconceived ideas; he breathes such life into a subject. It is so satisfying to explore a new era with him; together we are endeavouring to understand the rise of the Roman empire in the East.' She caught herself and patted Tamsyn's arm with her black silk mittened fingers. 'Now, I must not keep you, but I implore you, do not tell Lucinda that I have taken up with the Byzantines until I have had time to absorb them a little. She will give me no peace when she knows. My best love to her.'

She pattered away, with her Roman nose well to the fore and *The Times* tucked under her arm. Tamsyn was left feeling strangely redundant and empty, as if the baton had passed to other hands. Determined to shake off this momentary lowness of spirits, the aftermath, no doubt, of her recent illness, she ran upstairs and worked hard for the remainder of the morning, checking and re-checking her text, rearranging the tales in order to end on a cheerful note and touching up the colours on her drawing of the clown. Such solid accomplishment did much to improve her humour and it was with a very real sense of relief that she delivered her work into Mr Hatchard's eager hands at a few minutes before one o'clock.

'I cannot stay, I'm late already. Pray let me know if you like it,' said Mrs Elsworth, the author, at once proud and humble.

'Always in such haste,' chided her publisher, preserving his accustomed calm demeanour, as he escorted her to her carriage. 'And did Charles appreciate John Evelyn?'

'My dear sir, he is revelling in it. I cannot thank you enough for procuring it for me.'

'Not at all, not at all. It gave me much pleasure to serve you. I will not keep you waiting long for a word on your manuscript. Good day to you, ma'am.'

He closed the door and the carriage moved off at a sedate pace in the line of traffic. Hannah had remained at home to help Mrs Jennings and Tamsyn was grateful for the solitude. Now that she was liberated from her creative endeavours for the moment, she could give her full attention to the many developments of the weeks since the arrival of Mr Aylward and Mr Ferguson. She gazed out of the window unseeingly, but her inner eye was aware of many swirling currents and shoals which needed to be sifted and considered in relation to one another. She knitted her brows in intense concentration and checked off the various aspects on her fingers.

The heart of the matter, the root as it were from which all others stemmed, was the advent of John Aylward. In some ways she felt that she knew him quite well, in others he remained a mystery. He had declared that he loved her, but he had told her very little about himself, his family, or his plans for the future. What credentials could he offer to prove his claim to Oak Place? She suspected that her father knew something of the matter and perhaps Lady Lucinda too. She wondered if he knew himself what his intentions were. She began to feel confused and uncertain of her own mind and wishes in relation to Mr Aylward.

'That way madness lies,' she murmured, resolutely turning her thoughts to Alanna. What must be her friend's state of mind this morning after the revelations of Gabrielle St Marque (not yet proved, of course) regarding her betrothed; and how would Sir Robert react to the woman's charges? She searched her memory, pondering the extent to which Hawksmore might feel threatened already by his rival claimant for the Windlesham estates. She was obliged to admit that he had not appeared unduly alarmed; the most she could remember was Alanna's reference to 'polite hostility' when the two men met skating on the Serpentine. Would Alanna still feel bound to Sir Robert if he were to be disinherited by John – or proved indeed to be a 'vile seducer'? What would be Lady Molesworthy's attitude? Would she want Alanna to marry John instead? She grinned, but in truth it was no laughing matter. She hoped the news of Miss Lovett's transference of her time and attention to Mr Farrell would not prove the last straw; her ladyship's constitution was not as strong as she liked to suppose. Tamsyn sighed; so many questions, so few answers and her own case in such a tangle.

She arrived in Portman Square to be met by the one person whose position she had not considered – Oliver Hempseed; and it was clear to Tamsyn that he was in a very distraught state. He was ashen pale and his hands shook, while his clothes looked as if he had slept in them.

'Mrs Elsworth!' he stopped, his hand raised instinctively to straighten his cravat.

Tamsyn thought it best to behave normally. She untied her bonnet and glanced about for Josselin.

'Good morning, Mr Hempseed. I hope I am not late for our gathering. Where is Lady Lucinda?'

'There, there is no lecture today . . . did, did you not receive my message?'

He stammered in a way quite unlike his usual self. Thoroughly alarmed, Tamsyn shook her head. While she hesitated, relief appeared in the shape of her ladyship's butler, who made haste to help her remove her pelisse and fur tippet.

Observing her agitation with a trained servant's eye, Josselin spoke reassuringly, 'You find us all at sixes and sevens today, Miss Tamsyn, ma'am. Miss Gordon did send you a note, along with Mr Hempseed's, about the lecture, but ye must ha' missed it. It seems his Majesty is at death's door and her ladyship decided of a sudden to go to Windsor. Miss Gordon went with her and also the foreign person.'

The man-servant's expressive nose quivered in unspoken disapproval of Mademoiselle St Marque. Tamsyn exerted herself to respond with equal impassivity.

'I see. Thank you, Josselin. In the circumstances I will not linger, but I think Mr Hempseed is a trifle indisposed. Could you bring him some tea and perhaps a little brandy.' She turned to Oliver Hempseed. 'Where would you like the refreshments served, sir, in the morning room or the library?'

Mr Hempseed said urgently, 'Now that you are here, do stay and have some tea with me. I will tidy myself and be

115

with you directly. The morning room, if you please, Josselin.'
Not waiting for a reply, he bowed and hurried upstairs.
The butler looked at Tamsyn enquiringly. She smiled.

'I will stay a few minutes. It is cold and a hot drink would
be welcome. I need something to allay the pangs – I was
eagerly anticipating the literary luncheon – at least the
luncheon part.'

Josselin permitted his stern features to relax.

'Ye allus was one to enjoy your food, even as a little maid.
Mrs Talbot had begun to prepare for her ladyship's guests.
I'll see what I can do, after I set a taper to the fire.'

He ushered Tamsyn into a large, airy apartment on the
first floor, overlooking the courtyard garden and, greatly
condescending, bent stiffly to light the coals. Tamsyn sat
down on the elegant, uncomfortable chair which the butler
placed for her, facing the hearth.

'You are kind. Pray tell Mrs Talbot any kind of sandwiches
would be appreciated, but if she has a Cornish pasty . . .'

Josselin nodded. Lady Molesworthy's cook's pasties were
justly famed and the receipt was jealously guarded. The
butler withdrew and Tamsyn idly leafed through a new copy
of the *Ladies' Monthly Museum* while she waited for Mr Hempseed. He did not keep her long. When he rejoined her, she
was happy to see that his colour had returned and all trace
of his earlier dishevelment had gone.

Her expression must have been more revealing than she
intended, for he said wryly, 'Strange, is it not, the importance
attached to appearance? I usually strive for well-groomed
invisibility. A gentleman scholar, librarian, call me what you
will, leads a kind of half-life, rather like a governess, not
fully accepted either above or below stairs.' He sounded not
bitter, but simply matter of fact. 'My father was the vicar
of a small parish in Berkshire, a living in the gift of Lady
Molesworthy.' He seated himself, in response to Tamsyn's
gesture, and added conversationally, 'Her ladyship has been
a most kind patroness. 'Twas she who encouraged my studies
and supported my decision not to enter the Church. Perhaps
I have mentioned this before? I do not mean to bore you.'

Tamsyn disclaimed any such knowledge.

'You have always been most reticent, Mr Hempseed. I assure you I am interested; I suffer from incurable curiosity, my father says, but I try not to pry. I confess 'twas my inquisitiveness which brought me here today – at least in part. I do enjoy your lectures, of course – but after the events at the shelter yesterday evening . . .'

She hesitated and her companion intervened swiftly, 'You were there?'

Tamsyn nodded, surprised by his sharp tone.

He would have said more, but Josselin appeared followed by a footman, who set down a well-laden tray and retreated. The butler showed a distressing tendency to hover, after he had served their drinks and made up the fire.

At length Tamsyn said, 'Dear Josselin, do not let us keep you from your duties. I shall be quite safe with Mr Hempseed.' She sipped her tea meditatively. 'It is unlike her ladyship to depart in such haste. Did one of the princesses send for her?'

Oliver Hempseed shrugged.

'Possibly. She had some communication from the castle a couple of days ago. I expect she wanted to be a little ahead of the pack.'

Shocked by such disrespect and unable to think of any further excuse for remaining, Josselin stalked out and closed the door with an audible click.

Tamsyn probed gently, 'You do not think that was the real reason for Lady Molesworthy's departure?'

'No, I think she intended to go to Windsor, but the journey today was precipitated by Gabrielle St Marque.'

'You speak as if you knew her, Mademoiselle St Marque?'

He set aside his plate, adjusted his spectacles and toyed with a large gold signet ring before replying.

'I believe I once knew her, but I cannot be sure. I glimpsed her briefly in the servants' hall last night, but the light was dim and she was much changed. Mrs Talbot and the maids were clustered round her and she did not see me. I passed a sleepless night and fell asleep in my study about six o'clock

117

this morning. When I stirred it was too late for me to speak to her ladyship. She had already left town and Albert, the footman, was about to deliver Miss Gordon's note to you. I persuaded him to wait and myself scribbled a few lines to you. I gave Albert a list of literary society members and instructed him to call with a verbal message to cancel our meeting.'

Much intrigued, Tamsyn enquired, 'What did you do next?'

'I went to find some coffee and when I entered the kitchen, Mrs Talbot was just having a cup, so I joined her and we had a gossip. She was brimming over with news and delighted to have a good listener. It was most reprehensible of me, I know, to encourage her, but believe me, Mrs Elsworth, if this is the same woman that I knew, (and the name is sufficiently unusual to indicate a high probability that this is so), then Lady Molesworthy must be alerted regarding the character of this person who has so trespassed on her good nature.'

His former agitation was returning.

Tamsyn said, 'Her ladyship is a shrewd judge of people. I assure you Mademoiselle St Marque will not take advantage of her; my godmother offered assistance for her own reasons, not because the woman begged for help.'

As she spoke, Tamsyn remembered Alanna's stricken face on hearing of Robert Hawksmore's alleged involvement with the destitute woman. Mr Hempseed showed unexpected understanding of the situation.

'She would have been concerned for Miss Gordon, just so. But I must appear to you to be speaking in riddles. May I explain a little?' Tamsyn nodded and he went on, 'In the summer of 1814, during the temporary peace, I travelled to Paris to do some book purchasing on behalf of her ladyship and of Sir Jeremy Windlesham for the Oak Place library. The Continent had opened up and many people were travelling; Gabrielle St Marque, who is Belgian on her father's side, but French on her mother's, came to stay with her aunt, in whose hospitable house I also had found lodgings. Gabrielle was not a woman of easy virtue when I knew her, but she had a reputation as a rather fast young lady. She was very beautiful . . . or perhaps not, but she seemed so, with her silky dark hair, vivacious manner and provocative smile. Our temperaments were quite different; I was serious, studious, but somehow she was attracted. We were an ill-matched pair, but we fell in love. We were married secretly because of the difference in our religious faith. I had none; she was Roman Catholic. We continued to reside in her aunt's house and no one knew of our alliance, at Gabrielle's insistence – she said until she could speak to her parents. She was fascinating and infuriating by turn; I was obliged to travel to make purchases and while I was away she would encourage other men and then tease and tantalize me, when I returned.' He sighed and shook his head. 'I should not be telling you all this.'

'No, indeed,' agreed Tamsyn, disposing of her meat pasty with relish, 'but it is most fascinating. Thank you for your confidence.'

Mr Hempseed's eyes twinkled; Tamsyn had never seen him look so human and approachable.

She said, 'I had not suspected you of such a romantic past.'

'Hum,' he grunted, 'I suppose it may be considered romantic. In my humble opinion, romance is generally uncomfortable and frequently productive of unhappiness. In any event, by the spring of 1815, Gabrielle's infatuation was over and our marriage had become a torment. Then came the news of Napoleon's escape from Elba and arrival in Cannes, early in March. It was clear that he would soon be in Paris. All was chaos. Gabrielle refused to come with me to England and instead fled home to Bruges.

'With Napoleon almost at the city gates, I left for England. The books which I had shipped did not arrive for several weeks, but in late May I travelled to Oak Place with Sir Jeremy's consignment. He cordially invited me to dine and Sir Robert was also present, although he was on the point of departing to join the Duke of Wellington's Anglo-Dutch army in Belgium.

'I have always admired martial men. Unfortunately, my eyesight is too poor for me to serve usefully and her ladyship dissuaded me from volunteering. I had had no word from Gabrielle and I feared for her safety. I ventured to ask Sir Robert to be kind enough to send messages for me to Gabrielle. I spoke of her merely as a friend I had known in Paris. Sir Robert agreed to be my messenger, but had no opportunity to do so before the battle at Waterloo. He was wounded and my letter found upon him. In the general confusion, it was assumed that he knew the St Marque family; he was conveyed to their home and they cared for him. On his return to England some months later, he sent for me and told me that Gabrielle had asked him to say that she no longer wished to continue the acquaintance with me. He simply expressed his regrets, having no idea of the deep pain which he was inflicting, I truly believe. He congratulated me on my taste and said that his enjoyment of her favours had done much to speed his recovery. I was bitter; my love was unrequited, but Gabrielle was still my wife. I tried to contact her to ask for a divorce, but her father returned my letters and sent one of his own, saying that Gabrielle had run off with a wealthy lover and he had cast her out and forbidden her to darken his door again. He gave me no address. I do not know if the lover was Hawksmore or another. I determined to put all thought of love aside and buried myself in my books.'

Tamsyn cast around for some appropriate response.

At last she said, ''Tis odd, sir, that you and I were both married at about the same time, in the summer of 1814.'

'At least there was nothing clandestine about your marriage, Mrs Elsworth. For my part, I told no one of my own alliance, until this moment. I regret now that I did not speak of it to her ladyship. Of late, since Miss Gordon's attachment to Sir Robert, I have been tempted, but it seemed unwise to cast an unnecessary shadow on their betrothal.'

120

'Did you hear that Gabrielle has a child and she said last night that the father was Sir Robert?'

'There was some such rumour in the kitchen, but Albert's information was a trifle vague.' He saw the unspoken query in Tamsyn's eyes and added, 'For reasons of delicacy, I shall not elaborate, but I doubt if the child could be mine. However, much will be determined by the infant's age and appearance, if they can be reliably ascertained.'

He closed the subject, saying that he would write to her ladyship and in the meantime he would be grateful if Mrs Elsworth would keep his confidence and not discuss it with anyone. Tamsyn promised.

Then, to lighten the atmosphere, she enquired quizzically, 'You don't think 'tis better to have loved and lost, than never to have loved at all, I presume?'

'It depends upon the circumstances of the individual case – in your case, yes; in mine, no,' he responded judiciously. A thoughtful silence ensued, while they both gazed at the crackling fire. Then Oliver Hempseed resumed, 'I rejoice that you have been able to preserve your illusions. In the last few weeks I have observed a marked increase in your liveliness of spirits, but I fear I cannot flatter myself that I have contributed to your reanimation, if I may put it so.'

Dismayed, Tamsyn began to apologize for her teasing. He interrupted, saying, 'Pray do not misunderstand me, I like it. Now, let us talk of something else, before I say something I might regret. I am not quite myself today. Lady Molesworthy charged me with a message for you and it has slipped my mind, some commission . . .'

Relieved to be back on an impersonal footing, Tamsyn followed his lead and suggested, 'Perhaps it was about the invitations for the Valentine Ball. Does she wish to cancel them?'

'Of course, that was it,' he exclaimed. 'There can be little doubt, I'm afraid, that a ball will be out of the question in February. I hope your father's workshop has not already begun to manufacture the cards.'

'No, we expected something of the sort,' she reassured

him, as Josselin entered to enquire if they would like a fresh pot of tea.

Tamsyn declined, saying firmly that she ought to be leaving. She said farewell to Mr Hempseed and accompanied the butler downstairs.

'Please tell Mrs Talbot the pasty was delicious,' she requested, as she donned her outer garments. 'You should have one for your supper. Good day, Josselin.'

Albert assisted her into the coach and she drove home to George Street wrapped in profound cogitation. Strangely, it was not of Mr Hempseed that she thought, nor even of the poor King; it occurred to her – by a devious, sub-conscious mental process – that John Aylward had shown some jealousy of both Oliver Hempseed and Gil, but yet had appeared decided in his own feelings. She wondered if there was an American lady whom he favoured, or had favoured, with his friendship. That kiss under the mistletoe had not been the work of an inexperienced amateur.

An overwhelming aroma of Madras curry greeted her as she stepped into the hall, drowning the more usual scents of printer's ink, mingled with lemon polish, dried lavender, and vinegar. Her indulgence in meat pie made the prospect of curry seem less appetizing than it had when she'd ordered it that morning. Hastily, she picked up her letters from the hall chest and retreated to her sitting room. Here Tamsyn tossed aside her bonnet, rummaged for her paper knife and finally settled on the window seat, with Sam purring contentedly in her lap.

Following her invariable policy, she disposed of the apparently least interesting missives first. She set aside an invitation to an exhibition of Cornish landscape prints from Mr Ackermann – his Wednesday receptions for authors, artists, patrons and visiting foreigners were not to be missed. Perhaps James and John would like to accompany her. Next she skimmed the librarian's short communication cancelling Lady Molesworthy's literary luncheon. It contained nothing new. Alanna Gordon's note was more intriguing, her beautiful penmanship unimpaired by her evident agitation. She apologized for her haste and continued:

> . . . Grandmama's intentions are somewhat obscure. We go first to Windsor, but if his Majesty lingers some days, we may repair to Molesworthy Court as soon as the housekeeper has had time to air the rooms. Grandmama says Windsor is draughty and ramshackle, but she will do her duty if her rheumaticks permit! We will order mourning clothes in Windsor – so provincial, I cannot bear it! – and yet I must for there is no time to do anything before we leave Town.
>
> I will send word, darling Tammy, when our plans are fixed. Grandmama insists that the Belgian woman accompany us – but she will travel in the second carriage! I wish I could talk to you – but I will have time, no doubt, to write when we are settled. January in the country – and the prospect of a funeral. Pity your afflicted friend,
>
> Alanna.

Tamsyn sighed and turned to her last letter. It was no more than a single folded sheet.

My dear Tamsyn,

I regret that you were not at home when I called to take my leave. James and I feel restless amidst the approaching doom and gloom, so we have determined to flee the soot and grime of London for a while. We are going on a walking tour of the South Downs Way and hope to visit the boyhood home of our friend, Mr Clowes, in Chichester. It is also in my mind to view Oak Place, if the weather is clement and the occasion seems propitious.

I trust that you suffered no ill effects from the various shocks you sustained last night. I meant what I said, I do love you, but I think you need time and space – and that, my dearest, is the chief reason why I am going to tramp about the muddy countryside in the middle of winter.

Spare a kind thought for poor James, who has no desire whatsoever to leave the Metropolis and pray give my regards to Mr Farrell and my best respects to Lady Lucinda (what a redoubtable lady she is!) and Miss Gordon. I will write to you from time to time, so that you do not forget

Your most humble servant and friend,

John Aylward Windlesham.

'Well,' exclaimed Tamsyn, throwing down the letter and then jumping up to retrieve and reread it. The indignant Sam, thus dislodged, stalked over to the door and scratched it, meanwhile lashing his tail, his green eyes glinting ominously. Hannah nearly tripped over him when she came in to draw the curtains.

'Bless my soul, you'll be the death o' me, stupid creature.'

Tamsyn looked up and said, 'Don't scold him, Hannah, 'twas my fault. I had not noticed it was so late. You know how he likes to be fed on the dot of five o'clock.'

The maid suppressed a tart remark and lit the candles. She glanced at Tamsyn and, seeing her pale face, asked with affectionate concern, 'Can I get you anythink, ma'am? Ye look tired-like. Mr Aylward enquired after ye mos' perticular. Did you get his letter? He were that put out to ha' missed you – you'd only bin gone a few minutes.'

'Did he see my father?'

'No, ma'am, Mr Farrell and Miss Lovett were in the workroom, and Mr Aylward did not like to disturb them. He jest asked for pen and paper and sat down on the stair to write to you. It took him a long time, mos' of the time he sat gazing at the floor, chewing the end of the pen and spattering the ink about. I had to scrub hard with spirits of salts to get the stain out, but I didn't mind, 'cos he's a real gennelman, in spite of his easy manner an' I promised him faithful that you would get the letter the minute you came in – I knew you had it when I saw 'twas gone from the chest, otherwise I would ha' brought it up to you . . .'

124

'Yes, thank you, Hannah,' Tamsyn broke in to stem the flow, 'I can tell that Mr Aylward made a good impression and, no doubt, you envy the maidservants in Philadelphia where such masters are probably two a penny, but, unfortunately for you, we are in old London, where different standards prevail, so stop chattering, wench, and fetch me some coffee.'

With a sniff and a grin, the maid went to do her bidding, and Tamsyn read Mr Aylward's letter for the third, but not the last, time.

11

Correspondence

The last days of January were cold, misty and depressing. Troubles rarely come singly and Tamsyn had her share of minor problems, while the nation at large suffered from widespread commercial distress and labour unrest. Only Mr Farrell seemed immune to the prevalent mood, for he was cheerfully preoccupied with his budding courtship of Esmeralda Lovett. His daughter did not begrudge him his happiness, but his well-being emphasized her own loneliness; she missed Alanna to confide in and even Sam failed her, for he had developed an abcess following a catfight and was confined to the kitchen, where Mrs Jennings ministered to him with frequent applications of hot compresses.

In addition, Mr Hatchard requested 'adjustments' in several of her stories to 'improve the moral tone'. When Mr Farrell found Tamsyn fuming over her publisher's 'priggish suggestions', as she termed them, he was sympathetic, but not surprised.

'What else can you expect, my dear, of one who has the Clapham Sect in his back room? All those reformers of the evangelical sort, Wilberforce, Zachary Macaulay and Henry Thornton, they all read Hatchard's *Christian Observer.* John Hatchard has a reputation for extreme piety.'

'I know,' sighed Tamsyn. 'He is so respectable he even publishes Hannah More.'

Painstakingly, she rewrote the offending tales.

'If I were a child, I would not read them,' she muttered rebelliously, as she struggled to maintain the spirit, if not the letter, of the original characters. All too often, her mind would wander and her thoughts stray to the two Americans on their mid-Winter ramble. She had received no communication from John, but James Ferguson had written, in great delight to tell her that they had met Lady Montfort, the novelist, and her husband at morning service in Shawcross parish church and had been invited to dine at Huntsgrove Priory. How she envied them that experience. If only she were a man, well perhaps not, but she felt trapped and discontented in her present existence. Why, she brooded, had John felt it would aid his cause to leave her at this juncture? If he expected that absence would make the heart grow fonder, he was quite mistaken. She was much too busy to notice whether he was there or not.

She attacked her tales with redoubled vigour and, for a change of activity, she and Hannah went to the shelter and ladled soup and chopped vegetables until they were quite exhausted. Still, there came no letter from Mr Aylward, but the long-awaited word came by special messenger from Lady Molesworthy that the king had breathed his last on 29 January, at about 8.30 in the evening. She had written on Sunday, the 30th, but the accession of George IV was not proclaimed until the next day, the 31st, because Sunday was the anniversary of the execution of King Charles I, which did not seem a happy omen for the new king.

To make matters worse, his Majesty was attacked by an inflammation of the lungs contracted while listening to the proclamation in the cold air outside Carlton House. His doctors feared that the fifty-seven-year-old King might die of pneumonia or some other disorder in the first week of his reign. Meanwhile, his father was Lying in State at Windsor and his funeral was delayed until 15 February.

Alanna wrote to request Tamsyn to procure some broad black crepe for trimming, and a plume of black feathers for her ladyship,

127

. . . for there is none to be had in Windsor, though I have been much relieved to find there is a very tolerable milliner and dressmaker, a Madame Caley, who is patronized by the old Queen and the princesses.

Tamsyn reported this interesting information to her father, one morning in the following week, when he set aside his newspaper and enquired how she meant to spend her day.

'In other words, you are going shopping,' he observed acutely. 'I recommend you try the Burlington Arcade – I vow it must be the best place in London for such fripperies. Miss Lovett was in raptures over the choice and the quality of the merchandise.'

'I may, indeed, visit the Arcade, since price is no object to Alanna,' retorted Tamsyn, with somewhat unnecessary sharpness in her father's opinion. 'I will also call upon Mr Hatchard to give him my revisions, and if he is not satisfied this time – I shall offer the manuscript to Mr Murray.'

Mr Farrell was not unduly sensitive to atmosphere, but these words caught his attention. He drummed his fingers on the table and surveyed his daughter from beneath his bushy brows.

'You seem a trifle out of sorts, my child? Is aught amiss? I regret that you've been obliged to resume your mourning clothes so soon. Your new gowns became you . . .' he halted, aware that such remarks were not helpful and realizing, belatedly, that he had plunged into a seething maelstrom of suppressed anguish. Tamsyn gulped once or twice and dissolved into tears. Silently, Mr Farrell proffered his handkerchief. When the storm had subsided, he tried again.

'I suppose you're missing that minx, Alanna?'

Tamsyn nodded, blew her nose, dabbed her eyes and reached for some tea.

'That is only part of it,' she said reflectively. 'I fancy I was spoiled by all the Christmas entertainments. I had just begun to enjoy life again – and now Alanna is gone, and I resent having my pleasures snatched away so abruptly. Pay no heed to me, Papa, I am being selfish. It must be the after-effects of my recent indisposition – and my failure as an authoress.'

She gave a doleful sniff. Mr Farrell was not deceived.

'There's more to this than meets the eye, but I'll not pry, though why the devil he decided to go on a walking tour at this time of year is beyond me.'

Tamsyn hung her head sheepishly, but did not dispute this diagnosis. Her father wisely said no more on the subject, but dropped a kiss on her head and told her to buy some trinket in the arcade and he would pay for it. Then, having done his best to make amends, he dismissed the matter from his mind and went to work, while Tamsyn, inexplicably cheered by the prospect of shopping, summoned Hannah to help her get ready for her expedition.

The days dragged by and it was not until the middle of the month that Tamsyn's affairs took a sudden turn for the better. The first sign of improvement was a visit from Mr Hatchard, who called in person to inform Mrs Elsworth that he had no further fault to find with her tales and that consequently he intended to publish them in the late summer or early autumn if his terms were agreeable to her. Well-acquainted with the economics of publishing, Tamsyn assured him that they were most generous and they parted with expressions of mutual esteem. Jubilantly, she went to find her father and found him in his study, reading the afternoon post.

'Ah, Tamsyn,' he greeted her, 'Sit down, child. I was about to come in search of you. I have a letter from John Aylward and he encloses one for you, with a package.' He indicated the square box in front of him, neatly wrapped in brown paper.

She set the letter aside for the moment and began to untie the string with nimble, eager fingers. She did not quite forget the original purpose of her visit and described Mr Hatchard's reactions briefly, before examining her parcel.

She removed several layers of tissue paper padding and came at last to a soft leather case. Inside was a plain gold

129

locket in the shape of a heart and a fine gold chain, with a note which read:

> Doubt thou the stars are fire;
> Doubt that the sun doth move,
> Doubt truth to be a liar;
> But never doubt I love.
>
> (Shakespeare – *Hamlet*)

'Oh,' she whispered, displaying her gift for Mr Farrell to see. 'How beautiful. Should I accept it?'

He reached over his desk and took it to inspect more closely.

'A valuable valentine, indeed,' he commented. 'And do you mean to accept him, also?' He handed the chain back and regarded his daughter keenly.

Abstractedly she opened the locket, but it was empty.

She raised her deep blue, long-lashed eyes to meet his and said honestly, 'I don't know, Papa. What does he say in his letter to you?'

Mr Farrell adjusted his spectacles, held his correspondence at arm's length and paraphrased,

'His thanks, his apologies for departing in such haste – hum – his delight in the English countryside, which he finds much more attractive than he had expected at this season. The introductions given him by William Clowes served him well in Chichester and he has much new material for articles. He and young James were going on to Winchester and then turning inland and he asks that if any mail should come here for him from Adam Lindsay, his American lawyer, or from his friend William Pettigrew, I should forward it to "The Star and Garter" hotel in Windsor, where he intends to stay while visiting the environs of his ancestral home at Oak Place. He encloses a packet for you, his kind regards to Miss Lovett, Lady Lucinda and Alanna and he remains mine ever, etc., etc. He evidently has no idea that her ladyship has removed to Windsor. I believe he intends to renew his acquaintance with Charles Knight; Knight will be a useful contact for he has lived in Windsor all his life and he is editor of the *Windsor and Eton Express*. They will have journalism in common, if nothing else. Knight is a young man with radical notions – he believes in educating the masses through cheap literature. Rather earnest, but with a touch of humour if ye dig deep enough. He and Hatchard deal well together, in matters of both publishing and religion. Somehow I doubt that Mr Aylward is of an evangelical bent.'

Tamsyn said thoughtfully, 'Perhaps not, but he does support increased literacy. He told me that his mother teaches reading to children in a charity school and he shocked Mr Hatchard by suggesting they should read the same books as the offspring of the well-to-do.'

Mr Farrell grunted and said, 'Bound to have some republican notions with his upbringing. I won't hold it against him.'

Father and daughter smiled at one another with understanding.

'You do like him, Papa?'

'Aye, I like him well enough. I take him for a man of strength and character and if he loves my daughter that must predispose me in his favour.'

Tamsyn fingered her locket as if it were a talisman,

'How I wish America were not so far away,' she wailed dismally.

'Perhaps he will settle at Oak Place. Berkshire is no great distance,' suggested Mr Farrell. 'His credentials seem impeccable; I gather it is more a question of his choice, according to the lawyers' letters. Does he *want* to inherit?'

Tamsyn shook her head.

'I do not think he has made up his mind.'

'Well, perhaps he will when he sees the library. It is one of the finest collections of rare books in the country. Hempseed catalogued it and waxes eloquent in its praises.'

Tamsyn sighed, 'That may not be enough to entice him. We must remember that England is in many ways a foreign country to him.'

Charles Farrell regarded his daughter with compassion.

'God knows I do not want to lose you, my child, but I do

know that all else is dust and ashes if you lose the one you love.'

Tamsyn replied steadily, 'I know – have you forgotten Gil?'

'Do not let it happen again,' he retorted, 'For different reasons, but perhaps the same result. Do not put John Aylward off from a misplaced sense of loyalty or duty to me. I will do well enough with Esmeralda Lovett, if she will have me. It is not the passion of youth, but our attachment grows daily and we both need companionship. Now go and read your letter and let me get on with my work. Gossiping won't pay the bills.'

Obscurely comforted, Tamsyn did as she was bid.

The first part of John's letter was disappointing in that it proved to be strangely impersonal. He repeated much of the information in Mr Farrell's letter, adding only that he intended to visit Jane Austen's grave at Winchester. The second page proved more rewarding for he confessed himself 'pen-tied' when writing to her, being uncertain of her reaction to his 'ramblings' and observed that he had never had this problem before. He sounded low in spirits and this was confirmed when he ended that he was tired, cold, lonely and missing the bright sparkle and elusive charm of her presence.

She sat down at once and composed a cheerful reply, in which she thanked him for his gift, which she had decided to accept. She was fortunate that Mr Charles Knight called on her father that evening after dinner and kindly volunteered to take her letter to Windsor. He would not stay for refreshments, as he wished to be in Windsor in time to attend the King's funeral on the following day.

'It is good of you to be my messenger, sir,' she said, as he stood up to leave. He was a man of middle height, with finely-cut features and sharp, piercing eyes indicating a keen intelligence. Tamsyn thought he was probably in his late twenties, but he did not look robust and might be older.

'I wished to call upon Mr Aylward in any case, to give him a copy of my new monthly serial work entitled *The Plain*

Englishman – and so it will give me no trouble and indeed great pleasure to play Cupid.'

He gave Tamsyn one of his rare smiles and departed.

'Too late to change your mind about that letter now,' teased Mr Farrell, as Tamsyn resumed her chair by the fire, 'What do ye make of Knight? Not one to waste words, is he? At least, not in person. On paper he's prolific enough.'

'What is this serial work?'

'It's planned to be a work of original compositions and selections from the best writers. Cheap, good literature to counteract the two-penny trash. At least that was my understanding when he told me of the project last month. He's writing the part on current affairs and that brings him to London, to glean material. I shall subscribe, but I doubt if it will fly for long – too ambitious.'

'Dear Papa,' Tamsyn leaned forward to warm her hands, 'You're always soft-hearted. Is Mr Knight married?'

'I believe so. I've never met her, but I know Knight moved from the accommodation above his father's bookshop near the castle to a cottage by the Thames a few years ago. He suffers from chronic ill-health and it is a damp town with bad drains, but I cannot think a dwelling by the river would be much of an improvement. William Clowes told me he is an ardent social reformer and probably short of funds, in part because of his work as an overseer of the poor, which he performs in addition to his publishing ventures. His father, Knight senior, was appointed mayor of Windsor two years ago and both Knights are well-respected in the town.'

'How hard he must work, but I thought him very agreeable. Such a cold night for his journey – I hope it improves for the funeral tomorrow or many people will get sick. Would you care to play a game of dominoes, Papa?'

They played, as was their wont, with great concentration, and Tamsyn dismissed Mr Knight from her mind.

Her next news from Windsor came a few days later in the form of two letters, one from Lady Molesworthy and one from Alanna, delivered in person by Albert, her ladyship's footman. The purport of their combined communications was that having done their duty in attending the funeral service in St George's Chapel, they now proposed to remove to Molesworthy Court. Here Alanna needed some company to prevent her falling into a decline, and Lady Lucinda urgently required relief from the burden of chaperonage, so that she could nurse her aching bones (much exacerbated by the damp mists of Windsor) and be at liberty to deal with affairs of the estate; the two ladies joined in beseeching Tamsyn to join them. Albert would accompany her in the travelling carriage and she could share Alanna's maid, if Hannah could not be spared from George Street. They longed to see her and, as an afterthought, could she bring some black lace of various widths, for collars and cuffs?

'When do you return to Berkshire?' Tamsyn asked Albert, who was waiting for her reply.

'The day after tomorrow, if it please you, Mrs Elsworth, mum,' he said, briskly, springing to attention.

'Very well, I will send a note to Portman Square tomorrow, if I decide to come. At what hour should I be ready?'

'At half past eight in the morning. It's a slow journey with the traffic and her ladyship said I should make sure you arrive before dark.'

Tamsyn nodded.

'Thank you, Albert.'

The tall manservant strode back to the waiting carriage with a jaunty step and jumped up on the box. He was clearly enjoying his responsibilities.

Once again Tamsyn went to find her father and met him on the back stairs, carrying a cup of coffee and a pile of papers. The coffee was tilted at a precarious angle.

'Oh, Papa, give it to me. You're carrying too much. Can I speak to you for a moment?'

They continued upstairs to the little antechamber where she had first met John Aylward. As soon as they were settled, she began.

'Papa, Alanna and my godmother have invited me to stay for a while at Molesworthy Court, but I am in the middle of type-setting Alan Dean's manuscript on *The Sublime and the Ridiculous in Parisian Society* and I promised Miss Lovett to help her make over her best mourning gown in time for the concert next week. Should I go?' she finished breathlessly.

Charles Farrell gave a rumbling laugh and his whole body shook. Tamsyn grinned; he was an infectious sight.

At length he said, 'In Heaven's name, child, GO. Hannah can help Esmeralda with her sewing and Alan Dean's book can wait a little – it is a foolish topic anyway. No wonder he is paying to have it privately printed. A change of scene would be beneficial for you – you've been a trifle overwrought these past weeks. Young company and luxurious surroundings, the countryside in early spring – ye'll be set up in no time. Besides you're at a loose end with your book done; and don't fret, I'll send the galleys along when they come. Can you think of any other objections?'

Tamsyn jumped up and gave her father a warm embrace.

'Not one, dear sir. I love you very much.'

'. . . and pray give my regards to Mr Aylward,' he added slyly as she whisked away to begin her preparations.

That she was indeed ready on time, when Albert arrived with the Molesworthy second best carriage, was something of a minor miracle. She and Hannah had shopped and mended and sorted and sewed far into the night, but she felt awake and alert as she drove through the streets of the metropolis, unaware that a plot to assassinate the entire Cabinet, including Lord Sidmouth and Lord Castlereagh, at a dinner party on the previous night, had been narrowly averted. The Cato Street Conspiracy, as the revolutionary plot came to be called, was followed by a number of alarming incidents, in various parts of the country, but Tamsyn found Molesworthy Court and the neighbouring village of Windlesham as peaceful and tranquil as ever. It was some years since she had visited Berkshire and she donned her riding habit after breakfast on her first morning in a happy mood of expectation.

'I hope you have a gentle horse for me to ride. I haven't been in the saddle for at least a year,' Tamsyn remarked to

135

her friend, as they stood on the front steps in the bright sunshine, waiting for their mounts to be brought round from the stables.

'Moonlight is a sweet-tempered mare, about four years old and very steady,' Alanna reassured her.

They set off for the village at a sedate pace, with Albert's brother, Will, the groom, following at a discreet distance.

'I had forgotten how beautiful it all is,' said Tamsyn, as they rounded a bend in the drive and she looked back at the old, mellow stone house, with its formal lawns and beech-woods, enfolded in a cup of the Berkshire hills. Out of sight, she knew, there were stables and orchards and the kitchen garden, with a pretty little stream which meandered through the estate, and reappeared in the village near the black-smith's forge.

'Lovely, but tedious living in the country. Paradoxically, I find one has almost less freedom than living in town. How-ever, it will be better now that you are here. Thank you for coming to my rescue. You were too tired for me to tell you last night, but I am so pleased to see you. Now, tell me all the news. I'm starved for society gossip. The black lace is perfect for a half veil; where did you find such exquisite quality?'

The young ladies were still deeply immersed in conver-sation when they reached the village shop. Here they dis-mounted and Tamsyn renewed her acquaintance with Miss Pepperbox, the proprietress, who remembered Mrs Elsworth as a little girl. Escaping at last from the good woman's flow of reminiscence, they continued on foot past Diggles' alms-houses to the stagecoach inn, The Lime-burners, where Tamsyn gave directions about forwarding her mail to the big house.

Will was waiting in the courtyard with the horses. Tamsyn stroked 'Moonlight's' velvety nose while Alanna mounted, with the groom's help.

'My godmother appears in good health,' observed Tam-syn, shading her eyes from the sun. A thought occurred to her and she blurted it out without reflection. 'Whatever happened to Gabrielle St Marque?'

Alanna glanced at Will and shook her head. She waited until Tamsyn was in the saddle and the groom fell back a few paces.

'My dear, she drinks.' she hissed dramatically.

12

A Visit to Windsor

Tamsyn raised her eyebrows, but made no reply to Alanna's revelation until they had crossed the bridge by the forge and entered the lane which led past the church.

'Perhaps she drinks because she misses her child,' she suggested tolerantly. 'Has she seen the infant since you came to the country?'

'Not to my knowledge. She was so sick that Grandmama sent her directly to Molesworthy Court; we feared that she might contract some deadly fever in her weakened state. But her habit of over-indulgence is the talk of the servants' hall. Mrs Ryder, the housekeeper, is at her wit's end and no one dares tell her ladyship.'

They emerged from the shade of the churchyard elms and the horses startled a pair of magpies which flew squawking from the hedgerow. The vicar was standing at the gate of his abode as they rode past, a Celtic-looking man, small of hand and foot, with dark hair and deep-set impenetrable brown eyes. He raised his hand in greeting and they wished him good day, but did not linger as a child cried and his wife called to summon his help in a domestic emergency.

'Mr Davis is a kind man, but indolent,' reported Alanna, unconsciously repeating Lady Lucinda's trenchant criticism'. 'He is from the town and does not understand the cruelty, ignorance and cunning of the countryside. His poor wife has ten children already and another on the way.'

They had reached a fork in the lanes and paused to let the horses drink from a thoughtfully-placed trough.

'Is the living in her ladyship's gift?' queried Tamsyn.

'Oh no, she would never have appointed Mr Davis. It is part of the Windlesham estate. Old Sir Jeremy Windlesham chose him, or perhaps the estate steward when Sir Jeremy was ill. You recall that lane leads to Oak Place?'

Alanna indicated the way to the right with her whip; following her direction, Tamsyn regarded the bare, windswept fields with interest. She sniffed appreciatively.

'Air, sun and wind, so refreshing,' she murmured.

Alanna's expression was sceptical.

'That's because you only arrived yesterday. I'll warrant after a month you will not enthuse so; my delicate skin is red and sore after a little exposure to these bleak gales, invigorating though they may be. Let us be on our way. We dine early in the country.'

They moved on, bearing to the left and dipping down into a mossy track which followed the windings of the stream through a little wood. For a while they were obliged to go in single file, with Alanna leading the way; Tamsyn wished enviously that she could appear as slender, graceful and confident on horseback as her friend. Moonlight stumbled, but recovered; Tamsyn hastily recalled her wandering wits and gave her full attention to her mount. At length they emerged from the copse and entered the park of Molesworthy Court by the West Lodge. Will dismounted to open the gate for the young ladies; they proceeded slowly along the sweeping carriage drive.

'You don't care much for the country, do you, Alanna?' remarked Tamsyn, taking up the thread of their earlier conversation.

Miss Gordon reflected, her golden curls blowing in her eyes; she turned to face away from the wind and met Tamsyn's quizzical gaze directly.

'It depends upon the circumstances. I might like it, in summer, with congenial company, but sometimes it

139

frightens me. I hear an animal in one of those wicked traps, or see a child with a club foot and vacant expression. And people gossip so. It is always "they say . . .", but nobody takes any responsibility personally. Even the gentry are narrow-minded and superstitious, sentimental, but insensitive. All change, even for the better, is stoutly resisted . . .' She sighed.

Tamsyn was amazed.

'My dear, what has happened? You were not wont to take such a gloomy view of human nature.'

Alanna made a fluttering helpless gesture with her hand.

'I suppose it is the prospect of forming an alliance with a man who does not love me and being alone so much of late, with time to brood. The King's funeral was a very sad occasion. We sat in the organ loft near Mrs Arbuthnot, the Duke of Wellington's confidante, and it was very dark and sombre, but the music was uplifting and grand, yet somehow empty. Pay me no mind, Tammy, wearing unrelieved mourning always oppresses my spirits and my vanity.'

They had reached the front entrance of the Court. Will helped them down with easy strength and led the horses away.

'Did you enjoy your ride?' asked Alanna, as they ran upstairs to change.

'Very much, I thank you. Moonlight is a darling and very patient with my incompetent signals.'

'Yes, she is,' Alanna agreed, grinning, 'and you will be stiff tomorrow.'

They parted, but Tamsyn felt ruefully that her friend's prophecy was already beginning to be fulfilled when she joined her godmother and Miss Gordon for dinner. She winced as she sat down; for once her ladyship was sympathetic.

'A warm bath and an early bed will relieve the aches,' she pronounced, 'and tomorrow perhaps you would prefer a carriage ride. I intend to go to Windsor and would enjoy the company. You too, of course, Alanna. She's been rather peaked since we came into the country, Tamsyn. Left too much to her own devices. Now, tell us your news? I trust Charles was in good health?'

Lady Lucinda picked up her soup spoon and her guest took a deep breath.

'He was in excellent spirits, ma'am. He sent you his humble duty and Miss Lovett also asked to be remembered.'

Her ladyship choked on a crouton, took a drink of water and said sharply,

'Esmeralda has been prominent in your letters of late; she appears to have become almost a fixture in your household.'

'She has been most kind and attentive during our illnesses. Indeed, it is entirely owing to her good offices that I was able to leave Papa and join you so speedily.' Tamsyn smiled disarmingly.

Alanna asked curiously, 'Do you think they might marry?'

Trapped, Tamsyn shrugged.

''Tis in the lap of the gods, but I believe it is possible. Nothing is settled, but they are happy in one another's society and I have done all I can to promote the match.'

'Their characters are complementary; I imagine they will deal very well together,' pronounced her ladyship unexpectedly, pushing her plate away.

Tamsyn and Alanna looked at one another in astonishment across the table.

Correctly interpreting their expressions, the older lady observed tartly, 'Why should I object? 'Tis none of my affair and I am always in favour of commonsense solutions. Your father works too hard and needs a companion for relaxation and diversion; and Esmeralda deserves a better lot in life than has heretofore been her portion. In the nature of things, you will probably marry again before long; which reminds me – have you had word from young Mr Aylward, as he calls himself?'

Tamsyn laughed and said, 'Are you a witch, Godmama? Yes, I have heard from John Aylward. He sent me a letter and a valentine last week.'

'Oh, you sly puss. You didn't tell me. What did he send you?' exclaimed her friend.

141

'News of his walking tour with James Ferguson. He says James has grown a moustache which is very luxuriant, while away from civilization. He wrote from Winchester and I understand he may visit this neighbourhood quite soon. He also sent me this locket,' She indicated the chain she was wearing. 'There is nothing in it.'

Alanna peered between the candlesticks and Lady Lucinda lifted her lorgnette.

'Simple and elegant,' said her ladyship, dropping her glass and turning to select a wing of chicken.

'It may be one of the lockets with a hidden spring,' suggested her granddaughter, 'Try pressing in the centre on the right.'

Tamsyn did as she was bid and was delighted to hear a tiny click; the smooth surface thus released, opened to reveal a small compartment. She saw the initials 'J' and 'T' intertwined and the words 'Be mine' engraved below.

'Oh, how vexing that I did not know that was there when I wrote to thank him. What must he think?'

Her eyes clouded in dismay.

'Either he will think how modest you are; or he will divine correctly that you did not find the hidden compartment. It is no bad thing to keep him guessing,' said Alanna.

They ate in silence for a few minutes, each following her own train of thought. Lady Lucinda was the first to speak.

'It does not seem as if you needed a valentine ball to find a beau, Tamsyn Elsworth; but I regret being obliged to cancel it for Alanna's sake. This is not an opportune moment for us all to be in mourning.' She drummed the table with impatient, heavily beringed fingers.

Surprised, Alanna protested, 'But, Grandmama, I thought you wished me to wed Sir Robert Hawksmore.'

Her ladyship sighed and wriggled irritably in her chair.

'I'm not so sure now. I may have been hasty in encouraging you to regard him with favour. Until this question of the inheritance of Oak Place is settled between him and John Aylward, I must withdraw my consent to your betrothal. It was to have been announced at the ball,' she explained

142

for Tamsyn's benefit. 'Perhaps, after all, we shall derive some advantage from this court mourning; it gives us a space for these cousins to sort out their affairs. I regret that you are denied the youthful frivolity of the season, however, for once you are married life is never the same again.' She munched meditatively, 'And then there is the problem of the drunken St Marque woman.'

Once again Alanna's expression registered shock; her tight little curls bobbed furiously. Tamsyn was amused.

'Do you know everything, ma'am?' she enquired.

'If it goes on under my nose, in my household...' responded her ladyship, fixing the wooden footman with a fierce glare. 'Clear, Albert,' she commanded.

'May I ask, Godmama, if Mr Hempseed has written to you concerning Gabrielle St Marque?' Tamsyn ventured, when the covers had been removed.

'He did and a fine pother he was in, after he spoke to you. I told you, I believe, Alanna, that Oliver Hempseed may have been acquainted with our Belgian guest in the year of Waterloo? I have written and invited Hempseed to join us for dinner next week. I have also invited Sir Robert Hawksmore. I think perhaps Mr Aylward should be here too. I will leave a message for him when we are in Windsor tomorrow. The reason I wish to be in the town is to discover if various enquiries which I set in train have been resolved.'

She sat back with an air of satisfaction, her elbows resting on her chair, the tips of her fingers together; her bright eyes flashed from one puzzled face to the other.

'The woman's child must be found. It is unusual, you understand, for a foreign child to be fostered in a country parish and if Mademoiselle St Marque could no longer pay for her upkeep, she may be in some charitable institution. I cannot persuade her to divulge the child's whereabouts. I suppose she fears to lose her.'

'Mr Charles Knight is an overseer of the poor, he may be able to assist you,' offered Tamsyn. 'I met him last week, when he called on Papa.'

'You mean the mayor of Windsor?' It was Lady Lucinda's turn to look puzzled.

'No, ma'am, his son, who bears the same name. The younger Mr Knight is a journalist, and in that capacity (as well as in his public office for the poor) he has much local knowledge.'

'A journalist?' Alanna's lip curled. 'He cannot be a gentleman.'

'Mr Aylward is also a journalist,' Tamsyn reminded her, 'and they are both gentlemen, in the truest sense.'

Alanna acquiesced good-naturedly, 'Well, if you vouch for him, my dear Tammy, there is no more to be said.'

'Enough bickering, young ladies,' interposed her grandmother, rising from the table. 'Your suggestion is a good one, Tamsyn. I will certainly consult Mr Knight. Do you know where Mr Aylward intends to stay in Windsor?'

'His direction is The Star and Garter Hotel,' said Tamsyn, as she and Alanna followed Lady Molesworthy to the door. Here they parted. Her ladyship sought the comfort of her room, but the other two spent an hour before bed, drinking tea and browsing through the latest modes in the magazines which Tamsyn had brought with her.

'Black crepe flowers to trim a bonnet, ugh.' Alanna shuddered.

'Very distasteful,' Tamsyn agreed. She pointed to one of the coloured fashion plates. 'This is better, epaulettes shaped like a scallop shell. You would look well with a plume of black feathers on this bonnet, but it is not easy to contrive a becoming effect in bombazine. I have a new silk walking dress, with a full skirt and double flounce. I will wear it tomorrow, if it is fine.'

'We must go to bed,' said Alanna at last. 'Fanny will wake us very early and you must be tired after your journey and the ride.' She walked over to the window and looked out to the darkened garden, fitfully illuminated by a nearly-full moon. 'Wouldn't it be strange,' she mused, 'if you were to live at Oak Place instead of me? Of course, Molesworthy Court will be mine one day. We could grow old side by side.'

144

She turned to face Tamsyn.

'Do you intend to accept John Aylward?' she asked softly.

Mrs Elsworth looked down at her friend.

'Papa asked me the same question. I told him I did not know. He has doubts and so do I, as to whether John will decide to live in England. After all, his upbringing was American and his mother and sisters live there. Also, I like my independence. Lady Lucinda is quite right in saying that one's life changes after marriage.'

'You will have to decide whether to follow your head or your heart. I do not envy you that decision.'

'I cannot make any decision until John Aylward makes his.'

She gathered up the scattered magazines and her shawl and they quitted the cosy, panelled chamber and lit their candles in the hall. Alanna went ahead, carefully shielding the flame with her hand as she passed the landing window.

'Grandmama says in our station there are few really happy couples; one does not expect it,' she said over her shoulder.

'At least you are reprieved. She is no longer insisting that you should marry Sir Robert.'

Alanna lifted a finger to her lips, as they tiptoed along the upper passage.

'Hush, Gabrielle sleeps in here.'

At Tamsyn's bedchamber door, she paused and whispered, 'You will think me mad, but I am not sure I wish to be reprieved. Goodnight, sweet dreams.'

She blew a kiss and slipped into her own room before Tamsyn could reply.

As arranged, the ladies were up betimes the next morning. Fanny told Tamsyn, when she woke her with hot chocolate, that there was a keen wind, but the day promised to be dry. Accordingly, Mrs Elsworth donned her new black silk travelling dress and hoped the effect was not spoiled by the addition of sturdy half-boots, which she felt obliged to wear in case they should do much sightseeing. She completed her ensemble with a pelisse of fine black cloth, a small black bonnet, the brim lined with white crepe which she felt gave

145

a pleasing effect, and the inevitable black gloves. She was happy to note, when she joined Lady Molesworthy and Miss Gordon in the hall, that both ladies were sensibly shod in boots similar to her own.

They drove in state the few miles to Windsor in her ladyship's capacious barouche, which displayed the Molesworthy crest on side doors and boot. Their hostess pulled down her veil and dozed, while Alanna huddled in her corner, yawning and seemingly not disposed for conversation. Tamsyn seated beside the maid, Evans, had her back to the horses, but she enjoyed the drive nonetheless for her sharp eyes caught many hints of spring in the fields and hedgerows. She glimpsed the River Thames as they approached the town by the Maidenhead road but, seated as she was, she missed the view of the castle and was obliged to be content with the bustling townspeople and their shops. The carriage rattled uphill, over the cobblestones, until they arrived at the very heart of the town, the junction of the High Street and Castle Street. Here the ladies descended and Lady Lucinda directed her coachman to await them at The Star and Garter.

Then she turned to Alanna and Tamsyn, saying, 'I have some business to attend to in the castle. Evans can accompany me and you may explore the town a little. I am acquainted with Mr Knight's bookshop; you recall, Alanna, it is over there on the hill, opposite Henry VIII's gateway to the lower ward of the castle? I will meet you there at noon.'

'Very well, Grandmama.'

Alanna bobbed a dutiful curtsey.

She waited until the older lady and her maid had disappeared from view through the castle gateway and then observed mischievously, 'She treats me like a child. I have known Mr Knight's shop since I was ten years old, but I never thought much about the name of the proprietor. I suppose he must be the father of your Mr Charles Knight? A very respectable citizen, my dear, and very dull – he tells long stories about the times the old king would come and visit his shop and read seditious works by Tom Paine, or some such name.' She wrinkled her nose, 'Ugh, how it stinks when one is downwind of the ditches. Come with me, we'll go along Church Street and I'll show you the house where Nell Gwyn is supposed to have lived. We'll visit Madame Caley's, but she is expensive and there is also Miss Hudson's, by The Star and Garter, who sometimes has the same goods at lower prices.'

They spent a stimulating morning, patronizing the chief milliners and haberdashers in Windsor. As the hour approached midday, they trudged back up the hill, laden with a variety of small packages and one large hatbox. The latter belonged to Miss Gordon, who had been unable to resist a grey satin bonnet, topped by a plume of grey feathers.

'It will be perfect for half-mourning next month,' she remarked breathlessly, as they reached the brow of the hill and the grey stone walls of the castle loomed above them. She shivered delicately, adding, 'The castle looks so lowering and lifeless without the royal family. In truth, it is a miserable place, full of tunnels and passages and rooms that cannot be entered without going through other rooms. No doubt it is very old and grand, but in my opinion it needs a thorough renovation. Let us find a place to sit down out of the wind; we're early and I don't want to get trapped listening to one of Mr Knight's interminable tales.'

They found a sheltered spot, as she suggested, and put down their parcels with sighs of relief.

'We should have brought one of the footmen with us, but Grandmama does not think it necessary to "keep an army of servants eating their heads off in the country"'.

Alanna mimicked with her usual impish accuracy.

'Quite right,' responded Tamsyn, wriggling her cramped toes and wishing she had bought her boots a half a size larger. 'I like the unpretentiousness of Molesworthy Court; it is a comfortable house. Oak Place is renowned for its style and grandeur, I believe?'

'Oh, have you never been there? Yes, it is quite different from the Court, much newer. It was built by old Sir Jeremy's grandfather about a hundred years ago and is a most imposing residence, with plenty of pillars and porticoes; Sir Robert will be happy there, he prefers the classical style. But I keep forgetting, he may never live there. Don't look now but there are three men coming up Thames Street and one of them is pointing to us; how ill-mannered. He has a moustache and the others are in breeches and top boots and carrying fishing rods.'

Knowing that her friend was a little near-sighted, Tamsyn could not resist glancing over her shoulder.

She turned back hastily and said in a rapid undertone, 'My dear, I beg of you, do be polite. It is the younger Mr Knight and his companions are James Ferguson, with the moustache, and John Aylward.'

13

Lady Lucinda's Dinner Party

'I am a lady. I am always polite except when confronted with impertinence,' said Miss Gordon, rising with dignity.

Tamsyn stood up reluctantly, feeling windswept and shop-weary, and wishing very much that her boots would stop pinching more with each passing moment. Innate good breeding came to her aid and she presented a serene exterior to the three young men who made their bows and shook hands. Alanna was introduced to Mr Knight and gave him the tips of her fingers. She warmed a little when he apologized for his dust and the unmistakable smell of fish, which hung about him.

'We were resting a moment on our way to visit your father's bookshop, Mr Knight. We are meeting my grand-mother, Lady Molesworthy, and I believe there is a matter on which she wishes to consult you,' she said graciously.

'Then by all means let us adjourn hither; it is but a step,' he replied eagerly. 'We must not keep her ladyship waiting. I would offer my arm, but I fear that burdened as I am, that honour must fall to Mr Ferguson. Pray follow me.'

He leaped nimbly across the street, followed at a slower pace by Alanna and James, deep in bantering conversation. Tamsyn and Mr Aylward brought up the rear, carrying most of the packages.

'Why are you hobbling?' John enquired.

'My boots are too tight and I have a blister,' Tamsyn responded shortly.

These were not the first words she had dreamed of saying; she scowled.

'Hop,' he commanded. 'Or would you like me to carry you.'

'Neither, I thank you.' She stumbled and gave a cry of pain.

'Wait there, give me your parcels. Good girl.' She reseated herself on the bench by the wall; he soon returned. 'You remind me of my sisters,' he said, as he assisted her halting steps. 'Why are women so foolish and vain when it comes to footwear? Am I very fishy?'

Tamsyn tried hard not to laugh, but in the end she gave a giggle.

'That's better,' he said encouragingly, as they entered the bookshop to the tinkle of a little bell.

Tamsyn rejoiced in the familiar musty aroma of books and bindings. Mr Knight, senior, bustled forward and kindly ushered her up the stairs to his sitting room overlooking the Round Tower, where he provided a basin of warm water, a cloth and a court plaster. Then he discreetly retired. Ten minutes later, soothed and refreshed, Mrs Elsworth rejoined the company.

The younger Mr Knight also reappeared, looking more presentable. He stood on the threshold regarding the scene with an expression of contemplative melancholy remarkable in one so young Tamsyn thought. He was probably younger than John, but he appeared to have the cares of the world on his shoulders. Her ladyship was holding the floor, with the bookseller in close attendance.

'Do you live here with your father, sir?' she whispered.

Mr Knight roused himself to respond.

'No, ma'am. I live with my wife, Sally, in a cottage near the river. It is just off the Long Walk in a fairly isolated position. My mother died when I was a child and I lived here until I was married; I try to visit my father as often as possible. I came today to bring him some fish.'

'Ah, here is my son . . .'

The young man thus summoned went forward dutifully to be presented to her ladyship.

'A journalist, I understand, pray what is your opinion of our new Queen Caroline?' Lady Lucinda sat down in the bookseller's own high-backed, carved wooden chair, and bent on young Mr Knight a hard stare, which would have intimidated a lesser man. He did not hesitate. 'In my opinion she is an injured wife, but also a depraved woman.'

'Her ladyship does not believe in beating about the bush,' murmured John in Tamsyn's ear, 'but I think she may have met her match in Charles Knight. Come and sit down.'

He led her to a pair of stools set a little apart in the corner containing works of theology and sermons. Tamsyn noticed that he was wearing a black armband, presumably as a gesture of respect to the English king in whose reign the American colonies had forever severed their ties to the 'Old Country'.

'I had forgotten that little mole by the side of your mouth,' said John, observing her appreciatively. 'Country air must suit you, you look much better than you did when I saw you last.'

'A doubtful compliment, but I will accept it in a positive spirit.' Tamsyn rubbed the aforementioned mole with her finger and glanced at the shelves behind her. 'Do you intend to remain long in this vicinity?'

'If you do,' he returned promptly. 'I haven't had an opportunity to visit Oak Place yet. Knight tells me that the house is about three miles from Molesworthy Court. Do you know if there is a tolerable inn in Windlesham?'

'There is The Limeburner's. I believe they have a few rooms. It is clean, but very plain,' she said dubiously.

'I am used to simple rustic conditions.'

Tamsyn caught the hint of irony; she decided to change the subject.

'I hope you received my letter of thanks when you arrived in Windsor?'

'It was not at the hotel when we enquired at the desk,

151

and James will tell you I was like a bear with a sore head the whole afternoon, quite unimpressed by the antiquities around me. However, Knight called on his way home before dinner with your missive and my humour was vastly improved, so much so that even our earnest friend teased me about my lively spirits.' He craned his neck to see the others; satisfied that they were not missed, he continued, 'It is some years since I have sent a valentine token and never with such uncertainty concerning its reception. I could not trust my memory on the sonnets, although I wanted to write "Shall I compare thee to a summer's day" – but I dared not wait to search for it, knowing that I might miss the mail and be late with my valentine, an unpardonable offence. So I was reduced to *Hamlet*, which I was obliged to memorize in school, never dreaming how grateful I would be one day. And I like to buy gifts, I saw the locket in a little jeweller's near the market cross in Chichester – it was not intended to compromise you in any way. When can I see you again?'

Across the room, Lady Molesworthy stood up, looked round and beckoned imperiously to Mr Aylward.

'I believe she intends to invite you to dinner,' Tamsyn offered in an undertone, perceiving that John was disinclined to obey the summons. He smiled and threw out his hands in a gesture of resignation, then jumped down from his stool and turned to assist Tamsyn from her high perch. He gripped her elbows for a moment.

She added hastily, 'I will wear my locket if you come.'

They crossed the wooden boards together, Tamsyn's silk skirt swishing in a way most satisfactory to its owner.

'Ah, Tamsyn, my dear, are you ready? And Mr Aylward, perhaps you and Mr Ferguson will have the goodness to escort us to my carriage? We must not keep Mr Knight and his son any longer. I thank you both for your assistance, good sirs, you have been most patient and helpful with all my enquiries. Good afternoon.'

She swept regally to the door, which Charles Knight held open for her.

'Pray send me a copy of your new publication, young man,

152

I'm intrigued by the idea of a *Plain Englishman* and, as always, I am in need of some fresh reading material.'

Mr Knight bowed and said, 'I shall be delighted to send you the next copy. The March edition should be off the press any day now. Thank you, ma'am, and might I add, don't let your librarian read it, unless you wish to bring on an attack of apoplexy.'

His deep-set eyes twinkled with unexpected humour.

Lady Lucinda gave a cackle of laughter and departed, followed by the rest of her entourage. Tamsyn delayed to thank the bookseller for his hospitality; when she caught up with the others she found that the dinner invitation had been given and accepted by Mr Aylward for the following Wednesday. James, it appeared was unable to come, as he was returning to London earlier in the week.

'Do you have any message for your father?' enquired James, while they waited for Lady Molesworthy to settle comfortably in her carriage.

'Only my love, if you see him, I thank you. Will you be returning to Windsor, James?'

'Possibly. It depends on John; he needs time to be in the country and look at the estate, but I can be more usefully occupied in London.'

'You did not wish to leave the city in the first place, I think' Tamsyn teased gently.

James flushed and flung back a lock of hair, with a gesture of disgust.

'The country is so, so . . .' he searched vainly for the right word.

'Rustic, is that not so, Mrs Elsworth?' supplied John.

She smiled; Alanna leaned forward to the open door.

'For once I am in complete agreement with you, James. Goodbye. Kiss Uncle Charles for me.'

'Alanna, sit still and stop behaving like a hoyden. Mind your skirt in the door, Tamsyn. Good day Mr Ferguson. Until Wednesday, Mr Aylward.'

The door was closed and the well-trained horses began to move.

'A very satisfactory expedition,' pronounced her ladyship. Tamsyn thought of all that John had said and Alanna clasped the hat-box on her knee.

'Yes, indeed, ma'am,' they said together.

Not wishing to raise the subject before Evans, who probably knew everything anyway, Tamsyn waited until the evening after dinner to ask Lady Lucinda if Mr Knight had been able to give her any positive information concerning the whereabouts of Gabrielle St Marque's child. She and her Godmother were alone, as Alanna had gone to bed early complaining of a sick headache after the jolting carriage ride.

'He thinks it will not be too difficult to trace the infant, especially if she has a French accent. He did not say, but I know well, that there are many bored Ladies of Quality about the Court who bear illegitimate children and arrange foster homes for them in the neighbourhood. Strictly speaking, such a child would not come within the jurisdiction of an Overseer of the Poor, like your Mr Knight – at least not so long as she continued to be provided for in some discreet fashion. However, it may well be that the mother has defaulted in the the payments of late. If the child has come on the Parish, it will make the search easier; Mr Knight has promised to keep me informed. He is a worthy man, you did well to suggest him, Tamsyn.' She leaned back in her chair, something which she rarely did. Her god-daughter noted with concern her wizened appearance, accentuated by the dull black bombazine stuff of her gown.

'Why don't you go to bed, ma'am? Or would you like me to read to you? It has been a fatiguing day.'

'Looking hagged, am I? Well, I'll not deny I've been a trifle out of sorts since I was laid low by that feverish cold after Christmas. At my age one does not regain one's strength and spirits with the elasticity of youth. I'll go upstairs soon, but I need your candid opinion on a certain matter. Pour me another cup of tea, child, and tell me do you think I was wrong to forbid Alanna's betrothal to Robert

more? I did not think her affections were seriously
ed.'

syn felt a wave of sympathy for the old lady; she
l the tea thoughtfully.

1 Alanna, sometimes forbidden fruit is more
le.'

1in incidents from childhood rose vividly in her mind.
can be headstrong when thwarted,' Lady Moles-
agreed. Her shoulders sagged; she sighed and sipped
drink. 'My daughter, Alice, was much more amen-
1e married Richard Gordon at the end of her first
just as arranged. It was not a love match, but nobody
or that in those days. I did not discover until after
and Alanna were born that he was a cruel wife-beater.
as terrified of him, but she would not leave the chil-
do not wish Alanna to suffer as she did and I do not
ir Robert is always very kind to women. I fear I made
ke in promoting a union; it seemed sensible because
1tes run together, but the disparity in their ages and
:ts does not bode well for my granddaughter's
ess.'

lack of confidence in her own judgement was most
her ladyship's customary demeanour. Much dis-
, Tamsyn moved to seat herself on a little stool and
er Godmother's ice-cold mittened fingers in her own
1ands. A clawlike grip tightened painfully, while sharp,
eyes searched Tamsyn's face.

ink their characters may be complementary; perhaps
ld be best to let Alanna decide for herself.'

y Lucinda blinked at this novel idea.

es Alanna know about her father?' Tamsyn pursued.
vas she who first told me of it, but in her childish way.
1ay not recollect . . .' Her eyes dimmed at the memory.
oused herself with an effort. 'Pay me no mind, Tamsyn.
1n old woman and I miss my daughter. It's a sad thing
e after one's own child. 'Tis time I was in my grave.'
'is time you were in your bed, dear Godmama. Alanna

and I still need your wise advice and think of all those wh[o]
depend on you. You will feel better in the morning.'

She helped the old lady to her feet and stooped to ki[ss]
her leathery cheek. Evans miraculously appeared to esco[rt]
her mistress to her chamber. She was a lean, wiry woman [of]
indeterminate age, completely devoted to her ladyship.

'You're a good girl, Tamsyn, strong and comforting. Joh[n]
Aylward is a fortunate man.'

Lady Lucinda reached up and patted her cheek; then s[he]
grasped her cane and walked firmly across the room. Eva[ns]
and Tamsyn exchanged wry smiles, before the maid hurri[ed]
to open the door.

The next few days proved uneventful, apart from the arri[val]
of a note from Sir Robert accepting Lady Molesworthy's ki[nd]
invitation to dinner the following Wednesday. It rained [a]
good deal; confined to the house, the young ladies sew[ed]
and read and Alanna played the piano. When the ra[in]
stopped they rode or walked through the swampy fields a[nd]
miry lanes. One day they went up in the attic and explored [as]
they had done when they were children, rummaging amo[ng]
heavy gilt picture frames, broken furniture from centuri[es]
past and chests of motheaten clothing discarded by lo[ng]
forgotten Molesworthy ancestors.

'It is odd there are no letters or diaries,' Tamsyn co[m]-
mented.

'I think Grandmama had most of them burned when [my]
grandfather died. She said the papers were private, of [no]
interest to anyone but the parties concerned and in gene[ral]
tedious, repetitious and unworthy of preservation, when [I]
asked her about it.'

Trained from her earliest years to respect books a[nd]
manuscripts, Tamsyn's archival instincts caused h[er]
expression to register shock, but Alanna took a differe[nt]
view.

'Don't look so disapproving my friend, imagine if eve[ry]
one kept all their correspondence. The world would [be]
buried under a mountain of paper. I have always thoug[ht]

156

that it was a great blessing that some of the ancient libraries were destroyed; we suffer quite enough from outmoded treatises appropriate for remote countries in remote times as it is. I fail to understand why an acquaintance with classical authors is so widely regarded as adequate preparation for modern life. Thank heaven I was not born a boy.'

'Do you include the Bible in your strictures?' asked Tamsyn, sitting back on her heels and pondering deeply. 'How do we know what will be of interest to posterity?'

'The Bible is a special case,' acknowledged Alanna, 'but you must admit that there are parts of it which do not seem very relevant to life in the Nineteenth Century; our society is so very different. Who do you know who sacrifices lambs, for example?'

'We cannot take it too literally,' averred Tamsyn cautiously. 'Have you raised these thoughts with the vicar, or Sir Robert?'

Alanna's pretty lip twisted scornfully.

'My dear, do you take me for a fool?'

'No, but Sir Robert may,' retorted Tamsyn. 'Sensible men do not respect butterfly brains.'

'Tell me, then, why do so many clever men marry foolish women? Think of Mr Bennet in *Pride and Prejudice* or, alternatively, why has poor Miss Lovett been a spinster so long? – because men like to feel superior, physically and intellectually,' she finished triumphantly, shaking the dust from her skirts.

'It is better not to be married at all, like Miss Lovett, but to have a life of the mind,' said Tamsyn obstinately, but she recognized she was on slippery ground.

'Let's go downstairs, it's cold up here. My mind is very lively, I thank you, but I reveal it with discretion to my trusted friends.'

They closed the chests. A mouse rustled in the corner.

'Mice are very destructive little creatures. It's a good thing there are no papers up here,' Tamsyn observed pacifically as Alanna preceded her down the ladder. Alanna looked up; she had a smudge on her nose, cobwebs in her hair and

157

a grin on her face. Tamsyn wished that Sir Robert could see her now. She tried once more.

'Men of moderate intellect may be intimidated by clever wives, but I believe you underrate Sir Robert; how can he communicate with you if you do not share your thoughts with him?'

The argument and others like it, waged back and forth, during the week. By Wednesday they were both ready for diversion and a change of company. There had been no word from John or Mr Farrell, or from Charles Knight concerning Gabrielle St Marque's child. Gabrielle herself kept to her room, but would steal out in the middle of the night and drink anything alcoholic that Mrs Ryder had not secured. On Wednesday evening, the housekeeper's attention was elsewhere and Gabrielle was able to filch two bottles of wine and half a bottle of cooking sherry from the little cubby hole known as the butler's pantry, although these days her ladyship did not keep a butler in the country. Mademoiselle St Marque retreated with her booty to her room overlooking the stableyard. She uncorked the bottles and, cradling her glass, sat down on the window seat, from which vantage point she could watch the comings and goings in the yard below.

The first guest to arrive was Mr Hempseed in her ladyship's second-best carriage. Gabrielle did not see the librarian, because he had been let down at the front entrance. She did see the carriage and watched with interest while the horses were unharnessed and led away to their stalls. It grew quiet; the grooms and stable boys were having their dinner. One of the maids knocked on her door, but she did not answer and, finding the room locked, the servant left a tray with a clatter and retreated to the nether regions. Gabrielle ignored her food and continued to sip her wine. She may have fallen into a light sleep, for it was dark when she was roused by voices. There were lanterns bobbing about and three horses to be unsaddled. She opened the window and leaned out; in the fitful gleams of light she discerned a tall gentleman and two grooms. When he spoke, giving the

Molesworthy groom instructions about the care of his animal, she recognized Mr John Aylward. With a final wave of his hand, he strode off and she heard his boots crunching on the gravel as he made his way round to the main entrance. The well-trained grooms rubbed down the horses and left them contentedly munching their oats. The men settled on the bench below Gabrielle's window to blow a peaceful cloud and have a gossip.

''Tis queer right enuff, the way Mr Aylward resembles your gennelman, Davy. Like as two peas in a pod they be,' said Will, her ladyship's head groom. He tapped out his pipe on the water barrel and refilled it slowly. Gabrielle could see the top of his head, with its shock of curly fair hair. She strained her ears to catch Davy's reply. He ruminated for a while.

'Like enuff in appearance, I grant you. But Sir Robert would never come round to the stable yard in his evenin' clothes; 'ee stands on 'is dignity, does Sir Robert, an' quite right too, if yer was to ask me. I loike a gennelman to keep 'is place.'

'What time did he tell you to be ready with the horses?'

'Sir Robert said to bring 'em round at ten o'clock.'

'Good, that gives us time for a game o' cards. Bring yer glass and follow me, Davy.'

They tramped across the yard, two short, bow-legged men, and disappeared with their lantern into the tack room, leaving the yard in darkness. Meanwhile, Gabrielle, somewhat sobered by the information the grooms had unwittingly imparted, unlocked her door and crept downstairs. She could hear a hum of conversation from the sitting room; to her left the door was open and she could see the dining table laid ready, silver and delicate china on polished mahogany, sparkling glasses and in the centre a bowl of hothouse roses. The room was empty. She slipped in, still grasping the second bottle of wine which she had brought from her bedchamber. She gave a small hiccup and caught her breath; there came a sound of movement from across the hall and she glanced round desperately for some place to hide. A tall

159

Chinese screen had been set in front of the long windows; with not a second to spare she whisked behind the screen and crouched down. Lady Molesworthy and her guests filed in and under cover of the general scrapings and rustlings, Gabrielle found a small flaw in the silk fabric and cunningly contrived to make it larger with the top of the bottle as her implement. Then she took a fortifying swig and set her eye to the hole.

To her annoyance she could not see very much. Lady Molesworthy had her back to her, as she sat at the head of the table, resplendent in turban and nodding plumes. Sir Robert was on her right and John Aylward on her left; Gabrielle caught her sleeve on a splinter from the screen's frame and nearly toppled it in her excitement. Nobody noticed the screen rocking; cautiously, Gabrielle resumed her surveillance. Of the young ladies she could see very little beyond their slippered feet and another gentleman seated at the far end, nearest the door, was quite invisible to her and at first inaudible as well.

They began with oysters, followed by a roasted loin of pork and another of mutton. The cook had excelled herself with the accompaniments and for a while the conversation was rather muffled and indistinguishable to the listener behind the screen. Then she heard Tamsyn's clear voice raised to catch her friend's attention across the table, though she addressed her neighbour, Sir Robert.

'Alanna believes that the study of classical languages is an outmoded exercise, which could well be dispensed with in modern society,' she remarked, directing a mischievous smile at Miss Gordon.

'Do you indeed, Alanna? That is rather a heretical notion,' but he appeared interested, not shocked.

Alanna tossed her head and coloured becomingly.

'I merely implied that a knowledge of the French tongue was a more useful accomplishment for young ladies,' she said meekly.

Tamsyn shook her head in mock despair.

Sir Robert waited while some more vegetables were

160

heaped on his plate. He had a hearty appetite; Gabrielle wondered sourly how he had managed to keep his hard, lean, athletic figure.

As if in answer to her unspoken question, he observed, 'A day in the saddle does wonders for my appetite. I intend to spend a few days at Oak Place before returning to Town. Perhaps you would care to join me, Cousin John? You must be wanting to view your ancestral acres.'

'Thank you, Cousin. I'll not deny the comforts of the inn in Windlesham leave something to be desired. And I suspect the village folk are beginning to wonder if there is a touch of the supernatural in our resemblance. I arrived early this afternoon and I swear every soul in the village has made it his business to catch a glimpse of me.'

'Then that is settled. We will stop at the inn and pick up your traps on our way home.' He turned courteously to the ladies, and included Oliver Hempseed, silent and brooding at the end of the table, 'I hope we may have the honour of returning your hospitality at Oak Place. We have pineapples in the greenhouse, your ladyship. I know my gardener is longing to display them to an appreciative and knowledge-able person like yourself; And the library is famed through-out the land. Uncle Jeremy made some interesting additions in his later years; we even have a shelf of books about Virginia. It is interesting to speculate why, is it not?'

The conversation ranged widely and Sir Robert exerted himself to be agreeable. They talked about America and John and Robert exchanged good-humoured jibes about the recent war between their two countries, which had figured so largely in the consciousness of the United States and so little in England, preoccupied as she was with the situation on the European continent.

Replete at last, Sir Robert pushed aside his pudding plate and regarded Lady Molesworthy with an enigmatic smile.

'A capital dinner, ma'am. Almost worth the ride from Town. However, knowing your ladyship as I do, I suspect you had an ulterior motive, when you summoned me to join you.' He gave Alanna a fleeting smile and continued, 'Of

161

course, I realize that His Majesty's untimely demise must delay our plans for a happier event, but is the announcement of our betrothal to be made official?'

Before anyone could speak, there came the sound of a loud hiccup. Waving her bottle wildly, Gabrielle emerged from behind the screen, looking like a ghost, with her enormous eyes, pale tragic face and borrowed, billowing *robe de chambre.*

'You cannot marry him, Mees Gordon,' she spluttered, 'Madame, you must forbid it. I 'ave told you, 'ee is a faithless seducer, not worthy, not fit to kiss the boots of your granddaughter. I spit on you, Sir Robert 'Awksmore.'

Unmoved, their hostess looked round the table; every countenance registered varying degrees of stupefaction and amazement.

'You all know Mademoiselle de St Marque, I think,' said Lady Molesworthy.

14

Remorseful Sir Robert

Sir Robert sprang to his feet as if stung; he approached his accuser menacingly, then recoiled in disgust, lifting his handkerchief to his nose.

'Faugh! The woman is inebriated. Surely your ladyship does not credit this poor creature's slanderous insults? Let me summon the servants to remove her: Miss Gordon and Mrs Elsworth should not be exposed to such low company.'

He reached for the bell pull, but the movement was arrested when Alanna said distinctly, 'Wait, Robert. Have you thought that you helped bring her to this?'

Taken aback, he hesitated and pulled at his neckcloth as though it were too tight. Tamsyn had not seen Sir Robert since the night at the play, when he had offered her a slip on the shoulder and her feelings towards him were not precisely cordial, but she felt a certain sympathy with his predicament. He gripped the back of his chair, his grey-green-flecked eyes fixed on his betrothed. Tamsyn stretched to lay a restraining hand on his impeccably cut coat sleeve; he glanced down at her and she nodded in the direction of Oliver Hempseed.

Mr Hempseed had also risen. He had eyes for no one but the pale, tormented woman, who was swaying uncertainly behind Lady Lucinda. Her ladyship indicated the gentleman previously unnoticed by Gabrielle.

'Of course, it is some time since you have seen him, but I expect you recall your husband, Monsieur Hempseed.'

'How are you, Gaby?' he said.

Mademoiselle St Marque's eyes widened and she gave a little moan. Oliver moved with surprising swiftness to catch her as she crumpled and fell.

Lady Molesworthy stood up decisively. She addressed her librarian.

'We will leave you, Mr Hempseed, to your reunion. Your arm, Mr Aylward, I fear you must drink your port with the ladies tonight.'

Without a backward glance, she stalked across the hall, with John gallantly in attendance. Tamsyn poured some water into a glass and handed it to Oliver, while Alanna moistened a napkin and laid it on Gabrielle's forehead. Grateful for their compassion and concern, Mr Hempseed smiled at both ladies and said that he could now cope without assistance. Tactfully they retreated, ignoring Sir Robert, who trailed after them to the drawing room. They found their hostess already ensconced by the fire, with John bringing her a cup of tea. He volunteered to perform the same service for Tamsyn and Alanna.

'The decanters are on the side table over there, Robert, pray do not stand on ceremony – you look as if you needed a drink.'

Her ladyship waved her hand vaguely in the direction of a small Queen Anne side table set against the far wall, below an elegant oval mirror of the same period. Catching a glimpse of himself in the glass, Robert took a deep breath, straightened his shoulders and composed his haughty features to a mask of aloof disdain intended to indicate that he was not a man accustomed to being treated so shabbily and left to pour his own refreshment. When he joined the rest of the company, he found that the ladies had ostracized him, Alanna and Tamsyn being seated side by side on a sofa to the right of Lady Lucinda's chair. Having waited upon the ladies with cheerful good grace, Mr Aylward went to fetch his own postprandial port; his cousin watched him

164

over the rim of his glass, his expression impassive, only his nostrils flaring slightly. Tamsyn almost expected him to breathe fire.

'Well, Robert, what have you to say for yourself? I don't intend my granddaughter to contract the pox because you consort with low women,' said her ladyship forthrightly.

Despite the seriousness of the occasion, John's lip quivered. Alanna blushed rosily and the ladies presented a solid phalanx of female disapproval. Sir Robert spilled his wine and a dark red stain appeared on his snowy cravat. He swore.

'Am I then to be condemned without proof?'

An angry muscle twitched by the corner of his mouth.

'Mr Hempseed has furnished me with all the proof I need regarding the liaison between his wife and you, her aristocratic lover. Mr Hempseed has but just returned from Bruges. I sent him to interview the St Marque family; her father remains implacable in his attitude towards Gabrielle. He gave Oliver all the letters which you and she exchanged; she left them behind when she fled from her home to seek your protection. Monsieur St Marque could not understand the letters, but he kept them and willingly offered them to my emissary as a form of revenge for his daughter's dishonour. In addition, I have the names of others who can bear testimony to the truth of his assertions.'

Her ladyship folded her hands and waited tranquilly for his response.

Striving without success to keep the chagrin from his voice, he said sulkily, 'It grieves me, ma'am, that you trust the word of your librarian before mine. How do you know the letters are not forgeries? It is clear that he bears me a grudge. Why was I not informed of these charges before?'

Unperturbed, she replied, 'Stop blustering, Robert. Your reputation is well-known.'

She paused and glanced at Tamsyn; it was Mrs Elsworth's turn to blush. Lady Lucinda nodded, as if satisfied that she had not missed her mark, and continued, 'I did not speak of it earlier because I was waiting for the proof; Oliver Hempseed put the letters in my hands this afternoon. It all happened quite by chance when we found Gabrielle at the shelter in London. John was with us, he will tell you of it. She mistook him for you. I did not then discover Oliver's involvement, because we quitted London the next day. The king's illness made our journey to Windsor imperative.'

Robert stood up and towered over Lady Lucinda.

'If my reputation is so well-known, ma'am, I am puzzled that you countenanced our engagement in the first place. Why object now?'

Her ladyship shrugged.

'What will you? I am aware, we are all aware, that a double standard of conduct operates in our society. Men are granted more licence if their affairs are discreet, but in this instance, Sir Robert, it was thrust beneath our noses . . .'

Robert tried one Parthian shot.

'Very well, *mea culpa*, I acknowledge my guilt. However, I would point out that Gabrielle St Marque was not a "low woman". She was the daughter of a well-respected Belgian merchant – thoroughly bourgeois, ma'am. I didn't know she was married to Hempseed. She gave me no hint. Demmit, I like the man, I wouldn't have poached on his preserve. Ours was a fleeting relationship and she was handsomely rewarded.'

He sat down with the air of one who had acted honorably in every particular.

'With a child.' Alanna spoke for the first time, her clear blue eyes fixed on a point somewhere above Sir Robert's impeccably-groomed head.

'A child?' he echoed, blankly.

Alanna lowered her chin a fraction and confronted her betrothed with a direct, level gaze which he found uncomfortably disconcerting.

'You have a daughter, Robert. A little girl of four. Your affairs, even your proposal for a *ménage à trois* with Tamsyn, I could understand, perhaps tolerate. But how can I overlook the fact that you have ignored your own child and left her to starve or at the least, exist miserably at the expense of the Parish of Windsor?'

166

The two gentlemen looked stunned. Mr Aylward's lip was no longer quivering with amusement. He was biting it with suppressed fury. Robert recovered first and spared him a quick glance.

He said, 'Mrs Elsworth refused me, Cousin. Pray do not grow heated, one must expect a similarity of tastes in the family, after all.' He addressed Alanna. 'Whatever you may think of my character, believe me, I had no inkling of Gabrielle's condition when I quitted the Continent. I must assume your ladyship has proof that the child is mine?' he finished bitterly, turning his piercing, hooded gaze on Lady Lucinda.

He reminded Tamsyn of a stag at bay; perversely she felt a flash of sympathy once again. To Alanna he appeared younger and more vulnerable than she had ever seen him. Her grandmother was speaking.

'I expect to have proof positive within the next few days, but the circumstantial evidence is well-nigh incontrovertible. Gabrielle has shown me a miniature of the infant and she bears a marked resemblance to you, sir, both in feature and colouring. Her mother has been reluctant to reveal her foster home. I think she fears to lose the child, but she cannot afford to support her any longer. I have made every effort to have the child traced and I anticipate a successful conclusion to the search by the end of the week.'

Robert Hawksmore came to his feet and bowed to each lady in turn with awe-inspiring grace and dignity.

'Pray keep me informed, ma'am, of the progress of your researches. I thank you for your hospitality. I presume you wish to be released from the prospect of a distasteful alliance, Miss Gordon?' He kissed her limp hand with cold formality and swung on his heel, not waiting for a reply, 'Come, Cousin John. There is still the little matter of our inheritance to settle, is there not?'

He flung the words over his shoulder and was halfway across the room, when Lady Lucinda called after him. 'We will leave the matter of your betrothal in abeyance for the present, Sir Robert. It is always better to sleep on these

167

dilemmas in life and not rush to hasty decisions. Pray tell your gardener that I shall come and see his pineapples on Saturday afternoon at three. Goodnight, John Aylward.'

John bowed. The gentlemen departed in a profound silence. A door slammed in the distance. Tamsyn, Alanna and Lady Lucinda looked at one another and began to laugh.

'How are the mighty fallen. But we must not get hysterical my dears.' Her ladyship was chuckling and wheezing in turn. 'Laughter is a great relief after so much tension. Is the coffee or tea still hot, Alanna? Let us have another cup and think what is to be done.'

She kicked off her shoes and wriggled her toes luxuriously.

Alanna exclaimed, 'Grandmama, how could you speak so of Robert giving me the pox? I wanted the floor to swallow me up.'

'You're getting to be as prudish as the evangelicals. 'Twas not so in my day. I wanted to get his attention and to dent his pride, Alanna. By suffering a little one hopes he will become more sensitive to the feelings of others.' Her bright, sharp eyes shifted to Tamsyn. 'John was not much edified, I think, by my hints? There is something of the colonial puritan about him too. I would do much to hear their conversation now! But, to speak seriously, for a moment, we must establish our goal – do you still wish to marry Robert Hawksmore, Alanna?'

'Or *vice versa*, will Robert still wish to wed me after such humiliation?' retorted Alanna.

'That will be a test of his strength of character and perhaps his love for you: I think we need not fear on that score, he has always been one to strive for the unobtainable. You will become more valuable in his eyes now that obstacles have been set in his path.'

'He was so humble, yet dignified. I no longer fear his sarcastic tongue and the age discrepancy does not seem so wide.'

Alanna spoke wistfully, almost tenderly. The other two ladies looked at one another and raised their eyebrows.

168

'What of the child?' enquired Tamsyn.

'She will be cared for, you may be sure of that, Tamsyn. The precise provisions await other developments. We must not forget Oliver's role in this; we do not know if the marriage will be resumed or dissolved, that is for him and Gabrielle to decide.'

Mrs Elsworth pondered, chin in hand, then said, 'It will be very awkward for him. After all, she has been a woman of the streets.'

'I agree. It was perhaps foolish of me to take her in, although I never dreamed of the complication with Oliver. I merely felt pity for the woman and thought the connection with Robert should be sifted for Alanna's sake. The servants have been grumbling, Evans tells me. They resent the fact that Gabrielle is vocal in her hatred of the English aristocracy and yet is living at my expense.'

Lady Lucinda sighed.

''Tis Robert she hates, ma'am, and perhaps other men also,' said Tamsyn.

'If she resumes her relationship with Mr Hempseed, will you keep him as your librarian?' asked Alanna curiously.

Lady Lucinda plucked her sleeve fretfully, as she frequently did when vexed, and said, 'I don't know. I would miss him, but it may not be possible . . .'

Tamsyn said gently, 'Let us not worry about that problem tonight. The hour grows late. Shall I ring for Evans?'

Her godmother nodded. While they waited for the maid to appear, Alanna meditated.

'Dare we go on Saturday, Grandmama? Suppose Sir Robert bars the gates of Oak Place against us?'

'He won't do that,' said her ladyship confidently.

Her confidence was not misplaced. When they arrived at the stately mansion at the appointed hour on Saturday afternoon, the two cousins were waiting to welcome them. They mounted the steps between tall, neoclassical columns and entered a high, square hall, with a bare marble floor and an enormous chandelier. Their heels tapped loudly and Alanna's voice, chattering nervously, echoed back from the

169

domed ceiling. Sir Robert gazed at the collar of her dress, which was rather high and stood out from her throat in a full, double ruff, composed of white crimped crepe; it accentuated her smooth, swanlike neck.

'You must forgive me, ladies, if I do not talk very much. I had a tooth drawn this morning, after having suffered from an abscess for several days. In consequence my jaw is sore and I have intimations of mortality,' he concluded wryly.

'You should apply liquor ammonia to reduce the pain,' said Tamsyn sympathetically. The ladies regarded his well-defined lineaments more closely and observed some swelling and puffiness below the right cheekbone.

'He needs compound extract of colocynth, extract of jalap and Castile soap blended into pills. I will give your house-keeper the receipt.'

Lady Lucinda gave him a stern, yet kindly smile, which reminded Sir Robert of his old nurse.

Having removed their wraps, they followed their host to his famous library. John whispered in Tamsyn's ear,

'How very sly of Robert to contrive to enlist all your sympathies in this cunning way.'

Her eyes twinkled.

She whispered back, 'Fortuitous certainly, but I acquit him of contrivance. One does not choose to have the toothache.'

They had reached the entrance to an elegant apartment on the first floor. Tamsyn looked about her with delight. The library was a long gallery, with numerous alcoves and window seats over-looking the terraced rose garden at the rear of the house. A strip of Persian carpet ran the length of the gallery and Greek or Roman statuettes and vases occupied niches at the entrance to each book-lined alcove.

'The "fifteeners" or as some book people say, "incunables", from the dawn of printing and rare sixteenth-century Aldine Press books are in the glass cabinets beyond the fireplace,' said Sir Robert. 'And there are a few illuminated manuscripts which were acquired by my predecessor. Your ladyship might care to see my latest prize . . .'

He shepherded Lady Molesworthy and Alanna to a recess a little way down.

'What are "incunables", Robert?' they heard Alanna ask, as she disappeared from view.

'The Latin word, *incunabula* means "things in a cradle . . ."'

He also disappeared. John and Tamsyn lingered near the door.

'You must see this fore-edge painting by John Brindley. Robert keeps the pages slightly fanned out and held fast with a remarkable holder, so that the painting may be seen. I must tell Hatchard of it, next time we meet.'

He took her elbow and steered her past the others to a bay adjacent to the glass-fronted cabinets. Together they bent over the painting; Tamsyn was very aware of his proximity.

'How beautiful it is,' she murmured.

John's lips brushed the top of her head.

'How beautiful you are,' he rejoined.

Tamsyn half-turned, but could not move for fear of upsetting the little book stand. John looked down at her steadily; being a tall lady, she found it extraordinarily pleasant to be looked down upon. She could feel a little pulse beating in the base of her throat; John watched it too.

'I'm enchanted to see that you and your locket have become inseparable. At dinner the other night, I thought you might have worn it in common politeness, but to find you wearing it again today, that is indeed encouraging.' He smiled, his eyes crinkling at the corners in a most endearing way. They heard the others approaching. 'We must talk,' he said urgently.

However, the opportunity for further private conversation did not present itself; Lady Lucinda proved an all too conscientious chaperone and kept her two charges constantly beneath her eagle eye. Sir Robert led them to the shelves containing books about North America. He selected one and handed it to Tamsyn.

'John tells me he wants to wed you and waft you off to

the United States; before you make any irrevocable decision, may I suggest that you peruse Mr Fearon's account with close attention.' He glanced at the others and added, 'Fearon is a wine merchant who went to America in 1817 to examine the country with a view to emigration. He went at the behest of some forty families and sent them reports of his wide-ranging travels, which occupied almost a year.'

'I remember seeing the work when it was published, but I did not purchase it, for I had no special interest,' said Tamsyn repressively.

'Perhaps you should refresh your memory. May I?' Robert retrieved the volume and read aloud.

'"A Philadelphian (particularly a female) is as old at 27, as a Londoner at 40." and here, again, on p.377, about American females "and the universal neglect of either mental or domestic knowledge, which appears to exist . . . as compared with those in England." Do you agree with that assessment, Cousin?'

Their host's eyes glinted wickedly, as he handed the book back to Tamsyn.

John laughed and protested good-humouredly, 'It is the truth, but not the whole truth. You should read it, Tamsyn, in order that you may judge fairly. Each individual's experiences are very different and European arrogance may do much to provoke hostility and outrageous behaviour in certain quarters. As we have discussed before, America is a young country with many faults, but also many advantages over the Old World. In my view, it is for educated people to seek to overcome the mutual antipathies which exist on both sides, in order that we may cooperate for our mutual benefit. As for you, Robert, were it not for your current afflictions, which might impede your aim, as they certainly impede your judgement, I would suggest pistols at dawn as the best solution to our mutual differences.'

Robert rubbed his swollen jaw pensively and proceeded to the next alcove.

Tamsyn whispered to John, 'It is settled then, that you will return to America and not remain at Oak Place?'

'Nothing is settled,' he responded, grimly.

To Tamsyn's regret, after about half an hour, her ladyship demanded to leave the library to be shown the fruits of the greenhouse. Their host conducted them through the Conservatory, ablaze with exotic blooms, across a small courtyard, well-sheltered by a high, ivy-clad brick wall and into the greenhouse, damp and warm, where he handed them over to the presiding genius, a dwarf with a bald pate and neat, pointed beard, named Juggins. Sir Robert excused himself and retired to the house to seek an ice pack and order refreshments. Her ladyship soon won the man's grudging respect by her knowledgeable questions and Tamsyn, Alanna and John learned more than they really wanted to know about the difficulties of rearing foreign fruits, which, it appeared, were constantly under attack from their twin enemies, English bugs and the English climate.

Relief came from an unexpected quarter. John had retreated to the door opening on to the courtyard and was gazing up at the sky, wondering if it was about to rain, when a man came hurrying from the direction of the stables. It was Oliver Hempseed. He had his head down against the wind, but John hailed him. At the same moment, Sir Robert came from the house, in search of his guests.

'Gentlemen, thank heaven I have found you. I pray it is not too late. Where is her ladyship?'

'I'm here, man, come inside and tell me what is amiss.'

The old lady tapped her cane imperatively. Mr Hempseed edged past the trays of potted plants, stumbling in his haste.

He reached her side and gasped, 'Forgive me, ma'am, for alarming you, but Gabrielle has disappeared and I fear she means to employ desperate measures. Mr Knight came this afternoon to tell you that he had found the child; I offered him refreshment after his ride and Gaby must have overheard our conversation. While we were talking and the stable lads were at dinner, she stole Moonlight. She left me a wild note saying that she was going to take the child to a safe place. There was an empty bottle on her dresser,' he finished gloomily.

'Don't look so dejected, sir, she cannot have gone far. When did this flight take place?'

Lady Lucinda's bracing tone had its effect.

Mr Hempseed took a deep breath and said calmly, 'It must have been about four o'clock. She is a competent horsewoman and could be in Windsor by now. Fortunately, Knight was still with me when the groom reported the missing horse. He hoped to intercept her, but the wind is rising and it will be a dark, wet night. I fear much for the safety of Gabrielle and her child.'

His hands began to shake.

Sir Robert spoke decisively, 'John, take Hempseed into the house and find him a drink, while I go in and change. Then you can escort the ladies home, and follow me to Windsor, if you wish. Get the child's address from him and bring it to my dressing room, there's a good fellow.'

Lady Molesworthy opened her mouth to protest, but Robert seized her hands. Over her bonneted head, his eyes met Alanna's.

'She is my daughter. I must go.'

His eyes were pleading for their understanding, but his tone brooked no defiance. Alanna nodded and he gave her a warm smile, before he turned and ran back to the house.

Everyone did as they were bid. Mr Aylward ushered the ladies to the green Chinese sitting room and a footman served sherry and wafer biscuits. When he withdrew, John and Oliver Hempseed had a whispered colloquy; Charles Knight's direction and the address of the child were written down and conveyed to Sir Robert. The ladies sipped their sherry and muttered among themselves.

'Surely the child has a name. What did Gabrielle call her?' Alanna mused distractedly.

'Her name is Claire,' said Lady Lucinda. 'She told me when she showed me the miniature in one of her more lucid moments.'

Tamsyn glanced about her, at the heavy green silk hangings, lighter green brocade upholstery and Chinese tapestries depicting mists and rocks and waterfalls, which

174

decorated the walls. She shivered and reflected that green had never been her favourite colour. She thought of Moonlight's soft nose and gentle disposition. They sat a while in brooding silence.

Alanna broke it, saying, 'We cannot let Robert go alone. He is in pain with the toothache and, besides, Gabrielle will not trust him. Grandmama, will you allow Tamsyn and I to go with Mr Hempseed in the carriage? The journey would be too much for you, but we could take you home and fetch our travelling clothes at the same time. Molesworthy Court is on our way, but there is no time to be lost.'

Pleased by the prospect of action, Tamsyn chimed in, 'Dear ma'am, I think it would be for the best. Then John could ride with Robert and we would be quite safe with Mr Hempseed.'

Her ladyship demurred, saying that such matters should be left to the gentlemen. Tamsyn and Alanna set themselves to persuade her that their presence was a necessity for the success of the enterprise and by the time Sir Robert reappeared booted, spurred and in his greatcoat, she was convinced. John welcomed the opportunity for action and Robert welcomed his company and support. It was soon settled. In less than half an hour the two cousins rode off at the gallop down the darkening drive, followed by a groom. At a little after six, Lady Lucinda's carriage was brought round to the ladies, waiting impatiently with Mr Hempseed. The first drops of rain began to fall as they descended the steps of Oak Place and it was raining hard an hour later, when Miss Gordon and Mrs Elsworth set out for Windsor with their escort, having deposited her ladyship safely in her own home, where she sat up all night, anxiously awaiting news.

175

15

Dawn at Virginia Water

At first, Tamsyn and her travelling companions exchanged
desultory conversation, tacitly avoiding the uneasy thoughts
which were uppermost in their minds. Valiantly, Mr Hempseed followed Tamsyn's lead in praising the wonders of the
Oak Place library, while Alanna, half-bored and half-queasy
with travel sickness, fell asleep, with her head pillowed on
Tamsyn's shoulder.

The rain lashed against the panels and the atmosphere
inside the coach became inordinately stuffy. The talk lapsed
and Tamsyn began to worry about the possibility of becoming mired in a pothole. The driver was obliged to take a
detour for the road was flooded; then he lost his way. The
horses floundered on and eventually they emerged once
more on the toll road. The journey had a nightmare quality
which reminded Tamsyn of a similar night when she had
travelled up from Cornwall with Gil, just before he departed
for the Continent; they had had so little time together. She
sighed. Oliver Hempseed moved restlessly; he kicked her
foot, but was so absorbed in his thoughts that he did not
apologize. Tamsyn knew that after the first shock, Gabrielle
had taken refuge in silence. She had displayed no affection
for Oliver, maintaining a mask of indifference. It was Lady
Lucinda's opinion that the Belgian woman had long since
forgotten about her youthful infatuation and had dismissed

Oliver from her mind, although the marriage had never legally been dissolved. Her ladyship's librarian was equally reticent about his personal feelings, although Tamsyn, remembering their conversation before she quitted London, suspected that the flames of passion had not quite died in his bosom and could be rekindled were he to receive some encouragement.

In Windsor, the coachman paused to enquire precise directions, but they did not descend as it appeared that the Knights' cottage was only a mile or two on the far side of the town and they were anxious to hear news after their delays. Another fifteen minutes and the carriage came to a jolting halt. The coachman opened the door and Mr Hempseed jumped down, saying that he would knock on the cottage door and ascertain if it were indeed the Knights' abode. Alanna stirred and Tamsyn pulled down the window and peered into the gloom. She heard the click of a gate and footsteps receding. It was still raining. She sat back and a few moments later, the gentleman reappeared, carrying a bobbing lantern.

'Mrs Knight begs you will step inside and get warm, ladies. She says the men have gone in search of Gabrielle and her husband with them, to act as guide. Be careful you do not slip, the lane is very muddy.'

Oliver assisted them to the shelter of the porch and then went to help the coachman with the horses, for the Knights had no domestics save a little maid. When he re-entered the cottage by the back door, he passed through a scullery and stone-flagged passage, following the sound of voices. He found the ladies with their hostess and was obliged to dip his head to avoid striking it on the low-beamed ceiling. The room was clean, bright and cheerful, with fresh flowers on the round table in the centre and pots of aromatic herbs on the window sills. There were several shelves of books and papers by the chair where Alanna was seated, with a rug over her knees. Mrs Knight was applying the bellows to the smouldering coals.

'Come in, sir, come in,' she welcomed him, sitting back

on her heels, while she waited to see the results of her labours. 'I let the fire die down, as I was just going to bed.'

She was a comely woman, swathed in a voluminous shawl and wearing a nightcap frilled round her rosy cheeks and tied under her chin. A long brown plait hung down her back. Tamsyn thought she was about her own age, or a little older. She took an instant liking to her and wished she might have her for a friend.

'Can I help?' she asked.

'If you will be good enough to move that pile of papers, then you and Mr Hempseed can both sit down. Mr Knight is not very tidy, I fear, but then 'tis hard for him, with the children so small, and no room for him to write and be private. We hope to move to a bigger place soon. What a horrid night. Can I make you some hot chocolate?'

They assented eagerly, being chilled after the long ride. It was the first of several cups which they drank as the night wore on.

Mrs Knight told them all she knew, which was not much. Her husband had returned early in the evening and gone in search of Gabrielle at the house where her daughter was lodged. He found the woman who cared for the child distraught, because the foreigner had taken the little girl, but she looked very strange and talked very wildly, mostly in some heathen tongue which the good woman could not understand. The little girl was crying and she did not want to let her go, but the mother insisted, so she'd wrapped her in her warmest clothes, kissed her and put into her hand the wooden doll she loved and a bun to eat.

'Charles came home very angry that the woman had not summoned him, but after all, I said, the Belgian had a right to her own child. He ate his dinner and felt better, and we were just discussing what should be done, when Sir Robert and Mr Aylward arrived a little after nine. They agreed to go in search of her. The foster mother said the pair had gone off through the forest in the direction of Virginia Water and Charles knows the paths like the back of his hand, having been raised in Windsor. So he said he would go too,

178

or the gentlemen might get lost on such a dark night. He kissed me and bade me lock up and go to bed, which I was about to do when you arrived, my dears.'

She gave them a gentle smile. There was no servility in her manners, nor reference to her humble cottage, Alanna noticed, but rather a certain proud air of independence, which matched her husband's.

'How was Sir Robert?'

'Well, Miss Gordon, he was in pain, if that is what you mean, with the toothache. I gave him a mixture of my own devising, which worked like a charm with my own little ones, when they were teething. I hope it does not make him drowsy . . .'

Her voice tailed away. They listened, but there was no sound, save that of the elements. The hours dragged slowly by. Tamsyn suggested Mrs Knight should seek her rest, but she preferred to stay and care for the comfort of her guests as best she could. They drank tea, talked and dozed alternately and waited; as it grew light the rain abated, but the wind continued to blow at gale force.

'These March winds, 'tis no night to be at sea,' said Mrs Knight comfortably, as she returned with yet more tea.

At last the gate slammed and boots stamped on the path. Mrs Knight flung the door open. Oliver Hempseed, who had been on the point of saddling a horse and setting off on his own search party, despite the women's efforts to dissuade him, leapt to his feet to assist the tired wanderers. A puddle formed rapidly as they stood dripping and dazed with their exertions. Mrs Knight took charge.

'Come to the kitchen, sirs,'

Robert staggered and leaned heavily on John. Charles Knight thrust a round bundle into his wife's arms.

'Take the child, Sally,' he said.

She was soaking wet. With a cry of pity, Alanna ran forward.

'Give her to me, Mrs Knight,' she pleaded.

'Where is Gabrielle?'

Oliver's anguished voice penetrated above the general

179

hubbub. The confusion subsided; in the sudden silence, Robert raised his head.

'She's dead,' he said.

Oliver's eyes blazed and for a moment, Tamsyn thought he might lunge at Robert; then he groaned and put his head in his hands. Sally Knight looked from one to the other in puzzlement.

'The child's mother was Mr Hempseed's wife, my dear.'

Mr Knight laid a finger against his lips, forestalling further questions about the little girl. His wife understood; she bustled to some purpose, sending the three men to the kitchen to divest themselves of their wet clothing; Mr Hempseed was put to work fetching coals, wood and water from the well and she herself took little Claire and Alanna to her bedroom. The child refused to be parted from Alanna, clinging to her neck with desperate fingers. After a while, Mrs Knight returned and found Tamsyn alone tending the fire.

'She's taken a rare fancy to Miss Gordon, poor mite. She's dry and warm now and I'm going to heat a hot brick and some milk. She can sleep with my Mary.'

'You're very kind.'

'In Christian charity, one can do no less.'

The two women smiled at one another.

Half an hour later, somewhat physically restored, the whole party reassembled in the main room of the cottage, with the exception of the infant, who had fallen into an exhausted slumber in Alanna's arms. She was tucked up with the Knights' small daughter and Alanna, much shaken by the experience, trailed down the narrow wooden stairs. There were more shocks to come – it appeared that Robert had been injured; he was sitting in Mr Knight's chair, with one foot wrapped in bandages, propped up on a stool. He had another bandage round his head, with a gauze pad above his right eye.

'Robert!' she exclaimed.

He reached out a hand and pulled her down beside him, rejoicing in her evident concern.

180

'Don't fuss, little one, I'm an old campaigner. Superficial scratches, no more. Hush now, Knight will explain everything.'

They waited expectantly. Mr Knight clearly relished his task; he was a born storyteller.

'We went by way of the pine plantation and then across wild, open country. Here I almost missed the path, for although the ground is familiar as my own home, yet on a night such as this all is terribly changed. We found the track at last, but were much impeded by a tree which fell in front of Mr Aylward's horse, affrighting the poor beast to such a degree that it took much coaxing and skill on the rider's part before we could continue.'

The ladies beamed admiringly at John, who grinned and shook his head.

'At length we arrived at a rustic bridge, which spans the narrow neck of the lake. In summer this is a pretty spot, but tonight it was "romantic" in the most awe-inspiring sense. We decided to tether the horses and proceed on foot, for on the bridge we found Claire's wooden doll and a little further on we discovered footprints and odd hoof-prints, indicating that a horse had gone lame. For nearly a mile we followed a verdant walk beside the wide expanse of water. The lake is hemmed in by evergreens and big, old trees, beech, ash and the weeping-birch; the silent, dripping woods appeared sinister in the extreme.'

John and Robert nodded fervently, while their host took a sip of ale and looked from one to another in the circle of intent faces.

'We approached the cascade from the south bank of the lake. The gentle falls had become a rushing torrent and the rocks were treacherous and slippery. Imagine our dismay, as we came to this place, to see the woman we sought on the opposite bank, with the child in her arms, crying most pitifully. The first light of dawn illuminated the eerie scene; before we could retreat into the shadows the woman saw us. She gave a wild scream, such as I pray I may never hear again, and jumped into the water, with her babe.'

The ladies gasped and Oliver shuddered convulsively. John put a hand on his shoulder and gripped it.

'Sir Robert acted without hesitation. Bravely he plunged into the swirling waters, and Mr Aylward and I waded in to assist him. It was all over in less time that it takes to relate. Sir Robert managed to seize the child and swim back to us, then he returned to save Miss St Marque, struggling against the numbing chill, and uneven footing, choked by weeds.' He sighed. 'I fear she had no will to live and perhaps she could not swim. In any event, she made no effort to stay afloat and before her rescuer could achieve his object, she was swept over the waterfall and dashed to her death on the rocks below. She was still alive when we came up with her, but breathed her last without recovering consciousness. We retrieved the horses, including the lame one, and carried her body to the inn. The Wheatsheaf on the Egham Road – you remember, my dear, I pointed it out to you when we picnicked last summer?'

His wife nodded and answered. 'Yes, of course, Charles. The poor soul.' She turned to Robert, '' 'Twas bravely done, sir. I'm glad you saved the little girl.'

Everyone concurred in this assessment. Oliver Hempseed strode to Robert's side, shook him by the hand and left the room abruptly; Alanna gazed at him with profound adoration, which was a balm to his wounded spirits. Even Tamsyn smiled at him with approval, which did wonders for his self-esteem. There was a hint of self-mockery in his answering smile, but he was proud, also; he had delivered his small daughter from a terrible death by drowning.

'You are become a hero, Coz,' said John.

Modestly he demurred, 'I could not have done it without your aid, and that of our kind host.'

Amidst renewed praises and thanks, the visitors prepared to take their leave. John and Oliver rode ahead to relieve Lady Molesworthy's anxiety, while Tamsyn and Alanna accompanied Sir Robert in the carriage. It was decided that Claire should remain with the Knights until more permanent arrangements were made for her.

In the carriage it was Tamsyn's turn to doze. She dreamed uneasily of the Chinese pictures at Oak Place, which suddenly became real waterfalls and perilous, swaying bridges, suspended above ravines filled with jagged rocks. Alanna leaned forward and asked softly, 'Do you feel much pain, Robert?'

He was stretched across the seat, supported by cushions and covered by a blanket. His face was pale and gaunt in the harsh morning light and there were dark shadows round his eyes.

'Can't seem to stop shivering.'

'Here, take my rug, I don't need it.'

Unsteadily, she moved to lay the cover on his chest, the carriage lurched in a rut. He clasped her so close that she could not escape his eyes, which searched hers with dark, burning intensity.

'How beautiful you are. Why did I not see it before? And now I have lost you . . .'

He released her and she sat up indignantly.

'I'm not an object of art or a thing of beauty. You did not see ME before, because you took me for granted, without thought.'

She sniffed.

Robert seized her hand.

'I meant you are beautiful both inside and out. I did not express myself very well. I'm in pain, Alanna,' he finished, wincing.

'Then go to sleep, sir, and you will feel better,' she retorted, but her smile was warm and sympathetic.

He grunted, closed his eyes and clasped her hand more firmly.

'I'm in pain, too, Robert,' she protested.

He did not move. She examined his features and was startled by the resemblance between him and Claire. There could be no doubt of his paternity when his face was softened and relaxed; there was the same curve to the eyebrows, the high cheekbones, the shape of the nose, the hazel green eyes, hidden now by deep fringed lashes. She sat quietly holding his hand and brooding. Tamsyn viewed her beneath veiled eyelids and sensibly dozed again.

In the days which followed Gabrielle's death, Tamsyn was intrigued to observe the bond of friendship which had sprung up between the cousins. Charles Knight arranged a respectable funeral for the unfortunate woman, which Robert, John and Oliver attended. Then Oliver returned to town, to resume his duties as her ladyship's librarian, his kind patroness thinking it would be better for him to be occupied in familiar surroundings. With his departure the gloom of the preceding months suddenly lifted, the weather improved and Tamsyn and Alanna were much in the company of the two gentlemen from Oak Place.

Great ingenuity was displayed in devising numerous little excursions and diversions. With expert care, Moonlight recovered from her ordeal and Tamsyn was able to ride again. The two couples walked, played cards and squabbled; sometimes in the evening Alanna would play the piano and they sang, teasing John, who knew many of the same tunes, but with different words. Because of the court mourning there were no assembly balls and few private parties, which left the gentlemen at liberty to pursue their courtships unhampered by the usual demands of neighbourly social intercourse. Easter came and went, the hedgerows were alive with nesting birds and spring flowers and still the cousins lingered at Oak Place.

'John is learning about the affairs of the estate,' was Sir Robert's excuse when Alanna taxed him about their lengthy sojourn.

They were standing on the terrace with Tamsyn waiting for John one sunny morning in late April.

'I expected you to be gone long since, but the court mourning ends on the 30th of April and we can all return to town.' She sighed wistfully, her fair curls fluttering in the breeze. 'I vow I never thought I would miss the country, but it has been so pleasant on these warm days . . .' She gazed out over the park, her eyes a limpid blue which matched

184

the sky. She was wearing a grey dress, with pastel-coloured ribbons, while Tamsyn had borrowed a fashionable scarlet silk scarf, without a border, to relieve her black silk.

'You find the countryside entertaining? Good Lord, Alanna, what is the world coming to?' Robert spoke mockingly, but his eyes were serious. Tamsyn had remarked that of late Sir Robert paid flattering attention to Alanna's opinions. In consequence her friend was no longer intimidated and spoke her mind quite freely.

'A letter for you Tamsyn.'

John's arrival created a diversion. Like Sir Robert, he was dressed for riding in breeches and top boots, but he wore brown, more suited to his sallower complexion, while his cousin was in dark green. Tamsyn thought John looked at his best in this informal attire and his face was interestingly irregular, if not precisely handsome. These days the resemblance between the two men seemed less marked than it had formerly; now that she knew them better she was more aware of their differences in height, expression, demeanour and attitudes.

The letter was from her father. At her companion's behest, she seated herself on the nearest wooden bench to read it. After a few moments she looked up.

'Two pieces of good news. The most important first – my father writes that Miss Lovett has consented to be his wife and he considers himself to be a fortunate and happy man. He says he does not care for too much pomp himself, but does not want his bride to feel cheated, so he begs that I will return for the ceremony and help him organize a small reception.'

Alanna showed unexpected concern and sympathy for her friend.

'Well, Tamsyn, at least he is marrying a lady of his own age, more or less. Many men when making second marriages seem to wed someone young enough to be their daughter. And you are grown – it's not as if she could replace your Mama, but it is certain to be difficult when you have been accustomed to be mistress in your father's house. Oh, why do things have to change? I could shake Uncle Charles.'

Mr Aylward's ears pricked up at Alanna's words. He had not thought of this aspect of the situation.

Tamsyn laughed and protested, 'I have been expecting it, but it is always a shock when it happens. However, I am very happy for Papa, for both of them.'

Alanna sat down beside her. She giggled.

'Will you be able to call her Esmeralda, do you think? Darling, you are wonderful to take it so well. When is the date? Can I come?'

Tamsyn looked at the page again.

'Of course you can come. It will take place on the third Saturday in May.'

They talked a little longer and then Tamsyn said she would go in search of Lady Molesworthy to give her the news. John accompanied her, while Alanna and Robert went to the shrubbery to pick some trailing greenery for a floral centre-piece; Miss Gordon liked to do artistic flower arrangements. Her escort dutifully carried the trug. Tamsyn was pensive as they paced slowly back to the house.

'You did not tell us your second item of good news,' John reminded her.

'Oh, no, I forgot. But it *is* very encouraging. Papa had met Mr Hatchard at church and it appears he wants to publish my tales without any further alterations. He said he also likes the illustrations. He asked Papa for my direction, so that he could write to me and send me the proofs.'

'That is indeed good news. My felicitations. Now that you will be more at liberty domestically, do you intend to work on another book?'

'I suppose so. It is very selfish of me, but I confess I do feel dispirited.'

They had reached the morning room. Lady Lucinda looked up from her newspaper on hearing Tamsyn's last words.

'Come in, child,' she said, 'And tell me why you feel low. Is this young man responsible?'

She nodded to John. Tamsyn blushed.

'No, Godmother, but I have received a letter from Papa and while I rejoice for him, I find my own feelings are somewhat mixed.'

She explained. Lady Lucinda listened in silence, until Tamsyn had finished.

Then she said, 'Enough of this shilly-shallying. It is time some decisions were made. You know, Tamsyn my dear, that you always have a home under my roof, if you wish it. But we shall see. Send someone to fetch Robert. I want to see him and John alone in the estate office in ten minutes.'

She rose, adding that she had some papers to find.

'I will fetch Robert,' he offered when her ladyship had gone. He hesitated at the door. 'I had a letter also. From James. He grows impatient to return home.'

Tamsyn grew rigid.

'And you?'

'I too have some decisions to make.'

He was watching her closely. She gripped her hands, but remained mute. 'We must talk later.'

It was a statement, not a request. He swung on his heel and she heard him striding down the hall. Soon his voice came to her through the open window, calling his cousin. It grew fainter and ceased. Tamsyn ran upstairs to her chamber. She closed the door and leaned against it; then she burst into tears.

16

Lady Lucinda Disposes

It was late in the afternoon when Alanna tiptoed into her room, with a tray of chicken soup and thin toast.

'Tammy dearest, are you awake?'

The crumpled figure on the bed heaved and rolled over.

'I'm so unhappy.'

Alanna set down her burden on the little writing-table by the window and fetched a damp cloth and a towel from the washstand.

'I know,' she said, 'Grandmama said we must give you time because of Gil, but John said he did not think time would help; the decision would always be a difficult one. However, Grandmama was splendid and I think she has smoothed the way for us.'

Tamsyn sat up and bathed her flushed face. She peered at her friend over the top of the towel.

'How?'

Satisfied that she had captured her interest, Alanna arranged the coverlet and put the tray on Tamsyn's knees.

'You eat and listen and I will tell you all. It has been an eventful afternoon.'

She drew up a chair and employed her talent for mimicry to the full, while Tamsyn toyed with her soup.

'Well, to begin at the beginning, after you and John returned to the house, I was snipping merrily in the shrub-

188

bery and Robert was trying to help, but a clinging tendril of ivy caught in my hair and an enormous spider fell on my nose. I shrieked and Robert manfully dislodged the creepy creature; my eyes were quite crossed. Then he kissed my nose and my eyes and I think wished to do more, but he let me go abruptly and stood there looking absurdly hangdog and dejected. He declared that he loved me, but that he had no right to ask me to marry him in the face of grandmama's prohibition of our betrothal and his own doubtful prospects. Then we heard John calling and I said quickly that I would marry him, but on one condition, that we adopted little Claire and raised her in our own household. I added that my inheritance would be sufficient to support us, if we lived modestly. Robert's face was a study of conflicting emotions. We could hear John approaching, so he said in a rapid undertone, "Bless you, my darling, for your loyalty, but I cannot ask you to share my poverty, for your grandmother is the trustee of your estate. Your dowry and your eventual inheritance of Molesworthy Court will only come to you at her ladyship's discretion, if she approves your choice of husband. And, in any event, I will not foist my by-blow onto you . . ."'

Tamsyn was open-mouthed. Alanna grinned.

'I think John may have caught those last words, but he gave no sign, merely popped out from behind a laurel and delivered his message. So we repaired to the estate office. Grandmama was very cold and formal behind her huge desk. She was not best pleased to see me, but I insisted that the matter concerned me too and in the end she let me stay. She said that it was time the question of Oak Place was settled, Sir John. I jumped, but it is true of course, that he must be a knight, if he is the heir. John frowned, she screwed her face into a very tolerable facsimile of Mr Aylward's expression and went on, and said distantly, as if he resented Grandmama's interference, "There is nothing to resolve, ma'am. Robert belongs at Oak Place. I have always made my own way. Very few people in England know of my existence. I will simply disappear as quietly as I came and no one the wiser." Robert began to protest that he could not claim an inheritance to which he was not entitled. I thought of you, if John disappeared . . . The atmosphere was getting heated and then Grandmama banged on the desk with the big red accounts' book and we all subsided, like children in school. She opened a large wooden deed box and waved some papers at us. "These documents came to me from three sources: from John's lawyer, Adam Lindsay, verifying his parentage; from my childhood friend, Lady Angelica Windlesham, who married my brother-in-law, Gerald Molesworthy, and died without issue. She was Robert and John's aunt. Finally, from Jeremy Windlesham's lawyer, Jonathan Stubbs, who is also my lawyer. As you gentlemen both know, but perhaps Alanna does not, I was appointed by Jeremy as executor of his will, with Mr Stubbs. Angelica's correspondence, which I found in the box, with her elder brother Jeremy's papers, confirms that they had a twin brother and sister, John and Mary." I was getting mightily confused, so Robert kindly explained that John was our John's father and Mary was Robert's own mother. "The point is," Grandmama continued, "Mary was born first, but in general the preference is given to the male heir, being John's father, since both Jeremy and Angelica died without issue. It is, however, a debateable legal point. Now, gentlemen, I have a solution to put forward, which might save considerable legal costs. You were always a scamp, Robert, but I have a fondness for you and I think you have redeemed yourself of late. I therefore withdraw my objections and you may marry Alanna with my goodwill, if she will have you." Robert and I began to speak, but she was not finished. "John, you inherit the title, whether you will or no; Robert has his from the Hawksmore line anyway. I suggest that you let Robert caretake Oak Place for a year or two, while you return to America and deal with your affairs. If you then wish to claim your ancestral home, Robert and Alanna can move to Molesworthy Court and I will keep the London townhouse, if God spares me." I said the Dower House at Oak Place could be renovated. John asked what would happen if he decided to stay in America

190

and Grandmama said she would ask Mr Stubbs to arrange for a financial settlement after a specified period of time. John and Robert looked at one another, it seemed like forever, and then they shook hands and kissed Grandmama's hand and then her cheek and she said "Pish and tosh", but was pleased. She sent for some wine and we drank a toast to old Sir Jeremy. After a little John wanted to go in search of you, but Grandmama said he should think first, so he rode off, but Robert stayed for luncheon. He told Grandmama that I had agreed to marry him before the change in his fortunes, at which she raised her lorgnette and looked at me like a beetle, but not nearly so disapproving as she was when I told her I wanted to adopt Claire.'

She paused for breath.

Tamsyn set aside her untouched soup and asked curiously, 'Did you persuade her, and Robert?'

'Robert was no problem, I can always wheedle a man. I simply said Claire was his daughter and I would love her like my own. I had to speak forcibly to her ladyship. I said one must be realistic; that we might not be able to have our own children, not everyone can, and even if we were blessed, infant mortality is very high. Half the graves in Windlesham churchyard are little ones.'

'Alanna.' Tamsyn regarded her with laughing respect. 'You're quite outrageous.'

'I know, but in a good cause.' She jumped up and picked up the tray. 'You didn't drink your soup. Bad girl, you look pale and undernourished. That will never do. My matron of honour must be rosy and blooming.'

'When is your wedding to be?'

'In late June. Now, get into bed properly and rest. And eat your supper when it comes. I will leave you in peace and look in later.'

'I'm not an invalid.'

'You will be, if you go on like this. *A bientôt, ma chérie.*'

She departed, leaving Tamsyn to her thoughts, which were many and varied. She tried to read, but could not concentrate. It was depressing to read Mr Fearon, who wrote like a sensible man, and whose views on the United States had a ring of truth about them. She brooded – perhaps she would have different experiences and would be able to write her own, more positive, tome. She knew that there were a number of women printers in the former colonies and that they were treated on terms of equality with men; this was an appealing aspect to the situation. She realized that she was beginning to consider the possibility of living in America much more seriously than she had done hitherto.

True to her word, Alanna looked in on her way to bed. She was very excited.

'Grandmama and I have been discussing plans. We return to town almost at once – but you must do that anyway, for your Papa and Miss Lovett.'

Tamsyn tried to share her enthusiasm.

''Twill be the wedding of the season,' she said.

'Late June is really the end of the season, but it will take that long to make all the arrangements. You must help me choose my dress.' She pirouetted around the bedchamber, gave her friend a quick embrace and exclaimed, 'I wish you could be as happy as I am tonight.'

When Alanna had gone, Tamsyn brushed her hair one hundred times and prepared for bed. She felt very wideawake. The scent of blossom drifted through the open window as she leaned out, resting her elbows on the sill. Her room overlooked the small side porch leading to the kitchen garden and orchard beyond. It was a tranquil scene, with a clear starry sky and the night air filled with mysterious rustlings and creakings. She would miss the serene beauty and fragrant air when she returned to London. A barn owl hooted and she saw a flash of white tail as a rabbit ran for the shelter of its burrow. She leaned further out to make sure the little creature escaped; there was a movement in the shadows immediately below. A bunch of violets landed on the window seat beside her.

'Good Evening, Mrs Elsworth. May I come up?' said a well-known voice.

'John!'

192

With the aid of some vines and crumbling niches which offered footholds in the old stone porch, Mr Aylward displayed remarkable agility in scaling the height and soon swung his leg over the sill.

'My mother always said I could make my living as a cat burglar,' he observed with some pride. He took Tamsyn in his arms and murmured, 'I couldn't wait any longer to see you. England is so small and over-populated, it's almost impossible to get anybody alone.'

He bent his head and kissed her long and hard. At first she responded eagerly, but then she felt the warmth of his hand through the thin fabric of her nightgown and began to shiver. He thought she was trembling and stopped abruptly, his eyes searching her face.

'I'm not a virgin, John,' she reminded him softly.

Acutely aware of her every tone and action, he caught the hint of apprehension in her voice.

'You are to me,' he said firmly, taking her hand and leading her to the bed. 'Get in, you'll catch cold. I want to talk to you.'

He tucked her in and drew up a chair. Tamsyn watched him through narrowed lids, uncertain whether to be flattered or dismayed at his rejection.

'Shall I light the candle?' he enquired.

Tamsyn shook her head. 'I can see you quite well.'

'It's easier to talk in the dark. At home my family often sit outside on warm summer nights and listen to the crickets and watch the fireflies.' John leaned forward and gave one of her long, heavy tresses a little tug. 'I love your hair. Promise me you won't ever torture it into those ugly tight curls so many women favour. They look like bunches of grapes.'

'My looks are no concern of yours, sir.'

Tamsyn sounded more petulant than haughty. John laughed and took her hand.

'Darling idiot, everything about you concerns me. Now hush and don't distract me, which I admit it is all too easy to do. First there are some matters which must be settled between us. Did Alanna tell you of Lady Lucinda's proposals?'

Tamsyn withdrew her hand and said with as much dignity as she could muster in her recumbent position, 'Yes, indeed, Sir John. I must congratulate you on your inheritance.'

'Titles mean nothing in America, Tamsyn. Is it your desire to be Lady Windlesham?'

'I haven't been asked,' she retorted.

John smote his head.

'Give me patience. Don't be obtuse, woman. You know I want to marry you.'

She put her head on one side and said teasingly, 'Well, a widow with a modest competence and some facility with her pen must not give up her independence without good cause. A title would be just the thing.'

John clenched his teeth.

'Are you saying that you will only wed me if I remain in England and settle at Oak Place?'

Tamsyn meditated, then said, 'Of course, I would want to make some changes. I am used to occupation. Would you object if we changed the colours in the Chinese sitting room?' Mr Aylward drew a deep breath, but before he could speak, Tamsyn relented. 'Forgive me. Emigration is such a big step, but I do not believe we could be truly happy if I made conditions in a half-hearted way. I will come to America as plain Mrs Aylward, if that is what you wish, John.'

At this self-sacrificing speech, John gave a delighted whoop, which Tamsyn feared would wake the whole house and crushed her to him, his coat buttons pressing painfully into her ribs. After an interval, she wriggled and he loosened his hold.

She whispered, 'I have missed the feeling of being central to someone's happiness. I hope I will know you in another life, for existence without you is unthinkable.'

'And Gil?' he said, holding her gently and looking deep into her eyes.

'I loved him dearly, but it was a youthful love. This is a

194

more mature emotion. I shall not let his memory come between us.'

Unwilling to give free rein to the intensity of his feelings, John cleared his throat and resumed his chair.

'I want you to know America,' he said, 'and to meet my family and my friends. I suggest that we keep open the option to return to Oak Place, as her ladyship proposed. In Philadelphia I am called John Windlesham. I merely used my mother's maiden name in England to avoid attention.'

Tamsyn reclined comfortably on her pillows.

'What will your mother say when she hears you are marrying a widow?'

'She will be enchanted with you, my love,' he said promptly. 'Mama likes intelligent women. Besides, she was a widow herself when she married my father. Her first husband died of typhus, when she was eighteen. They had been married two years.'

'Oh! No children?'

'None that lived.'

John watched the changing expressions which flitted across his beloved's face.

'I'm frightened. It is such a leap in the dark and Mr Fearon . . .'

'Ah yes, Mr Fearon. Curses be on Robert's head,' broke in John. He spoke with good-humoured resignation. 'Fearon is accurate in so far as he goes, but it is not the whole story. It is good to go with open eyes, but books are no substitute for experience and I will be there to protect and interpret for you. You are a tolerant and civilized lady and you will find much to criticize, but also, I hope, much to admire and enjoy. We are not going for ever. Transatlantic transportation is improving all the time.'

He talked on, describing his home, his sisters and their young families, the climate and the larger world of culture and politics. It was far into the night when a drowsy Tamsyn pronounced herself much reassured.

'I had intended to make a tour of the Continent before

195

returning, but if you wish we could have our wedding journey in America instead.'

Tamsyn pondered.

'It seems a pity for you to miss the grand tour. Perhaps we could do a curtailed version,' she offered.

John smiled.

'I have a fancy to visit the Low Countries,' he admitted, 'But I want to have you safely in America before the autumn gales. I have not forgotten the discomforts of a winter crossing and, if I do, I'm sure James will remind me.'

'I will be able to write articles about my first impressions of the United States,' said Tamsyn, her eyes sparkling mischievously.

'Your revenge. But to be serious a moment, it must be your choice whether you become a lady of leisure and fashion, as your position in English society as the mistress of Oak Place would dictate, or whether you prefer to share the hazards of a literary life with me on an equal footing, writing, printing, publishing and bookselling. It will be interesting to discover how you finally decide.'

'The decision will not be mine alone. Perhaps we can find some way of incorporating the best of both worlds in our lives.'

She yawned mightily.

'Perhaps. We'll let the future decide. I must leave, the servants will be up soon and your reputation will be ruined if I am discovered when they bring your morning chocolate. I left my horse in the orchard. I hope the ivy holds for my descent. Goodnight, my darling. Don't cudgel your brain for any more coherent thoughts – just surrender yourself to sweet dreams.'

He kissed her, a very assured, not to say possessive, kiss. Tamsyn's eyes opened very wide.

'You'd better not tell her ladyship of this nocturnal visit,' he advised, kissing her hands and retreating to the window, 'I will return to London and wait upon your father formally next week.'

He disappeared from view. She heard an ominous tearing

196

sound and a heavy thud, accompanied by muffled curses. She lay still and relaxed, listening for the soft beat of horse's hooves, faint and distant, but unmistakeable. She closed her weary lids.

'Silly John,' she murmured, 'How can we possibly keep our love a secret when we're both glowing with inner radiance.'

She was sound asleep when the maid entered quietly with her drink. Fanny pulled open the shutters, puzzled to find them half-swinging on their hinges, and discovered a posy of wilted violets on the window seat. She filled a toothglass with water and set the flowers on the nightstand; sometime later Mrs Elsworth woke up to the sweet scent of fresh spring blooms. She sipped her cold drink with a contented air and from time to time she touched the delicate flowers to make sure that they were not a figment of her disordered imagination.

17

The Wedding of the Season

'Only think, my dear, a crocodile couch and a sphinx sofa. What execrable taste.'

Overhearing this snippet of conversation as she waited for Alanna in Mrs Bell's fashionable dress shop in Charlotte Street, Tamsyn grinned. Hoping to hear more she moved to exchange her copy of *La Belle Assemblée* for another of the periodicals laid out on the heavy mahogany oval table, which occupied the centre of the room, but the two ladies put their bonneted heads close together and lowered their voices. Disappointed, Tamsyn retired to a chair by the window and leafed idly through yet another article on summer modes. Alanna's fitting was taking a long time.

She read with interest that the colours most likely to be fashionable in June were lilac, rose colour, green, azure, straw colour and pale slate colour, while the Parisians favoured pale pink and citron. Her eye was taken by a tinted engraving of a half-dress in jaconaut muslin, embroidered in light green sprigs and tied behind with a broad white ribband, edged with green. The waistline was lower than it had been for many years, which was an intriguing development.

She dropped the magazine in her lap and gazed out at the sunny street. London in springtime was not so depressing as she had feared; indeed the end of the official mourning period, coupled with a marked improvement in the weather, had caused the ladies of the metropolis to deck themselves in all the colours of the rainbow. The delicate pastel hues and gossamer fabrics gave a light-hearted butterfly aspect to the grey city pavements and reflected Tamsyn's own state of mind.

It had been difficult to hide her happiness from her godmother and her sharp-eyed friend, but in the bustle of packing and removal from Molesworthy Court they were less observant than usual and Tamsyn had held her peace, feeling a superstitious reluctance to say anything before John had called on Mr Farrell. This he had done last week and her father had appreciated the courtesy and had granted his permission for their betrothal. Although not strictly required by etiquette, Tamsyn felt happier with his blessing.

For the first two weeks after her return home, Tamsyn had seen little of her friend, who was swept into a whirlwind of social engagements, including his Majesty's first levee on 10th of May, which was very numerously and splendidly attended according to the newspaper reports. The gossip columnists were much preoccupied with the possible advent of the new queen; her hapless husband was in daily dread of her arrival from the Continent. However, space was made for the announcement of the approaching nuptials of Miss Alanna Gordon and Sir Robert Hawksmore and the polite world learned that there would be a quiet, family ceremony, followed by a grand wedding breakfast, at Lady Molesworthy's house in Portman Square.

Tamsyn had also been much engaged with her own affairs. Her galley proofs required her urgent attention; to her relief they needed little amendment and had been returned to Mr Hatchard that very morning.

Hannah had been overjoyed at her mistress's news and had bravely volunteered to accompany her to the New World, which was a great source of comfort to Tamsyn. John called every day and had proved a tower of strength, enlisting Mr Farrell's help in making book and equipment purchases for use in Philadelphia, and relieving the ladies of his fidgeting presence, while Miss Lovett, Tamsyn, Hannah and Mrs Jennings planned his wedding. In one of their rare moments alone, John and Tamsyn had agreed that with her father's marriage in May, and Alanna's in June, they would wait until July for their own ceremony. Unfortunately Alanna would be on her own bridal tour during this last celebration, Tamsyn did not relish the prospect of telling her friend this news! Today they had met by appointment at Mrs Bell's for the first time since their return to town. Tamsyn's selection of a gown to wear as Miss Gordon's matron of honour had been a relatively simple task; she intended to make more modest purchases for her American trousseau in the Oxford Street shops, but it was pleasant to have one grand dress, which was to be Alanna's gift to her attendant. She had chosen a cream-coloured lace dress over a lilac satin slip, with short round sleeves and a full skirt, embroidered in a pattern of flowers, mixed with leaves. With this ensemble she planned to wear a lilac satin toque headdress, cream kid gloves and satin shoes. She wondered if she dared wear the dress again for her own wedding, for after all, very few of the same guests would attend both functions.

Alanna appeared before her and placed a small parcel on top of her magazine. Tamsyn looked up.

'What is this? Are you ready?'

'It is a present, because I've kept you waiting so long. Open it and then we will go and sit in the carriage in Berkeley Square and get Albert to fetch us ices from Gunter's.'

Obediently, Tamsyn untied the string. The two ladies had stopped their gossiping and were watching her across the room with birdlike curiosity, while Mrs Bell herself, very upright and stiff in corsets of her own invention, looked on from the curtained opening, which divided the antechamber from the inner mysteries of fitting and sewing rooms.

Tamsyn shook out a kind of hooped hood.

'It is a *chapeau bras* of my latest design. Also called a Calash. It can be folded and carried in your reticule.'

Tamsyn put it on and the proprietress came over to twitch

200

it into place. She stood back and viewed her client with justifiable pride.

'Very ingenious, Mrs Bell,' said Tamsyn sincerely. 'And thank you, Alanna. It is just the thing for a sea voyage.'

'A sea voyage?' repeated Miss Gordon, her blue eyes suddenly intent.

'I will tell you about it in the carriage. We must not delay Mrs Bell any longer. Good day, and thank you for your patience.'

Tamsyn smiled and made a hasty exit, not pausing for Alanna, who lingered to make arrangements for her next fitting.

'Oh, how tedious they are, these sessions with the dressmaker. Such exquisite relief to sit down,' exclaimed Miss Gordon, a few minutes later, as Albert closed the carriage door and put up the steps. 'And that reminds me, I need your support to dissuade Grandmama from arraying herself in jonquil satin for the great day. I do not wish to be unkind, but you will understand if I tell you it is truly a case of mutton dressed up as lamb. I can only think it is an attack of spring madness, for she always wears strong, dark shades, purples, oranges, brown and black.'

'Miss Lovett has had a similar attack. Bright pink, with a scarlet sash.'

'At least she is to be the bride.'

'Yes, I know, but think, my dear, in scarlet.'

The two young ladies shook their heads and chattered happily about the odd behaviour of those older, and presumably wiser, than themselves. Alanna waited until Albert had procured the ices, which were refreshing and delicious, before tackling the question uppermost in her mind.

'Now, tell me about this sea voyage,' she demanded.

'Such a treat. I wonder if they have ices in Philadelphia,' Tamsyn said, savouring the taste, her pink tongue extended to suck the spoon.

Alanna received this intelligence calmly.

''Tis all settled then? You are to go with John?'

Tamsyn nodded, dabbing daintily at the corners of her mouth.

'I could not tell you before, because John wanted to speak to Papa and then to Lady Lucinda. He went to call on her this afternoon. He and Robert have agreed to her ladyship's suggestion; you will live at Oak Place, while we go to the United States. If we come back, then my dearest, I shall turn you out of house and home, I hope you will not hate me when the time comes.'

Careless of the dish, Alanna flew up and kissed her on both cheeks.

'I should have known; you are in such good looks and spirits today. Oh, Tammy, I shall miss you, but I'm so happy for you, and I promise to look after the house as if it were my own. Oak Place is very grand, but it will not be a wrench for me to leave it; Molesworthy Court has always been my true home, so, I beg you, do not hesitate to come back on my account. Nothing would please me more than to have you as my neighbour.'

Alanna repeated this sentiment even more vehemently on her wedding day, when the hour for separation was almost at hand. As Tamsyn had anticipated, her friend had been most distressed to find that she would be unable to be present when Mr Aylward and Mrs Elsworth were united in matrimony. She had been only partially mollified to learn that she would be able to see Tamsyn once more, at Southampton, before the couple sailed.

They were in Alanna's room, whither the new Lady Hawksmore and her matron of honour had repaired to tidy themselves before the wedding breakfast. Alanna sat at her dressing-table, while Fanny rearranged her floral headdress; she looked very beautiful in a gown of white muslin threaded with silver and a trailing lace veil, draped loosely over her bare arms.

'Sit still, miss, I mean, milady,' said Fanny, her mouth full of pins.

In the looking-glass, Tamsyn's eyes met Alanna's; the realization dawned that life would never be the same again.

'Write to me. Why do you have to go so far?' Her expression lightened. 'At least you won't have to contend with any old antiquities.'

Tamsyn tweaked a stray curl firmly back under her toque.

'No, my problems will be rather different,' she agreed.

She looked so wistful that Alanna jumped up and hugged her fiercely. Then she sat down again.

'Don't be frightened of John's mother. She cannot be any more intimidating than Grandmama. I expect she will be kind to you for John's sake and if not, you can always come back to Oak Place.' She swivelled round on her stool so that she was facing Tamsyn and smiled, 'Will I do Robert credit in the receiving line?'

'Yes, you know you're quite perfect.'

They walked to the door arm in arm.

'I wish little Claire could have been a bridesmaid, but Robert said he had to draw the line somewhere, particularly since the likeness between them is so great – and John, too, of course. So I have had a doll dressed in a bridal gown exactly like mine and I will send it to the Knights for her, with some bride-cake. When we come back from Paris we will spend the winter at Oak Place and she can become accustomed to her new family.'

'You are a dear, generous soul, Alanna,'

'Nonsense, my dear. Now let me take a deep breath and we will go down. Thank you, Fanny, go and eat a good English meal while you can – I know how you detest French menus.'

The maid accomplished the difficult feat of grimacing and giggling at the same time.

'Lady Lucinda looks . . .'

Tamsyn searched for the right adjective.

'Remarkable,' supplied Alanna. 'Yes, doesn't she. I am more grateful than I can say that you persuaded her to wear that becoming amber silk; I only hope the springs in Mrs Bell's elegant new corsets can stand the strain. She insists on having the tapes much too tightly tied and Evans confided to me that she fears they will bring on a spasm.'

'Perhaps she will be too much occupied to eat.'

Laughing, they peered over the curved banister; by some sixth sense, Sir Robert heard them above the din of arrival. He looked up and waved imperatively. Lady Hawksmore joined her spouse, with Mrs Elsworth on her left, dutifully holding the bridal bouquet of trailing red rosebuds, which matched the floral headdress. The guests filed by and Alanna's cheek grew rosy with the many salutations. From her vantage point, Tamsyn observed the dazzling throng with fascination; the gentlemen were almost as brightly garbed as the fairer sex in striped or embroidered waistcoats of infinite variety and coats of plainer, but scarcely sombre hues. Josselin, the butler, was in his element, having established his position of supremacy after a slight altercation with Mr Gunter, the caterer. Between them, the two men and the army of Molesworthy servants, shepherded the new arrivals to the library, where they found Lady Lucinda, wearing an awe-inspiring array of diamonds, flanked by Mrs Charles Farrell, regal in deep blue satin, as befitted her married status. Having greeted their hostess, they were invited to partake of a sumptuous *déjeuner*, which had been set out on tables, under a striped awning in the little courtyard.

'Do you think it will rain? Where is Charles? Where is Oliver?'

Her ladyship fussed and fumed and enjoyed herself tremendously, while Esmeralda Farrell patiently soothed and reassured, secure in the knowledge that when the party was over, she and her husband would return to their own home and she would never again be at anyone's beck and call.

Most of the guests had now arrived and Sir Robert proposed that they wait five minutes and then abandon their posts in the hall.

In the momentary lull which followed, Alanna murmured to Tamsyn, 'My cousin George sent us a most hideous Greek vase. I suppose it was a kind thought, but it is chipped. We cannot possibly have it on display.'

Sir Robert overheard and said in tones of affectionate despair, 'My dear little ignoramus, Lord Byron's gift, which you so despise, is a rare Attic urn, with a most unusual motif. We will most certainly have it on view, in that empty niche in the library, where it will be appreciated.'

'As you wish, Robert, so long as it is not in the drawing room.'

Alanna's meek tone, was belied by her dancing eyes.

'Squabbling already, that will never do, *mes enfants*.' John appeared and offered his arm to Alanna, saying, 'Come with me, Lady Hawksmore, it is time you had something to eat.'

Tamsyn heard Josselin announce sonorously, 'Sir John Aylward Windlesham,' and a buzz of conversation.

Still clutching Alanna's bouquet, she smiled at Sir Robert rather tremulously.

Moved by a sudden impulse he said, 'John tells me we are soon to be cousins by marriage. I hope that we may also be friends?' He held out his hand and Tamsyn laid hers in his. They shook solemnly. Then he summoned a passing waiter to put the flowers in water and tucked Mrs Elsworth's hand on his arm. 'Let us follow their excellent example and seek sustenance. One day, Tamsyn, you will like me in spite of yourself.'

'I have always liked you – in spite of *your*self,' she retorted, revived by the prospect of food.

The bridegroom was diverted by well-wishers before they had trodden half the length of the library. Tamsyn inched forward alone, exchanging smiles and greetings with her acquaintances. The blue-stocking ladies of the literary circle were grouped around Mrs Farrell, enviously admiring her ring.

'It is interesting, is it not?' she heard her new stepmother say. 'That the custom of wearing wedding rings appears to have taken its rise among the Romans? The ring was a pledge and the man put it on the woman's fourth finger of her left

205

hand, because it was believed that a nerve reached thence to the heart.'

Tamsyn slipped past. In the next recess, where she had once sat with Robert, recovering from the shock of his likeness to John, she found Mr James Ferguson, dressed with unnatural care for a romantic hero, expatiating on the wonders of his native country to a flock of Alanna's fellow debutantes. She waved to him over the nodding curls and feathers, but did not dally, for the mingled scents of flowers, food and fragrances of warm humanity were overpowering. She glanced longingly towards the open door and had almost attained her goal when she was intercepted by Oliver Hempseed, looking very much his former self, aloof and impeccable in dark grey, with his spectacles perched on the end of his nose and a book in his hand.

'Taking refuge, for shame sir,' she teased, indicating the open door of his inner sanctum.

He favoured her with his rare, engaging smile.

'There is no refuge to be found in this house today, Mrs Elsworth, but I must not repine for it is a happy day and peace will soon be restored when Lady Hawksmore departs on her bridal tour.' He regarded Tamsyn thoughtfully and added, 'May I say how charming you look today? You have a sparkling aura about you which, I believe, owes little to artificial aid. I should like to offer you my felicitations. I understand you are soon to become Lady Windlesham.'

'We are to be wed on my birthday, the 15th of July. The invitations will be sent out next week. I hope you will come, Mr Hempseed?'

His expression was enigmatic, but he said he would be delighted. She chattered on, hearing herself talking too much, in her sudden nervousness. 'It will be quite a simple affair and in America I shall be plain Mrs Windlesham. I shall miss our literary talks and your wise advice on the book world.'

'My advice, such as it is, is always at your disposal, ma'am. Send me a line, whenever you have a query. The quality of our discussions will be much diminished by your absence.'

Tamsyn blushed, but met his eyes directly.

'Thank you for the compliment, sir. I know you are not one to flatter. I will perhaps start a similar circle in Philadelphia and I will not hesitate to ask for assistance. Shall I address my correspondence here? Now that you are free you may have other plans?'

Oliver Hempseed did not pretend to misunderstand her.

'It is many years since my life revolved around Gabrielle, but in a technical sense, of course, I was not free. My present liberty will change little, for the only lady I might have considered is betrothed to another.' Observing Tamsyn's stricken face, he said lightly, 'No pity, I beg. In sooth, I value my bachelor existence and scholarly pursuits too well to make a good husband. I am content. Sir Robert and I will cherish the Oak Place library against your, and Sir John's, return.'

Tamsyn's eyes filled with unshed tears.

'Dear Oliver,' she said and kissed him quickly on the cheek, then fled before her sympathy should overwhelm her.

It had been an emotional day.

She joined John and her father at one of the tables. Sir Robert escorted Lady Molesworthy to the head table, where Alanna was waiting with various relatives in town for the occasion. The repast began. Mrs Farrell slipped in beside her husband and gave him a quiet, affectionate smile and a soft word. He squeezed her blue-mittened hand and winked at Tamsyn across the board. The wine flowed, toasts were drunk and the company became jovial. Everyone had remarked on John's likeness to his cousin and in one final burst of zeal, Charles Farrell toasted both gentlemen and their ladies, and wished them health, long life and happiness. Even Lady Lucinda was beginning to droop with weariness by the time Alanna, assisted by Tamsyn, had changed into her travelling clothes and departed with Robert for Paris.

'Heaven be praised, I have a month to recuperate before your wedding, Tamsyn.' Her ladyship pecked her god-daughter's cheek and pressed into her hand a box containing a gold brooch, in the shape of a circle, inlaid with sapphires. She waved aside Mrs Elsworth's thanks.

'A trifling memento. John helped me choose it – said the stones matched your eyes or some such nonsense. Now, get Evans for me, there's a good gel. She's laced me far too tightly; I shall burst or expire if I don't get relief soon. Come and see me after the weekend; I shall be lonely without Alanna.'

Tamsyn promised and went in search of the maid. Her duty done, she glanced around for John, but was waylaid by Josselin.

'You and the other servants did splendidly, not a hitch,' said Tamsyn.

The butler beamed and preened himself, chest well out.

'Thank you, Mrs Elsworth. A few small mishaps, a broken glass, some scratches to the furniture and a torn curtain cord, nothing to speak of. I was wondering, ma'am, hif you needed assistance on the day of your nuptials? Her ladyship has given her permission and I should be happy to hoblige.'

'Josselin, how kind. But my wedding breakfast will be a very modest affair, nothing like Miss Alanna's.'

'Quite proper, ma'am, in your widowed circumstances an' all, but I should like to be there jest the same, to give you a proper send-off. After all, you will be the mistress of Oak Place one day, after your tour of the United States, Mrs Elsworth, ma'am.'

Tamsyn bit back a smile; clearly the grapevine in the servants' hall was in good working order.

She said graciously, 'Thank you, Josselin. That would be very nice.'

And so it came about that Lady Molesworthy's butler presided over the catering arrangements for his second wedding within a month.

Mr Farrell gave the bride away at a simple ceremony and then the book and printing fraternity of London, with much genuine warmth and affection, gathered in the familiar workroom in George Street for the reception, bearing gifts

208

of a distinctly literary nature: pens, pencils, paints for the bride and a journal, bound in leather with a stout clasp. Mr Hempseed proferred *The Monastery* by the author of *Waverley* with a rueful smile as he pointed to the title. *The Life of Richard Edgeworth*, father of the famed Maria, and Southey's latest tome, on Methodism, were among the many volumes which they received, hot from the press.

It fell to Mr Gunter, with the unlikely collaboration of Mr Hatchard and Josselin, to produce the *pièce de résistance*: a bride-cake topped by a small, but beautifully fashioned wooden book-press, holding an advance copy of Mrs Elsworth's *Animal Tales*. The company stood in an admiring circle, Josselin made sure that every wineglass was filled and Mr Hatchard proposed the toast.

'To the Printer's Daughter and her husband. Sir John and Lady Aylward Windlesham.'

The words echoed round the room.

Tamsyn's heart was full. She smiled mistily. Mr Hatchard placed the slim volume in her hands and she opened it at random. Mr Farrell produced his handkerchief and said gruffly,

''Tis unlucky to cry on your wedding day. Watch out ye don't smudge the tinted plates. It looks very fine. I'm proud of you. Happy Birthday, and many happy returns.'

Tamsyn sniffed and blew and smiled radiantly.

'Oh, Papa, how can I cut that exquisite cake?'

John came to her assistance and under cover of the lively conversation, for unlike most weddings, almost everybody knew everybody, he whispered, 'Well, my darling, do you think you will ever be able to abandon the book world for the polite world?'

Tamsyn shook her head.

'The love of books overcomes all social barriers,' she said confidently. 'There is my godmother in close converse with father's chief compositor and Charles Knight arguing with Oliver Hempseed about the value of popular education and books for the masses. I'm sure I shall find congenial bookish souls across the Atlantic as well.'

A shadow of doubt crossed her husband's face and Tam-syn said, 'If not, I shall become a literary missionary and Mr Knight can keep me supplied with suitable material, until I can set up my own press.'

The light of reforming zeal was in her eye, John looked alarmed. 'I trust I shall not regret my marriage to a printer's daughter', he said – and then he silenced her laughing protests with a kiss.